FORGOTTEN SOULS MC BOOK ONE

KIRA JOHNS

WARNING:

The characters in this story overcame horrific neglect and abuse, both mental and physical, and have taken extreme steps to survive during their journey through the darkness into the light.

Due to graphic content and mature subject matter (explicit language, acts of violence, sexual content both consensual and not, drug use, prostitution and sex-trafficking), this book should not be purchased by readers under the age of 18 or the faint of heart.

Prologue

Alana

"Lana!" Jax shouts as he enters my room, slamming the door closed behind him. He rests the full weight of his body tightly against the wooden barrier, his chest heaving. "We have to go!" Reaching out, he grabs the worn wooden chair from my desk and lodges the back underneath the doorknob.

"What's going on?" I ask, rubbing my eyes. It feels like I have just fallen asleep.

"Phil!" Reaching under my bed, he pulls out my backpack and begins dumping the contents on the floor.

My eyes widen at the mention of his name. He's back? I had been certain he wouldn't make bail, but I shouldn't be surprised. With his pull, he could literally get away with murder without as much as a slap on the hand.

I throw the covers off, tossing them into a heap on the floor as I scramble from my bed and rush to the window. I lift it with such force shards of glass shower around me as I pull myself up and through the window. Stepping onto the roof, I reach my hand inside for Jax just as my bedroom door splinters under the impact of Phil's shoulder.

Phil's eyes are reddened and filled with pure fury as he rushes towards the window. "Jax!" I scream, yanking on his arm in an attempt to pull him through the window. As soon as he jumps to his feet, we rush towards the trellis, making our way down to the ground.

"Run!" Jax yells, just as my feet hit dirt. I don't hesitate as I take off towards the wooded area adjacent to the house, stopping when I realize Jax isn't following me.

Turning around, I see him lying face down on the ground and I stop breathing. He doesn't appear to be moving as Phil straddles him, pounding his fists into the back of his head over and over. The need to run falls away, overpowered by seeing Jax's limp body being pummeled and I know what I must do.

Running back towards the house, I scream at Phil. "Stop it! Leave him alone!" He continues beating him until I am within arm's reach. Only then does he stand, tightly grabbing hold of my arm.

"Where were you two going, Alana?" he asks, his eyes cold and filled with unbridled fury.

I do not answer him. Anything I say will only anger him more. Closing my eyes, I wait for him to unleash his rage on me, making me pay for trying to run. When his fist collides with the side of my jaw, I cry out in pain as I drop to my knees on the dew covered ground. Hovering above me, he strikes me again and again until I am lying on my back, drifting in and out of consciousness.

I manage to whimper when I feel his callous hands on the bare skin of my stomach. Bile rises in my throat as he tugs at my shorts, swiftly pulling them down my legs. *Please make this end*, I silently beg, knowing that no matter how much I plead, he will never stop. This is our punishment for an unknown crime and Phil will be forever in our lives.

"Phil?" Janet's voice should give me a sense of relief, but it doesn't. She will do what she always does, look the other way as if ignoring it makes it all go away. If his anger is taken out on Jax and me, she reaps the benefits. That's the game she plays, and I hate her for it.

"Go back inside!" he orders before I hear the sound of his zipper being lowered. Hearing the door close, I know she has abandoned me, just as she always does. She may have never laid a hand on me, but I blame her just the same.

He spits into his palm as I clench my jaw, waiting for the pain that is sure to come. Squeezing my eyes shut, I try to zone out, my mind focusing on anything but what is about to occur.

"You're so beautiful, princess. You know that, don't you?" he whispers into my ear. "Happy birthday."

I've known for a long time that this day was coming. Since we arrived here a little over three months ago, Phil has made his intentions clear. The beatings I could handle, even him touching me was something I could bear, but not this.

When I feel him pressing himself against my entrance, fear consumes me. This shouldn't be happening. Instinct should tell me not to fight, to take what I know is coming, but I can't. To lay here and take his abuse would be him defeating me, making me a victim, something I refuse to be.

Summoning every bit of strength I have within me, I draw my hand back before thrusting it forward, my palm colliding with his face. "You fuckin' bitch!" he growls, his hand clutching his face as blood pours from his now broken nose. This is my only chance of escape.

Thrashing my body from side to side, I am able to move out from under him. Scrambling backwards, I get to my feet and rush over to Jax's still unconscious body. I refuse to leave him behind but am unable to carry him. Frantically I look around, trying to find some way to escape. Just as I roll him over, I am rammed from behind. Falling face first, my head collides with the ground, my forehead splitting upon impact.

Suddenly I am lifted from the ground, being jerked backwards again by my hair. Screaming into the silent night, I plead for someone, anyone, to help me but the only person who cares is lying unconscious a few feet away.

"You think anybody's gonna save you? You're worthless, both of you. Your own parents didn't even want you! Nobody cares if you live or die!" he spits at me, mere inches from my face. Shoving me hard onto the ground, he reaches behind him and pulls out the six inch blade he always carries. "You have a choice, princess," he says, walking over to where Jax lies. "And I'm tired of playing nice. You can either give me what I want, when I want it, or..." he lifts Jax's head off the ground, revealing his battered face illuminated by the full moon out tonight. "I'll slit his fuckin' throat. The choice is yours."

My shoulders sag in defeat. I can't win. All of this has been for nothing. I should have stayed in my room and just let him have his way with me. I shouldn't have let my fear of this man override my judgment. It always came down to this moment and I am done fighting.

I nod slowly. "Just leave him alone," I say, motioning towards Jax.

"You give me what I want, and I'll never lay a finger on him again." I have no choice but to believe what he says is true. We are out of options. There is no place we can go, nowhere to run and hide. He will always find us like he has in the past.

Carelessly he releases Jax's head, letting it land with a thud on the ground. He drops the knife as he reaches down to free himself again. Gripping himself roughly, he strokes his length as his eyes bore into me.

Swallowing hard, I do what I know I must: protect Jax. He is all I have in this world, the only person who has or will ever truly care about me. Slowly, I nod and begin walking towards him completely defeated. He grins at me, revealing his stark white, perfect teeth. He knows he has won.

Grasping my hand, he leads me inside the house passing by Janet who is standing immobile and silent in the entranceway to the living room. There isn't even a hint of remorse in her eyes as he leads me down to the basement.

Chapter 1

Alana

Five Years Later

Dropping my backpack on the hard ground, I plop down beside it deciding this is as good of a place as any. It must be close to three in the morning, and after wandering around for hours I ventured towards the empty park since every place that looked like a good place to stay warm for the night was already occupied.

Curling up into a ball, I try to conserve as much of my body heat as possible. It is getting colder now that November is here. I know if I don't find shelter soon, I am going to freeze to death.

Turning eighteen had been a milestone. After being released from the juvenile detention center, there was no chance of being placed in the foster care system again. As soon as I walked out of those doors, I breathed a sigh of relief. My past was just that, and I had my future to look forward to.

What a fool I had been. I was alone, not even having a friend to turn to. Abandoned in a cruel world full of violence. Instead of going home to a warm bed, I had to settle for the streets, a terrifying option.

Rolling over, I look up into the night sky using my backpack as a pillow. As always, it's breathtaking. The stars are bright in the evening sky and there isn't a cloud in sight. It would be perfect if this wasn't what my life had become.

Living on the streets will tear you down. Trying to stay warm, finding food, and remaining safe have been my main priorities. I have been lucky, but I've had a few close calls.

I hear voices nearby, causing me to knife upright. One thing I've learned is to stay out of sight as much as possible. An eighteen year old girl on the streets becomes prey to the monsters that lurk in the darkness. I am all too familiar with evil and have no intention of acquainting myself with it once again.

Phil Martin could be the poster child for evil. Sadistic, cruel, and uncaring doesn't fully define the monster he was. The things he did to me I will never forget. He ruined my life,

taking everything from me including my pride
and dignity.

You did it for Jax, I remind myself. I would go
through every bit of torture all over again if it
meant he remained safe. After that first night,
Phil kept his word and never laid a hand on
him again. I wasn't proud of what I had done,
but my priority had been protecting the boy
that meant more to me than anything. And
then he left me, abandoning me with that
monster. No phone call, no note - nothing.

Then it all ended. Two men broke into the
house one night and brutally killed both Janet
and Phil, slitting their throats. By some miracle
they spared my life, not harming a single hair
on my head. The night is still a blur, only bits
and pieces are clear. I remember wanting to
run, but I couldn't bring myself to do it.
Instead, I called the cops out of fear. When the
police arrived, I became their primary suspect.
At the age of sixteen, I was arrested and
charged with murder.

"If you change your mind, you know where to
find me," a man calls out, bringing me back to
the present. I watch as one man continues
walking in my direction while the other heads
for the opposite side of the park. I pull my
knees up to my chin, trying to stay
camouflaged against the tree as the man
approaches, silently praying he doesn't see
me.

He is just about to pass by the tree when he stops. Turning, he looks directly at me. "Hey," he says quietly.

I pull my legs up tighter, hoping he will just go away. Instead, he walks closer to me, stopping inches from me and crouches down. "What are you doing out here?" he asks.

I lift my eyes to his, feeling nothing but fear at this moment. "Nothing," I mutter.

"Nothing, huh? You look cold."

"I'm fine," I reply, my teeth chattering.

He nods, looking around. "You don't look fine. How old are you?"

"None of your business!" I snap.

"OK, I'll give you that." He sits down beside me, and while looking straight ahead, he begins to talk to no one in particular. "I remember being out here on my own too. I had run away from home and thought anything was better than being there with my fuckin' parents and I was right. It was better to freeze to death than to deal with the things they did to me, but the longer I stayed out here, the harder it got. I was hungry, cold and starting to get sick. Luckily, there was this guy that came along and offered to help me out. I didn't know him so I damn sure didn't trust him and he saw it. He sat down beside me and talked for hours until finally I had heard enough and decided to take a chance. What was the worst that could happen? He took me home that night. Gave me a hot shower, a warm bed, and food, never asking for anything in return."

"Why are you telling me this?" I ask.

"Because I believe in paying it forward," he says, turning his head towards me. His eyes meet mine and there isn't a hint of malice in them. "My name's Paul by the way. That story was about me when I was sixteen. A man named Jasper took me in."

"Good for you," I mutter, turning away from him.

"So that didn't work, huh? Well how about this? I can offer you the same thing he did for me, or I can stay here with you all night and make sure you don't freeze to death."

"I don't need your help," I tell him, wishing he would just go away.

"Bullshit! You need someone's help and trust me, I'm a lot better than some of the people you're gonna meet out here. When's the last time you ate?"

I sigh, trying to remember. I stole an apple the other day. Was that three or four days ago?

"I'd guess it's been at least a few days if not longer," he says, as if reading my mind. "Look, let me at least feed you."

My stomach rumbles at the mention of food. I am so hungry, but I can't trust this guy. For all I know, he could be a serial killer.

"Here," he says, pulling a pistol from the back of his pants. He drops the magazine and shows me the bullets inside before closing it and racking a load. "You hold onto this," he says, passing the gun to me. "I'll take you to my place, let you clean up a little and get something to eat. If you want, you can sleep on my couch for the night. If I try anything, you can shoot me. Deal?"

Did he just tell me I can shoot him? "Are you serious?"

"Dead serious. Look, you're a young, pretty girl sleeping in the park. There are some people out here that would love to get their hands on you. I don't want that to happen to you, so yes, I'm serious. Let me help you, even if it's just for tonight."

His eyes bore into mine, and my gut is telling me I can trust him. Slowly, I nod my head. He smiles at me and then stands, reaching his hand out to me. Reluctantly, I place my hand in his and he lifts me off the ground. He bends over to pick up my bag and tosses it over his shoulder. "You might want to stick that in your pocket for now. Don't want anybody throwing you in jail for holding me at gunpoint," he nods at the pistol I have pointed straight at him.

Quickly, I shove the gun into my coat pocket and follow him as he walks me towards his place.

Chapter 2

Hawk grins as soon as he sees me walk through the front door of the club, no doubt seeing dollar signs. "You got good news for me?" he asks as I take the vacant seat across from him.

"When do I ever have bad news?" Yeah, I'm a cocky bastard but I have every right to be. If it wasn't for me, this entire operation would have shut down a long time ago.

"I'm waiting," he says, leaning back in his chair, a smug look on his face.

Reaching into my jacket pocket, I pull out a wad of cash, slamming it onto the table in front of him. "Fifty G's. Not bad for a week's worth of work." I can't help but smirk. No way in hell was he expecting this kind of turnaround. "I've got a couple leads on potential buyers. Gonna be meeting with them tomorrow and that will be doubled."

"Is that all?" he asks, raising his brow at me.

"Actually, I've got a present for you." As if on cue, the door opens and Chuck leads the three girls inside.

"Well, well, well..." he says, eying the girls as they approach. "What have we got here?"

"You want me to take them to the room?" Chuck asks, stopping a few feet from the table.

"Except for Nina," I instruct him, smiling over at the blonde girl. Chuck walks away with the others, leaving Nina standing alone. "Nina, sweetheart, this is Hawk, the man I was telling you about."

Her face instantly relaxes, no doubt remembering the story I handed her. I have many that I tell the girls, and not once have they let me down. Maybe I should have thought about becoming an actor instead of settling on a career as a human trafficker and drug dealer.

"Paul said you could help me," she says, looking frightened.

"I sure can, darlin' and I will. Why don't you head into my office? Third door on the left. Make yourself comfortable and when Paul and I are done here, we'll talk," he says, the smile on his face kind. Damn, he's good. Not as good as me, but a close second. She nods her head, looking at me one last time with gratitude before she walks down the hallway.

When we hear the door shut, Hawk leans forward in his chair. "You've been busy."

"Always," I chuckle. I pride myself in bringing in at least five girls a month, and with the addition of these three, I may just break my all-time record this time.

"What can you tell me?"

"Nina, the blonde, she's a runaway. Thinks mommy and daddy are unfair. Need to get her shipped out as soon as possible." She would have made one hell of an addition to the club, but not at sixteen and definitely not with her parents actively searching for her.

"Virgin?"

"No," I say, shaking my head. "Gives one hell of a blowjob for her age and I a natural submissive. Should be able to get a good ten to fifteen grand for her."

"Liking the sound of that. What about the other two?"

"Cheryl's the redhead. Junkie by trade. Will do anything for a quick fix. Thinking we could put her on the south side. Got a gaping pussy and ass from selling herself already, so won't be much of an adjustment."

He nods his head in agreement.

"Tami I found outside the shelter with her six year old. Desperate for money and a roof over her head. Husband beat the shit out of her and the kid. Think she'd be suited to work in the north. Put her up in an apartment and give her enough supply to get her going. She's got a natural ability to draw 'em in so she can dump the shit at higher than retail. Isn't opposed to putting out either. She's not a great lay, but pussy is pussy." Sometimes I luck out, like with Nina. Cheryl and Tami will bring in cash in the long run, but we won't be seeing an immediate return.

"Sounds good. Put it in motion," he says as he counts out three grand, passing it to me. "You'll get your cut off the other two when they start delivering. In the meantime, what about the other girl? You said she'd bring in a few grand a week."

"Alana's gonna make this club," I tell him with confidence. She's not only gorgeous, with her raven colored hair and bright blue eyes, she's got a porn star body: tiny waist, big tits and the tightest ass I've ever seen.

"That's what you keep telling me, but so far she's costing me money, not making me any. Is there a reason I have yet to see this girl?"

I let out a ragged breath, unsure how I should explain this situation. Normally I am not affected by any woman, no matter how fuckin' hot she is, but Alana is different. She's damaged in a way I can relate to. She hasn't told me her entire story yet, but she's opening up to me, beginning to trust me, but I know enough without her uttering a word.

"Alana's different than the other girls. She's gonna take a little more work." *That's an understatement.* We've been living under the same roof for nearly three months and I have yet to get lucky. In fact, she refuses to sleep in the same bed as me, opting to slumber on the ragged couch in that shitty ass apartment instead. I've never spent more than two nights in that place before meeting her, and now I find myself calling the place home.

"You losing your touch?" he asks, raising his brow.

"Fuck you," I mutter, but deep down I am wondering. I've never had to wait to test out the merchandise before, so this is a first for me. The problem is that it doesn't bother me like I thought it would. Alana's... different. I don't know how else to explain it.

"I'll give you a week to get her in here or we're dumping her for what we can get. Ain't no pussy worth this much bullshit."

A deadline? I've never been given a time frame to complete any task, so this is all new to me, but I am confident in my abilities. I'll just need to up my game a little. "Alright," I say as I rise from the chair. "I can have her onstage in a week, but the backrooms will have to wait."

"I won't wait forever. If she can't handle it, we'll find someone who can," he calls out as I head for the door.

Chapter 3

Alana

"Hey," I mutter as I step inside our tiny apartment, my eyes landing on Paul as he stands at the kitchen counter, his back to me. "What's wrong?" I ask when he turns, a worried expression on his face.

He says nothing, passing me the slip of paper in his hand. I take it from his grasp, unfolding the sheet and staring down at it - an eviction notice.

"What are we gonna do?" I ask, looking up at him with pleading eyes. This is all my fault. If I hadn't moved in with him, this wouldn't be happening. He's taken on too much and now he's paying the price.

It's not like I haven't been trying. My days are spent pounding the pavement looking for any kind of work, but so far I've come up empty handed. No one is hiring, at least they aren't hiring me, but what did I expect? I've never even had a job.

"We'll figure it out," he says, but the look in his eyes tells me we are screwed. Opening the cabinet door, he pulls out a bottle of liquor and two glasses. He nods towards the table in the corner, prompting me to join him. He fills both glasses to the rim, passing one to me. "I take it no luck today?"

"No," I whisper, before taking a sip of the amber colored liquid. "Gah! What is this?"

"Bourbon," he chuckles. "Don't tell me you've never drank before."

I shake my head. "I wasn't allowed to go out much," I admit. The truth is that other than school, I was pretty much a prisoner in the Martin's home.

"Your dad must've been strict," he says, downing half his glass.

"My father died when I was six," I whisper, trying to fight back the surge of emotion that swells within me.

"Shit Lana, I'm sorry," he says, taking a seat at the rackety kitchen table.

"It's OK," I reassure him as I take a seat across from him. Losing my father wasn't a bad thing. He was a mean man who treated my mother like shit.

"I hate this," he begins, his eyes boring into mine. "We've lived together for three months and I barely know you. Then I say shit like that..."

"Paul, don't worry about. It's not like it just happened yesterday." Yet I can still picture everything as if it did. "But you're right. We don't know a lot about each other."

"How about a little drinking game then? To get our minds off our problems. We can get a buzz and learn about each other. I tell you something about myself and you drink. You tell me something, and I'll drink. Sound good?"

I'm hesitant about revealing much of my past but reluctantly agree. I can always bow out if I get uncomfortable. "Sure," I nod. "You go first."

"Alright. Let's see..." he pauses for a moment, looking deep in thought. "I don't know where to begin. How about you ask me something, to get the ball rolling. Nothing's off limits."

"OK," my mind is reeling. I don't want to ask anything too personal for fear that he will return the favor. "Who was your first love?"

"Aw man, you had to go there," he chuckles. "I've never been in love, Alana. Love causes pain and heartache, something I prefer to steer clear of."

"So you've never had a girlfriend?" I ask in disbelief. Paul is a good looking guy. I take that back, he's drop dead gorgeous. Standing six-three, he's the epitome of hot. Dark blonde hair with piercing blue eyes, he's quite the catch. Match that with his rock hard physique and boyish smile, and he's downright perfect.

"No, I never saw the need."

"So you're a..." I can't even form the words, I am so shell shocked. "You've never...?"

"I've had sex, Lana. Many times actually, but no girlfriends. In all honesty, you're the first friend I've ever had, aside from Jasper."

"The guy who took you in?" I ask, remembering the night Paul approached me in the park. Jasper had been to him what he is to me, a protector, saving me from certain doom.

"Yeah," he says, smiling. "He taught me a lot in the short time we knew each other."

"Wait, I thought he was still around."

"No, he died a few months after taking me in. Like I told you, I ran away from a bad situation. My father and mother... let's just say that their idea of parental love was different than most."

"They abused you." The words escape my lips without me even thinking.

"Neglect in the beginning. I was completely ignored for the first ten years of my life. Then I became their punching bag. That lasted about three years. I didn't think things could get any worse, but then I realized how wrong I was." He stares off into space, his eyes glazing over as he relives a moment in his past. "It hurt so damn bad," he whispers. "I remember looking over at my mother and pleading with her to help me, but she just laughed and told me to take it like a big boy."

A knot forms in my throat as he speaks.

"I tried to ignore the pain, pretend it wasn't happening, but I couldn't. The next time, he tied me down so I couldn't fight him. Before long, she started joining in. It took nearly three years for me to plot my escape, and I never looked back. I lived on the streets until Jasper took me in and that's when I learned life's not fair. My parent's prepared me for it without even knowing."

I feel tears welling in my eyes, and it takes everything I have to hold them back. What are the chances that Paul was the one to find me in that park, a kindred spirit, who had gone through an almost identical childhood? Fate had brought us together for a reason, perhaps so we could heal one another.

"I think that's worth a drink or two," Paul says, nodding towards my glass. I lift it to my lips, taking two huge gulps before placing the glass back on the able. "So how about you? Who was your first love?"

My mind wanders to Jax, wondering what has become of him. No matter how hard I try to forget about him, I can't. He left a hole in my heart that can never be replaced.

"Jackson Cade," I admit, my mind drifting back to the day we first met. Being in foster care was hard, but having no friends was even harder. "He and I were placed in the same group home. He showed up a few months after I did. He was angry at the world and wanted to be left alone, but I wouldn't have any part of it. There was something about him that drew me in. It didn't take long for him to warm up to me and we became the best of friends."

"That doesn't sound bad at all. You two keep in touch?" His question isn't out of malice, but it kills me just the same.

"No," I begin, thinking back to everything we went through together and remembering the day he just up and left. "He left me," I whisper, the hurt of his abandonment resurfacing.

"Hey," Paul whispers, lifting my chin with his fingers. "I'll never leave you."

"Don't say that," I say, turning my head to the side. "Nothing lasts forever."

"Except you and me," he whispers, and just like that he gains my trust. There is sincerity in his words, and for the first time in a long time, I believe that I have found the one person who will always be a part of my life and never let me down.

Chapter 4

"You weren't kidding were you?" Hawk says, taking the seat beside me. The Lap Room is filled to capacity, thanks to the snow storm that shut down the nearby airport. "That girl of yours is a looker."

He isn't telling me anything I don't already know. Alana has it all – looks, personality and compassion, three things that rarely go together. I almost feel guilty for tricking her into doing this, but my ass was on the line. If I don't deliver, I will lose everything, including the protection Hawk has given me over the years.

"So how'd you do it?"

"Eviction notice," I say, cringing. As luck would have it, Alana wasn't able to find a job in town, partly because I had hit almost every place of business and made a few threats. I couldn't take the chance that someone would hire her. If that happened, all of this would have been for nothing. We need her in the club and I have a feeling she'll bring in the crowds without partaking in the events that take place in the back rooms.

"Good call," he says, slapping me on the back. "Bet she's an animal in the sack. That innocent look is always deceiving. Behind closed doors, they become an insatiable beast."

"I wouldn't know," I grumble, feeling my cock begin to harden at just the thought of burying it deep inside her wetness.

"Yep, you're definitely losing your touch," he chuckles, obviously more amused than I am. "At least you have plenty of pussy at your disposal," he adds, looking around the room. Although his statement is true, the thought doesn't appeal to me. There is only one place I want to bury my cock and that is between Alana's thighs.

"I can help you out with that," Ginger says from behind me. "It's been a long time since you made me scream out your name." She takes a seat in the empty chair between Hawk and I, her eyes glued to me.

I shake my head, uninterested. Ginger and I have hooked up on more than one occasion, and I've never been disappointed. She's beautiful with her dark red hair and porcelain skin, but it is those full lips of hers that have always intrigued me. There's a reason Hawk refers to her as a vacuum.

"How's Paul's new girl coming along?" Hawk asks, interrupting my thoughts.

"I think she's ready, or at least as ready as she'll ever get," Ginger explains. "Gave her a couple Xanax to try and relax her though. Thought she was gonna have a panic attack when I told her this was a fully nude club.

Biting the inside of my cheek, I fist my hands at my side. It took a lot of convincing to get Alana here, so I can only imagine what was going through her mind when she realized how far she would need to go. "Is she alright?"

Ginger and Hawk both turn to me, their faces contorted in disbelief. "Are you worried about her?" Ginger ask, her voice lace with sarcasm.

"Hell no," I say, rolling my eyes. "I'm just worried she might chicken out." That's partially true. If she bails, I'm totally fucked. My agreement with Hawk is set in stone. He keeps my secrets and provides me a living and in return I make him money, no matter what it takes. I like Alana, more than I should, but I come first.

"Well don't worry," Ginger says. "That fake eviction notice you gave her was all the motivation she needed. I've got to hand it to you, you're good. Glad we're on the same side."

"I think I better go check on her, just to see for myself," I say, quickly excusing myself from the table.

I make my way backstage, coming to a stop outside the dressing room door. *Why do I feel so damn guilty?* The answer is simple. If things had been different neither of us would be in this situation today.

Letting out a rushed breath, I knock on the door. "Come in," I hear her sweet voice call out from the other side, making me smile.

I peer inside to see her seated in front of the small mirror, applying her makeup. "I wanted to see how you were doing," I say as I step inside, closing the door behind me.

She looks up at me, causing my breath to catch. Alana is a naturally gorgeous woman, but nothing prepared me for seeing her this way. "You're so beautiful, princess," I whisper.

Instead of beaming at me like most girls do, she flinches, lowering her head in shame. "Please don't call me that," she says in a hushed tone, her voice wavering.

"Hey," I crouch in front of her, lifting her gaze to meet my own. "What did I say?"

She shakes her head, internally battling an unforeseen demon from her past. When she finally speaks, I can hear the torture in her tone. "He used to call me that."

"You have to stop letting him win. He's gone. He'll never be able to hurt you again," I tell her, wishing it were true. The things he did to her will remain with her the rest of her life. "It's time for you to take control of your life and stop letting him win."

"I know," she begins. "But this feels so wrong." I swallow hard, trying to come up with something to say that will convince her otherwise. "How did you do it?"

No one knows the full extent of my past, including Hawk. I have told stories to girls, to lure them in, depicting my past to be similar to their own. I have a gift, as some would call it, the ability to read people. I can hone in on their weakness, use it to my advantage so that I can gain their trust, and then manipulate them in a way that is beneficial to me. That wasn't the case with Alana.

Our pasts are mirror images. The abuse she suffered was real, not unlike my own. Maybe that is why I cannot walk away from her, why guilt has an unbreakable hold on me.

I push aside those feelings, concentrating on the here and now. "I refused to let them control me any longer. I threw aside the pain, burying it any way I could so that I could survive. I became the master of my own world, making them my pawns." I pause for a moment, trying to crawl inside her mind. "They abused my body and made me ashamed of what had happened. I believed I was everything they claimed me to be. Worthless. Good for nothing. That is what they wanted, for me to be theirs alone, to never realize pleasure and joy. Now I am in control."

She says nothing, absorbing every word I have said, but she is not convinced. "So by doing this, I should feel liberated?"

"No, but it will come in time. Think of this as a hurdle. Your foster dad wanted you to be ashamed of your body because he wanted it for himself. By you taking this first giant step, you are defying him, taking charge. I'll be with you every step you take and I promise, I won't let you fall."

Her eyes fill with tears and I know I've won. "You've already done so much for me..."

"Don't," I say, pressing a finger to her luscious lips. "We are in this together."

She nods her head, giving me a shy smile. "I'm starting to feel better," she admits.

As I stand, flashing her a genuine smile, I feel relieved. "That's what I'm here for." I turn to head for the door, breathing a little easier than before as I reach for the handle and exit the room.

Stepping into the hallway, I lean against the door, hating myself for what I have just done.

Chapter 5

Alana

One Year Later

Staring at my reflection, I decide to apply a little more concealer under my eyes. Makeup does wonders, but the bags under my eyes are still quite noticeable. Rubbing in the thick paste, I watch as the discoloration quickly disappears. After applying a little powder and downing a few pills, I am ready to go.

Pushing my way through the dressing room door, I head to the stage with only a few moments to spare. I adjust my leather halter one last time before I hear Kyle start my intro.

Taking the stage, I move my body in time to the music. I start off slowly and seductively, wrapping my leg around the pole in time to the music. I don't waste much time playing the games the new girls do. I've been doing this for a while now, and the men in this audience aren't here to be teased. They want a show and that's what I give them every fuckin' time. That's also why I'm the one walking out of here with more money in my pocket than the rest of them every single night.

I slowly unzip my halter until my breasts are free, tossing the scrap of clothing to the side. Groping them roughly, I snake my tongue out, flicking each nipple into rigid peaks. Turning around slowly, I bend over, giving the men a glimpse of my ass cheeks before standing upright and removing my skirt completely. Now that I have their undivided attention, it's time to have a little fun.

Wearing only my bright red thong, I wrap my legs around the pole, working it hard until I know every man in the room is good and ready. When I final peel off my G-string, I toss it directly at the blonde man sitting closest to the stage, the one I have had my eyes on all night. He's a big spender and the one who's going to pay my rent that's due tomorrow, if I can pull this off.

Some of the other girls won't go to the extremes I do to make a few extra bucks, but they don't have as much at stake as I do. A few of the girls are stripping their way through college. A few are just needing extra money. A couple of the girls are foolish enough to believe this is the way they will meet some rich bachelor who will fall instantly in love with them. I don't live in a fantasy world. This is how I survive.

Crawling across the stage on all fours, I make my way closer, teasing him. His eyes are locked on me and I know I have him exactly where I want him. Pulling myself up so that I'm kneeling in front of him, I rub my hands all over my body until my fingers reach the apex between my thighs. Biting my lower lip, I wink at him before dipping my finger into my sex and then bringing it to my lips and sucking it into my mouth. I watch his eyes dilate and know he's mine.

Standing up, I turn around, gyrating my hips knowing he is imagining what it would be like if I was impaled on his cock doing the same thing. If he is willing to fork over a few hundred, he can find out. I just need to reel him in. Bending over, I spread my legs, giving him an unobstructed view of my freshly waxed pussy before standing again and peeking over my shoulder.

As the song comes to a close, I end my act by giving him something to think about as I drop to my knees once more and lay back, my legs gaped wide. Spreading my lips with my left hand, I use my right to show him where his dick can be if the price is right.

I wink at him one more time before exiting the stage, praying my antics worked. Hawk stands at the base of the stairs, rolling his eyes at me as I come to stand in front of him. "That was one hell of a show," he says, his eyes locked on my tits.

"Hopefully, it'll pay off," I tell him as I walk towards the dressing room.

Having just changed into a black lace bra and matching thong, I hear Hawk calling to me from the other side of the door. Peeking his head inside, he tells me exactly what I want to hear. "Hook, line and sinker," he winks at me, letting me know my plan worked.

"Which room?"

"Number one, same as always," he smiles.

I nod at him and then turn my attention back to my reflection in the mirror. Just a quick touch up and I will be ready for action.

There is nothing I hate more than looking at my reflection in the mirror and seeing the person I have become. Never had I planned on this life, but you have to play the hand you're dealt. With my history, you wouldn't think I would go to such levels to make ends meet and if things had been different, I wouldn't be.

Paul has taught me a lot in the time we've known each other. Gone is the naive girl I once had been. I am now in control of my actions.

When I first overheard Hawk and Paul talking about the private rooms, I hadn't given it much thought. It wasn't until I saw the kind of money that some of the girls were walking out with that I decided to question what went on behind closed doors.

Sometimes it's simple - a one on one private dance. Other times, the men wanted a little something extra. Consensual sex was a foreign concept to me and I wasn't sure I could go through with it, but I wasn't given much of an option. It was do this or be without a home. Paul and I were doing whatever was necessary to make ends meet.

Paul has reverted back to his old lifestyle so that we can survive, selling his body, drugs, whatever he has to do to make sure we keep a roof over our heads. I wasn't willing to let him be the only one to make sacrifices. He had already done enough for me.

Sex is nothing but mechanics unless there's emotion behind it. Easy for someone like me. I can let men fulfill their sick needs with the use of my body.

There is never any pain involved, at least not on the outside. Inside, it tears me apart every single time I allow a man to touch me. Just the thought sickens me, something I have learned to push aside a little too easily. They get pleasure, and I get cash. A simple exchange that no one could possibly understand if they haven't walked in my shoes.

I take one last look at myself in the mirror before darting out the door towards the private rooms in the back, hoping the man I pegged earlier will be the big spender I need him to be.

Stepping inside the room, I see him seated in the chair positioned in the center. "Hey baby," I say, sashaying inside. "You wanted a private dance?"

He eyes me as I run my hands down my body. "Uh huh," he mutters.

Glancing down, I see the bulge in his pants and take that as my cue. "Looks like you might be up for something more than just a lap dance, sweetie." I bite my lower lip hoping he is going to come through for me.

"I'm up for anything you're willing to give, sweetheart."

"Is that so?" I ask, stepping closer to him. I reach out, letting my fingertip touch his chest before trailing down to his covered hardened cock. "What did you have in mind?"

"Um... what are my options?" He reaches out to touch me. Instinctively, I grab his hand and lift his finger to my mouth, sucking it slowly and seductively into my mouth, twirling my tongue around the digit before releasing it.

"Blow job is seventy-five." I move his hand slowly down to my breasts, allowing him to feel their firmness through the barrier that conceals them. "Touching is an additional fifty." Moving his hands down slowly, I let his fingertips graze the fabric covering my pussy. "I'll fuck you hard for two hundred, and…" I move in closer, bringing his hand around to my rear, "anal will be another hundred fifty. All of the above and more for five hundred."

I release his hand and step back, hoping my instincts are right and he has that kind of cash on him. I've gotten good at reading men, and don't think I'm off my game. His eyes are hooded and I know he wants me, but everything depends on what he has in that wallet of his.

He doesn't hesitate as he reaches around and pulls out his wallet, gripping five one hundred dollar bills in his hand, he passes them to me. "Deal," he says, rising from his chair.

Pushing open the apartment door, I'm surprised to see Paul seated on the worn green sofa in our tiny living room. "Long night?" he asks, as I plop down beside him.

"Yeah, but I made the rent," I say, pulling the cash out of my pocket.

"Well at least that's one thing off our minds," he says, gripping the cash in his hand. "Electricity is getting cut off tomorrow," he adds.

"Fuck," I mutter, sagging my shoulders. If it isn't one thing, it's another. We can't seem to get ahead no matter how hard we try.

"Good news is I got an extension for the car payment, so we've got an extra three days on that."

That doesn't make me feel any better, and I can't see us getting out of this mess anytime soon. "It's something at least."

"We'll get through this, Alana. I've been putting in applications everywhere during the day. Someone's bound to call soon. In the meantime, we'll do what we always do."

Which means he'll continue dealing and both of us will whore ourselves out just so we have a warm place to sleep and food in our stomachs. Neither of us is happy about it, but at least we have each other to lean on. I can't imagine doing this on my own.

It isn't like we are living in the lap of luxury. We live in a rat hole of an apartment, barely six hundred square feet. Every piece of furniture is second hand at best. Our diet consists of ramen noodles and on occasion we splurge and get a package of hotdogs. The only thing decent we own is the 2000 Ford Focus we financed through one of those buy here pay here places. The payments are killing us, but we need a vehicle, even if the car is on its last leg. With close to two hundred thousand miles on it, we are lucky if we can get it to start. Yeah, we are living the high life.

"We always do," I tell him, forcing a smile. I know he can see the pain in my eyes, but it's been present for as long as I can remember.

"You up to a little three way action tonight?" he asks hesitantly.

No, I'm not, but I will never tell him that. This is code word for bill money and I know he wouldn't ask if there was another option. Luckily it doesn't happen too often.

A desperate man or woman wanting to fulfill a fantasy is usually willing to pay big dollars to make their dream a reality. They can always head to downtown Langley and pick up a few hookers that would suit the bill, but the people we deal with have a little more self-esteem. Paul is a good looking guy with a great body.

Being a stripper I have to stay trim as well, and I know I'm far from ugly. With a lot of makeup and the right outfit, I am exactly what they want. Put us together and it is a dream threesome, and a high dollar one.

"Sure. What's the game plan?" I listen intently for a few minutes while I get the details before I start to tune him out, wondering how I got myself in this predicament. The answer is simple. I can list every single monumental moment in my life in vivid detail, which is what brought me here to this moment. Closing my eyes, I relive each of those events that have scarred me for life.

Watching my drunken dad pull out his revolver and point it at my mother. Her begging him not to pull the trigger, but he wouldn't listen, accusing her of being with another man. Me screaming at the top of my lungs as he pulled the trigger, her blood showering me as she collapsed on the kitchen floor. Sobbing over her body, looking up at my father in disbelief as he put the barrel of the gun in his mouth. The loud boom that echoed through the empty house as he ended his own life.

The group home I was sent to, the same place I met Jackson Cade. He had become my best friend the same day of his arrival. We were inseparable, moving from home to home together as if we were brother and sister.

Arriving at the Martin's home, believing Jax and I were finally getting a family. The first time Phil laid his hands on me. The first time I watched him beat Jax unmercifully. And the deal I made with Phil to protect Jax, followed by every single time the man degraded me.

Jax leaving me. I had never been given an explanation other than he ran away. I just knew he was there one day and gone the next. I had expected him to call or write - something, but instead he had just forgotten I even existed. It devastated me more than anyone could ever know. That was the moment I realized you can't depend on anyone but yourself.

The night the two men entered our house and brutally murdered Janet and Phil. The time I spent in jail. Being released and living on the street. Finding Paul and learning to trust someone again.

And now I am living day to day, just trying to survive but I am no better off than I was before except now I have someone I can depend on. Someone who will never let me down like Jax did.

"We need to go meet him soon," Paul says, bringing me back to the present. He looks down at me with a concerned look. "Or we can just stay here." He knows the effect this has on me, even though I try my best to conceal it.

"No," I say, pushing my thoughts aside, becoming the shell of a person I am. Forcing another smile, I stand on my tiptoes and kiss him gently on the lips. "Let me go clean up real quick and I'll be ready."

He nods before I turn and head towards the bedroom. As soon as the door closes behind me, I break down. As I strip the clothes from my body, I sob uncontrollably. I am nothing but the whore Phil had always called me, only now, it is true. If I had more courage, I would have ended my life a long time ago but I am a coward. Too afraid to end this misery I call life.

I grab the brown bottle off the worn dresser and down a few pills quickly, hoping to calm myself. I am using more and more just to cope and it isn't helping our financial situation any, but I can't do it without them.

Making my way into the bathroom, I shred my clothes, tossing them aside. Standing in front of the mirror, I avoid my reflection as I begin to quickly wash away the remnants of the man from earlier just to go out and do it all over again.

Swallowing hard, I take in my reflection in the mirror. "You are nothing. You will never be anything but the whore you are, so suck it up and get over it," I say to the image looking back at me.

Drying the tears from my eyes, I quickly touch up my makeup and head for the door, leaving Alana Jacobs behind. She is dead and has been for a long time.

Chapter 6

Staring out into the yard, I watch in amusement as Tiny approaches Deuce. Fucker has a lot of balls thinking he can take on a man like Deuce. He may be slightly smaller than Tiny, but he is twice as fuckin' strong and there's no doubt who's gonna win. Plus, I always have Deuce's back and everyone in this place knows it. Fuck with Deuce, and you have me in your face and vice versa.

They exchange a few words, making no hostile movements to alert the guards. Neither of them is willing to take a chance out here. Too many witnesses, but it will eventually go down and my money is on Deuce. He's taken down every fucker that has gotten a wild hair up their ass and thought they could take him on. Fools, every last one of them.

Tiny walks away, glaring at Deuce over his shoulder as he crosses the yard. Shaking his head, Deuce makes his way over to me.

"What's up?" he asks as if nothing just happened before taking a seat beside me.

"Just thinking," I mutter, looking at the ground. Only Deuce knows the real me, the person I truly am on the inside. I am practiced at putting on a front, one that everyone is fearful of. No one knows that behind this killer's eyes is a man that is filled with pain and regret.

"We're outta this joint in a few months," he reminds me. Lucky for me, Deuce has been with me every step of the way. He has been my partner in crime from day one.

"Yeah," I say, not looking forward to our release as much as I should.

"The club's throwing us one hell of a party when we get out," he reminds me. Booze and lots of pussy. Every fuckin' man's dream but it isn't enough.

"Can't wait," I tell him, although my tone says otherwise.

He looks over at me, shaking his head, before rising to his feet. "You gotta quit beatin' yourself up. We ended it and she's safe now. She's probably living the high life while we're sittin' here countin' the days till we're outta this joint." He walks off, leaving me alone with my thoughts.

He is right. Alana is probably living out her dreams, far away from this place. She has probably long forgotten about me. That's good, at least for her. She deserves happiness more than anyone I know.

"Lana?" I call out as I walk into the kitchen. It isn't like Alana to miss school, even when she is deathly ill. She is the only person I know that has, or at least had before today, perfect attendance. Worried about her, I decided to skip out on my last two classes of the day, needing to make sure she is alright. What started as mere friendship between us has developed into more, although I will never let her know that. She sees me as a brother and best friend, and if that is all I can get from her, I'll take it.

I make my way up the stairs, pausing outside her bedroom door. I can hear her inside, sobbing. My first instinct is to leave her alone. I've never been good dealing with tears, especially where Alana is concerned. I start to walk towards my room when I hear her trembling voice.

"Please..." she begs.

"I love to hear you beg, princess. Makes me so fuckin' hard." I freeze at the sound of Phil's voice. "Bend over or you know what will happen."

"You promised!" she cries out.

"And you made promises too. Or are you going back on our little agreement?" His voice is cold, unlike anything I've heard from him in a very long time.

"No!" she sobs. "Just don't hurt Jackson!"

He laughs, the sound echoing through the hallway. "I won't touch the little bastard. Bend over and spread your legs."

My life changed at that very moment. The hatred I had felt for Phil multiplied exponentially in an instant. How could I have been so naive to think the abuse we both had suffered had just stopped? In my young mind, I honestly thought he had received therapy or some shit. Instead, he had focused on Alana alone, abusing her in the most unthinkable of ways. I knew I had to get us both out of that place, I just didn't know how. Running away wasn't an option because he had always stopped us or found us. So I chose my only option. Going to the counselor at school seemed like a good idea, but my plan backfired. I quickly learned who I was dealing with. Phil Martin's pull in town was indescribable. Not only did they ignore my cry for help, they yanked me away from Alana, labeling me as nothing more than a troublemaker.

When I was placed in the Wilke's Group Home, I met Danny, or Deuce as he likes to be called. He was different from the other kids, having never been beaten, mistreated, or abandoned. He was there for an entirely different reason. Both his parents were locked up and with no immediate family, he was placed into foster care. It was only temporary, he had told me.

I listened to him for hours telling me about his dad's club. The Forgotten Souls MC were notorious and stories of them spread across town on a regular basis, but none of them were as he described. He spoke of loyalty and brotherhood, something I had never experienced.

I had been at Wilke's a week when I broke down and told Deuce my story. When I described what I had overheard Alana going through, he had been enraged. "*People like that don't change,*" he had told me. I knew he was right, but what could I do? I had tried to get help, and look where it had gotten me.

"*Sometimes, you have to take matters into your own hands.*" *His gaze was cold and heartless.* "*There's only one way to stop a monster like that.*"

I swallow hard at his words. He doesn't have to tell me what he means. I hate Phil Martin more than any one person in my life, but I'm not a murderer. Could I go through with killing someone in cold blood?

"If he's doing the things you say, it's only gonna get worse. You can end this. You have to," he says, his eyes locked with mine. "We will end this."

I nod my head, but am still reluctant. To be honest, the idea scares the hell out of me. All it takes is one simple question from Deuce to settle it. "You love her, don't you?"

I'd been in love with Alana Jacobs since I first laid eyes on her. She means everything to me. "I do," I admit.

That day, we formed an unbreakable bond. We became brothers in every sense of the word and there was no turning back. I looked to him for guidance, knowing what had to be done but unable to go through with it alone.

The trek to the Martin's house takes us close to an hour. It is warm outside and I am sweating profusely, but it's not because of the weather. My nerves have gotten the best of me.

I stare up at the two story house that looks like the perfect home in the dim moonlight. This could've been paradise for Alana and I, but instead had become a living nightmare, more so for her than me. Tonight, that all comes to an end. She will be free and she will heal in time, never knowing I had anything to do with what is about to occur. I, on the other hand, will live with this for the rest of my life.

The faint light from the lamp in the living room is the only illumination coming from inside the structure. It is well past midnight and I expect everyone is asleep.

"You still wanna go through with this?" Deuce whispers. I nod my head, not trusting my voice. "Alright. Best point of entry?" he asks.

I motion towards the back of the house as I step forward, taking lead, stopping only when I reach the back steps. Reaching down, I lift the pot containing an array of flowers and pull the spare key out. Slowly, I climb the steps, vaguely aware that Deuce is inches behind me.

Silently, I unlock the back door and step inside the kitchen, the pungent aroma of tonight's dinner still wafting in the air. Pot roast, I think to myself, before brushing the thought aside. Deuce closes the door behind him and comes to stand beside me.

"Well?" he whispers, urging me to lead the way. I am frozen in this one spot, unable to move. Fear grips me for what I am about to do. "If you're having second thoughts, we can bail."

I vehemently shake my head. No. Walking away won't change anything for Alana. Taking a deep breath, I take a step forward, freezing at the sound of Alana's whimpers. I turn towards the basement door, gazing down at the faint light coming from underneath.

"Take it you fuckin' whore!" Phil's voice carries into the kitchen, sounding as though he is in the room with us.

I jump back as the basement door opens and Janet steps through the threshold, her eyes landing on me in shock. Before I can react, Deuce steps forward, clamping his hand over her mouth. "Make a fuckin' sound and I'll slit your fucking throat!" he says as he presses his blade against her neck.

Her eyes are wide with fear as she nods. Janet Martin is just as evil as her husband. She stood by watching her husband beat Alana and me unmercifully, and now she is allowing this to happen. She is as much to blame as he is. Fear is no excuse for what she has done, or what she has refused to do.

Anger takes hold. Pulling out my knife, I lunge towards her, pushing Deuce aside. "At one time, I felt sorry for you," I whisper as I press the serrated blade against the tender flesh of her throat. "I thought you were his victim too, but you are just self-absorbed, only looking out for number one. You stood by and watched him beat me until I was unconscious, never making a move. And now this? Do you get your thrills watching your husband rape her over and over?"

She opens her mouth to speak, but I don't want to hear her excuses. Slowly, I drag my blade across her flesh, the warmth of her blood coating my fingers as the life begins to drain from her. Stepping forward, I throw her towards the stairs, inwardly laughing as I release her and watch her tumble down the steps in slow motion. She lands with a thud at the base as I slowly make my descent, pulling the ski mask down over my face.

"What the fuck!" Phil roars, walking over to her crumpled body laying lifeless on the ground. He is completely naked as he kneels down and touches the blood still draining from the wound to her neck.

"Go," Deuce whispers from behind, pushing me forward.

Racing down the stairs, I come to a stop when I am face to face with him. His eyes land on me and he immediately rises to his feet, arms raised in the air. "What do you want?" he asks, his voice wavering.

Looking past him, I spot Alana blindfolded, gagged and restrained on a wooden table seated in the center of the room. The tears *staining her face only fuel my anger for this man. I want to run to her, hold her in my arms and tell her everything will be alright, but I can't. I am frozen in place, taking in the image of her brutalized form, something that will forever be burned in my mind.*

Her wrists are cuffed, attached to eye bolts drilled into the head of the table. Her blood streaked legs are spread wide, affixed to chains that limit her movement. She is trembling with fear, not knowing that I am here to free her. She will never again suffer at the hands of this man or anyone else.

I refuse to answer him, the reason for our presence apparent. He backs away as I step forward, fueled by hatred. With my blade extended, I lunge for him, driving the knife into his gut. He screams out in pain as I twist, my eyes never leaving his. I want him to suffer just as she has.

Deuce steps forward as I withdraw the blade, my eyes lowering to my blood stained hands. When I am able to raise them again, I watch as Deuce drives his knife into Phil over and over again in a rage I have never witnessed before.

It wasn't until later that I found out that Deuce's sister had been brutally raped, tortured, and killed by her boyfriend. Deuce's father, Ace, had been put in prison for putting a bullet between the boy's eyes when the justice system had failed. His mother, charged with being an accomplice, suffered the same fate. Deuce was more than familiar with brutality and because he was unable to exact revenge on his sister's behalf, he took the next logical step by ending the life of a man who had done the same thing to someone I loved.

We knew we had to leave, but first I had to free Alana. I can still feel her trembling in my arms as I pulled her to me. She was so traumatized that she did not even notice my blood stained hands as I held her close, never revealing who I was. When Deuce and I fled the scene, we felt certain the cops would look at it as a case of self-defense, but it didn't work out that way.

When I saw the news report of Alana's arrest, I lost it. She was being charged with their murder. Luckily, Deuce got in touch with Brent Douglas, the club's attorney and told him the facts. What he told Deuce was simple. Unless we stepped forward, admitting that we were the only ones involved, nothing could be done.

Deuce and I went to the detectives and confessed immediately, Brent by our side. Somehow, Brent managed to get us one hell of a plea bargain. We pled guilty to involuntary manslaughter and were sentenced to the maximum - five years.

Just a few months away from freedom, life has new meaning. I will be leaving this place and taking my rightful place as a member of The Forgotten Souls. I won't officially be patched in until I am outside these four walls, but I have already proven myself worthy of the colors. Unknown to outsiders, The Forgotten Souls aren't a group of outlaw bikers, they are brothers, all of whom have suffered some kind of torment in their lives. Together, they have formed a family and I have been accepted into their fold.

In less than ninety days, I will begin my new life but my past will forever haunt me.

Chapter 7

Alana

Taps is my least favorite place to visit. Being the closest bar to both the airport and the main highway, it is always filled with people from out of town, which is exactly why we are here. Flights are almost always delayed, if not canceled, this time of the year. It is a frigid twelve degrees outside this evening, the recent ice storm cancelling all ingoing and outgoing flights at least until morning.

Businessmen are the easiest of prey. Travelling does something to them, turning them into sex fiends. Maybe it's the fact of being trapped on a small aircraft for hours, or being away from their loved ones. In any case, they are always up for something adventurous and willing to pay top dollar for it.

If we pull this off as we have done so many times in the past, our bills will be covered for the remainder of the month. If not, we will be out a hundred and fifty bucks, the cost of the hotel room I have booked for the night. Sometimes you have to spend money to make money, but in this case, if we don't find a buyer, we are screwed.

When I step inside Taps, my eyes land on Paul immediately. He is talking to a man seated beside him, oblivious to my arrival. We've played this game so many times before and this time will be no different. His job is to find someone that is safe and willing to spend top dollar. Mine is to lure them in for the kill.

Our story changes only slightly each time, but the premise is always the same. A travelling couple, stranded in this remote town until the weather clears up, just like our prey.

I make my way over to them slowly, pulling my long coat around me tightly. "There you are," I purr as I come up behind Paul.

"Tom, this is my girlfriend Alana," he says motioning to me.

The guy looks over at me, trying to figure out if what Paul has told him about me is true. Before I make a move to reveal the goods, I need to know this is a go. "Hi," I say, biting my lower lip and extending my hand to him.

"Nice to meet you, Alana. Paul was just telling me you would be stopping by," he says, eyeing me up and down.

Paul and I used fake names in the past, but quickly learned that there is no need. The chances of us ever meeting any of these people again is slim, so we decided to forego the aliases.

I glance over at the abandoned booth in the back corner, seeing it as the perfect stage to begin our little performance. "I'll let you two finish talking and wait for you over there," I motion towards the table.

"Alright, babe. We'll be over in a minute," he says, cuing me that tonight is a go if I can seal the deal.

I slowly make my way across the room, coming to a stop at the table before untying my coat and peeling it off to reveal the ridiculous outfit I am wearing underneath. There is hardly any fabric to the dress, only strips of material that barely cover my bits and pieces. As I go to toss my coat on the nearby empty chair, conveniently dropping it to the floor. My dress is so short, I know that he is getting an eyeful as I slowly bend over and pick up the coat, laying it gently on the chair before taking my seat in the booth.

Moments later, Paul comes to sit beside me, Tom taking the seat across from us. "Here's your drink, babe," he says, sliding the glass in front of me. Sex on the Beach always seems to set the mood.

"Thanks," I say, placing the straw in my mouth. As I slowly suck the liquid into my mouth, my eyes lock on Tom.

"Paul and I were just talking about you," Tom says, his gaze lowering to my barely covered breasts.

"Oh yeah?" I ask, raising my brow. "All good things I hope."

"Most definitely," he murmurs.

"Tom was telling me how his flight was delayed just like ours."

"I'm so sorry," I say, batting my eyelashes at him. "It sucks being stuck in a small town like this."

"Don't be. It happens a lot this time of year." His eyes are full of hunger and need.

"I'm gonna hit the head and make a phone call," Paul says, rising from the booth. He looks at me over his shoulder, winking, before leaving me alone with Tom.

"How long is your flight delayed?" I ask, not really interested because I already know the answer. All flights are delayed until at least nine in the morning, when the temperatures warm up.

"Until ten," he replies. "How about you?"

"Same here," I smile. "We managed to find a hotel close by, so at least we'll have a warm bed for the evening." All the nearby hotels are completely sold out and chances are that since he is here, he hasn't gotten one.

"Lucky you. I called every place in the area and there are no vacancies."

"Luck is my middle name," I purr. "So, tell me about yourself Tom. Are you travelling for business or pleasure?"

"Business, actually. I'm heading home from a sales convention in St. Louis."

"Oh, that sounds interesting," I say, biting my lower lip. I don't know why this simple gesture has an effect on men like him, but it always does.

"Not really, but it's part of the job," he shrugs.

"Being away from your family must be tough," I add. It doesn't matter if he has a family or not, but it usually gives me some insight into what is missing in his life. "Your wife doesn't travel with you?"

"No. She's too busy living it up with her friends to be bothered with what I'm doing," he grumbles. Bingo. A wife at home that isn't fulfilling his needs. He doesn't need to say the words for me to know that is the case.

"That must be hard." We sit in awkward silence for a few moments, his eyes ravishing me. "Paul takes me everywhere with him. I think he's just worried about what I'll do when he's not around."

"Why is that?" he asks, his interest piqued.

"I don't know. I think he just doesn't want to miss any of the action."

His eyes dilate and I know Paul has filled him in, in graphic detail more than likely. "He mentioned that you like a little... diversity. He isn't bothered by that?"

Hook, line and sinker. "Not at all, as long as he gets to join in. I don't mind. There's nothing hotter than having two men ravishing my body and each other." He swallows hard, trying to maintain his composure. "Of course, not everyone is up for something like that."

"You mean a threesome?" he whispers.

Shrugging, I lean forward. "It can be very exhilarating. Imagine having two people worshiping your body. Taking you to new levels." I lean back against the booth, closing my eyes. I lift my hand to my collarbone before slowly trailing it down to my breast, dragging the remnant of fabric down so that my hardened nipple is exposed for only a moment before I continue downward, under the table. "Just thinking about it makes me wet," I whisper, opening my eyes and affixing them to his.

"It sounds unbelievable," he manages to choke out.

Taking that as my cue, I slide out from the booth and come to sit beside him. "Believe me, there's nothing like it," I say as I reach out and let my fingertips trail along the outline of his engorged cock straining against his dress pants. "Some people are too afraid to live out a fantasy. I believe you only live once," I whisper, bringing my lips mere inches away from his.

His gaze lowers, looking over at my scantily dressed figure and watching as my fingertips lightly graze over my exposed thighs. "You can definitely only live once," he murmurs, repeating my words.

"Am I interrupting?" Paul asks, arriving at the booth right on time.

"Not at all," I smile up at him. "Tom and I were just getting to know each other."

"That's good baby," he says, taking the seat I recently abandoned across from us. He begins talking to Tom, acting oblivious to the conversation he knows we just had. I suck down my drink as my hand rubs against Tom's raging hard on. "You want another?" Paul asks, when I set the empty glass on the table.

Shaking my head, I tell him, "No, I'm gonna hit the little girl's room." I rise from my seat and take the few steps necessary to lean over and plunge my tongue into Paul's mouth.

His tongue collides with my own, filled with passion and lust, while his hand trails between my legs. I moan loudly when his finger penetrates me with ease. He pulls back, gazing up at me with a hunger in his eyes, plunging his wet finger into his mouth. "Hurry back."

I walk towards the restroom slowly and deliberately, putting forth a little more effort in my movements. When the door closes behind me, I walk to the mirror and stare at the person looking back at me. *Filthy whore*, my mind screams as I fight the urge to shout back that this isn't what I want, but the words are meaningless. My wants are irrelevant.

I turn away, unable to look any longer, my reflection sickening me. Leaning against the wall, I stare at the tiles on the wall and begin counting them out loud, as I wait for the inevitable. When I reach a hundred, I push myself towards the door, leaving behind my conscious to focus on getting through the remainder of this night.

Hovering over Paul's swollen cock, I slowly slide myself down onto his rigidness, moaning as he fills me. His hands snake around from behind, tugging at my hardened nipples as I slowly begin to reverse ride him. Tom is perched on his knees, stroking his length as I rise up again, agonizingly slow, before slamming down onto Paul's length, burying him deep inside my pussy. With hunger in his eyes, Tom lowers his head, his tongue snaking out and flicking my clit.

Grabbing his hair, I pull him towards my nub. "Make me come," I moan, needing my release. With his flattened tongue, he begins frantically licking me but it's not enough. Rising slowly off of Paul's cock, I move back until my pussy is only inches away from Paul's awaiting tongue. As he sucks my clit into his mouth, Tom begins to lift his head but I won't allow him.

Gripping his hair tightly, I force him down until he is face to face with Paul's massive cock, urging him to take it in his mouth. "Suck him," I groan. His heated gaze meets mine before he parts his lips and lowers his head onto Paul's enormous cock, taking him as deep as he can into his mouth. Paul moans against my clit, as Tom begins sucking him hard, his head bouncing up and down on his cock that is soaked with my juices.

Paul releases his hold on my clit, his tongue diving into my core, eating me in a frenzy. I feel the tension between my legs rising, but I need more and as if on cue, Paul moves back even further until his tongue is circling my ass. I cry out as he dips his tongue inside, his fingers plunging into my wet pussy. I feel my orgasm approach at the same time Paul tenses and I know we are finding our release together.

I scream out as my body trembles, watching Tom swallow Paul's load, his gaze locked with mine as I come hard. I am panting hard as I crawl off of the bed. Dropping to my knees at the foot, I reach out and grab Toms' cock, taking him fully into my mouth. His eyes flutter, rolling into the back of his head as I deep throat him.

Paul watches from the head of the bed, his cock coming to life again as I fuck Tom hard with my mouth, taking him deeper than he thought possible. My left hand reaches out, gripping his ass cheeks tightly and spreading them slightly. I allow my right hand to gently graze his nuts as my finger trails towards his virgin ass. Slowly, I circle his hole, his moans telling me he's enjoying what I am doing to him.

Effortlessly, I slide a finger inside, letting him adjust to the feel of having a foreign object there as I slowly release him from my mouth. Slowly, I pull my finger out, plunging it inside again over and over, stretching him slightly. He doesn't protest, so I add another one slowly, stopping when I feel him tense.

Looking up at him, I bite my lower lip as I withdraw my fingers. He needs a little more coaxing, but we have all night. Rising to my feet, I crawl onto the bed, my ass high in the air. I can feel his eyes on me as I lower my mouth onto Paul's length. He arches his hips, causing me to take him deeper, moaning loudly as my finger penetrates his hole.

Paul has been on both the giving and receiving end of anal and knows there can be immense pleasure in the act. Not done correctly there is only pain, but in the right hands there is nothing but satisfaction.

I begin fingering him as I go down on him, his moans echoing in the room. When I pull back, I see Tom watching us, his gaze even more heated than before. "Watch," I moan as I rise to all fours, giving him an unobstructed view of my ass. Rising onto his knees, Paul dips his fingers into my drenched pussy before bringing them to my tight bud.

He starts slowly, one finger entering me with ease. He works it in and out, agonizingly slowly before adding a second. I match his movements, rocking back and forth as his fingers impale my ass, my own fingers feverishly working my clit. "You want inside her ass?" Paul asks.

Peering over my shoulder, I watch Tom step forward, his cock in his hand. Paul reaches over and grabs a condom from the nightstand, passing it over to Tom who quickly rips open the package with his teeth and slides the rubber over his rigidness.

I scoot back, inviting him in and he doesn't hesitate plunging inside my pussy first before lining his drenched cock with my ass. Paul reaches over and grips his cock firmly, guiding him inside slowly until he is fully seated deep inside. He doesn't move for several minutes, but then begins to pull out before pushing back in again.

My fingers feverishly working my clit, Tom plows into me, over and over again, groaning loudly as I take every inch of him. His pace slows and I peer over my shoulder to see Paul standing behind him, rolling a condom over his length while his fingers begin working Tom preparing him for what is to come. As Paul pushes his own cock into Tom's ass, he plunges into me hard, groaning loudly as Paul seats himself deep inside of him.

I awake the next morning, aching from the previous night's activities. Sitting up, I see Paul seated at the table in the corner, staring at the wall.

"Hey," I grumble, tossing the covers from my naked body. I need a shower more than anything and then a pot of hot coffee, but there is something I need to take care of first. "You OK?"

"No," he murmurs, his eyes still affixed to the wall. "I don't want to keep living this way."

"It won't always be this way," I tell him as I walk towards him. "You've said so yourself. We're just in a rut."

"A never ending one." Paul looks up at me, his eyes filled with shame and regret. "You deserve so much more."

We both do, but he never sees it that way. His concern is always for me and it breaks my heart. We are a team and have been for years now. He's told me more than once that I should leave, move on to bigger and better things. It seems easy enough, but that's not what friends do. They stick by each other, through thick and thin. I know all too well what it is like to have someone you trust implicitly walk away from you, and I will never do that to Paul. I will stand by him until he gets tired of me.

It is bound to happen. Everyone I have ever cared for eventually leaves and Paul will be no different. He needs me now, but one day that will change and he will walk away, never looking back.

"I'm not going anywhere," I tell him, my voice strong and firm.

"What would I do without you?" he asks, pulling me to him.

I hold onto him tightly because he is all I have in this world, the only person who cares about me and my existence. I depend on him more than he will ever know and I don't know how I will survive when he does decide to leave.

Pulling back, I smile down at him. "We will get through this, together."

He nods his head, releasing his hold on me. I stand, gazing down at the man that has become more than just a friend, he has become my reason for existence. Call it a weakness, but knowing he needs me just as much as I need him forces me not to give up. I will continue doing as I always have, becoming his protector and saving him from himself and the outside world.

Chapter 8

JAX

One Year Later

"Where you goin' baby?" Trix asks as I toss the covers aside and rise from the bed.

"Takin' a piss. Be gone by the time I get back," I call over my shoulder as I head to the bathroom. I hear her huff as I shut the bathroom door. Laughing to myself, I wonder why she isn't used to this by now. Trix is nothing but a whore and will never be anything but. She had hopes of becoming someone's old lady but no one will have her. It takes someone special to be an old lady, especially for one of The Forgotten Souls, not just gapping your legs for each and every brother in the club. She never understood that and there's no turning back now.

After relieving myself, I walk back into the bedroom to see Trix gone. She's probably already getting fucked by one of the other brothers knowing her. At least I always use protection unlike some of the guys. No way am I putting my cock in jeopardy by fuckin' that cesspool of a pussy.

Grabbing the pair of jeans I tossed on the floor earlier, I pull them on before reaching into the dresser and pulling out a shirt. I had plans on calling it an early evening, but now I am wound up and ready for some more action.

I descend the stairs quickly, stopping when I enter the main room. The party is still underway and my chances of going another round seem pretty good. Walking over to the bar, I motion for the prospect to grab me a beer.

"Watch the teeth!" Red snarls. I turn to see Monique perched between his thighs, going down hard on the old man. It still baffles me how a twenty something attractive young girl could do anything with Red. In his early fifties, he is a nasty old man who believes hygiene is unnecessary. "You want some of this?"

I turn to him, seeing he is talking to me. "Don't think so, old man," I chuckle.

"Suit yourself. She may have a canyon for a pussy, but her mouth is all hoover," he chuckles. Monique lifts her head, glaring at him. "I didn't tell you to stop!" he barks.

Shaking my head I walk off just as Monique begins taking him in her mouth again. Scanning the room, I look for any sign of Deuce. "He's in his office," Blaze calls out to me, before burying his face in Lexi's cunt.

Curling my lip in disgust, I make my way to the back of the club, stopping when I reach the wooden door of Deuce's office. I still chuckle when I see the bright shiny President sign he has affixed to the door. Getting the title wasn't good enough, he has to announce it to anyone that would stop and listen. Just in case you haven't heard, he wants to make sure you see it. From the sign on his office to the patch on his cut, there is no mistaking who he is.

It was a sheer honor for the brothers to vote him in. With his father locked away for life, the club was in need of another leader, and everyone was in agreement that Deuce was the clear choice.

I tap on the door twice before I hear him call out for me to enter. When I step inside, I shake my head. I'm not even sure who the fuck he has laying completely naked on his desk, but she is oblivious to my appearance, too busy enjoying having Deuce finger her wildly. "Meet Bunny," he says, reaching down and pinching her nipple roughly.

"I'm goin' on tomorrow's run," I tell him, rather than asking. Deuce may be President, but being his newly appointed VP has certain advantages. That and the fact that we are best friends.

"Show me what you're gonna do to my cock," he mutters as he removes his fingers from Bunny's cunt, shoving them into her mouth. "You sure you want to go back to that place?"

Langley holds a lot of bad memories, but that is all in the past. I've gotten over it, or at least I'm trying. There is nothing left for me there anymore. Besides, I don't trust Blaze and Nix to close this deal on their own. Hawk is notorious for driving a hard bargain and we need someone with enough balls to stand up to the fucker. He needs us, and it is my job to convince him of it.

"I'm good," I tell him. "Anything I need to know?"

"Just that Hawk drives a hard bargain. He's got runners in a hundred mile radius of Langley. He's got plenty of suppliers available, so it's all about purity and price with him. This could mean millions if we get this deal."

The Forgotten Souls may have started under a different premise, but there was a need for funds and drugs were easy money. "I'll convince him."

"Another bargaining chip for ya. He's lookin' to expand. Just so happens we just acquired The Lusty Lady. It's exactly what he's lookin' for."

I nod, knowing this may be what closes this deal. "I'll go over the numbers with you later," I tell him, turning towards the door.

"Where you going?" he asks.

"Letting you get on with your business," I say, turning towards him smirking.

"Last time I checked, this bitch had three holes. Ain't that right?" he grins down at the girl who nods her head excitedly. "You in?" He raises his brow at me.

The girl rises to her knees on the desk, pointing her ass right towards me inviting me in. My dick twitches inside my jeans at the mere thought. Shrugging, I stalk towards them, catching the condom Deuce tosses in midair. She climbs off the desk and bends over, spreading her legs.

Rolling it onto my length, I waste no time before lining it up with her wet entrance. She moans as I slowly enter her, rotating her hips as I plunge the rest of the way inside. I pump her a few times before pulling out.

"Climb on," Deuce says, lying flat on the desktop. She doesn't hesitate, crawling on top of him. Straddling him, she slowly lowers herself onto his rigid cock. Gripping her hips tightly, Deuce holds her in position so I can line myself up with her opening. I enter her slowly, closing my eyes as I push myself into her fully. She cries out as I seat myself deep inside her ass.

All gentleness ends at this moment as I pull out and plow back into her over and over again, Deuce matching my movements. She is like all the others, taking everything we give her without complaint.

When I feel my orgasm approaching, I pick up speed, slamming into her before groaning as my release takes hold.

I pull out of her just as Deuce tenses, and I know he's had his fill of her too. My eyes are glued to her gaping ass as he slams into her one final time, wondering if this is all my life will ever be. I'm not complaining. I have the club and all the pussy I want, but it somehow isn't enough. I need a challenge, or at the very least something that makes me feel again.

Peeling the condom off my cock, I toss it in the trash before shoving my softening cock back into my jeans and raising the zipper. Things could be worse, I think to myself.

I leave the room without a word, heading upstairs to my room. One day I'll feel again, I just don't know how long I'll have to wait.

"So what's your bottom line?" I ask, my eyes locked with Hawk.

Instead of going in with the premise of being his supplier, I made the decision to approach him as a buyer. That way I know what I am up against and can make him a deal he'd be stupid to refuse.

"Twenty per kilo." His gaze doesn't falter, thinking he's offering me an unbeatable deal. Twenty thousand definitely includes markup, but knowing where he is getting his supply, his cut isn't as high as others.

Shaking my head, I rise to my feet. "I can pick it up for ten," I say, turning to leave. Blaze comes to stand beside me, following my lead on this one.

"Wait!" Hawk calls after me. "If you can get it for that price, what are you doing here?"

"We're always looking for better options," I call over my shoulder. The fact is that we can pick up a kilo for four g's straight from our distributor in Colombia, and turn around and sell it for ten. A six thousand dollar profit is no joking matter, especially when your distributors order a minimum of ten kilos at a time. Multiply that by hundreds of drug lords throughout the country, and The Forgotten Souls are rolling in the dough but we are always up to make more.

"Maybe we can still do business together," he says, and I know I've got him right where I want him.

"What kind of business?" I ask, turning around.

"I've got mules. Lots of 'em. Perhaps you'd be willing to partner with me."

"The Forgotten Souls aren't looking for partners," I say, biting back a smile. "But, we are always interested in opportunities." I make my way back over to him, Blaze on my heels, and take a seat. "What are you offering?"

"Langley is a small town, but business here is booming. Just in my club alone, I net over six grand a week. Each of my mules brings in an easy ten to fifteen, more when product is good. More pure, more sales."

"What quantity are we talking about if we did cut a deal?"

He shrugs. "Fifteen kilos a week easy, just in powder. You add some herb, smack or pills into the mix, I can guarantee you one hell of a profit margin. You'll be making the bucks and so will I."

Easy as fuckin' pie, I think to myself biting back a grin. We continue talking numbers and by the time we are ready to shake on it, he is eating out of my hand. "What if we expand your market? What are we looking at then?"

"Expand? I'm already peddling in a hundred mile radius of my home base."

"What if we had an additional base to offer? Could you handle that?" The strip club we recently picked up could provide him with an entirely new area and an all-new client basis. If anyone can pull it off, he can.

"I'm listening," he leans back in his chair, looking at me intently.

"It just so happens that we recently acquired a strip club back home. Nice place, newly renovated."

He nods his head, raising his brow. "I see where you're going with this." He leans forward, tapping his finger to his top lip. "I think we can work something out. How much are we talking?"

"For you, one-twenty. We'll even allow you to make payments." Considering The Lusty Lady didn't cost us a dime, this is just easy money.

"Deal. I've got a guy who runs for me. Bouncer at the club part time. He might be willing to relocate and run it for me."

"Can he be trusted?"

Again, he nods. "Never had an issue with him. Get more sales from him than anyone else."

"Good." He sounds like just the person we need to run the club. "Like I said, club's already set up. Just needs a new name and staff. Plenty of girls in the area looking for work, so dancers won't be an issue."

"I'll talk to him tonight, but if he agrees he won't be coming alone."

I'm not keen on bringing too many outsiders into the operation. "No can do."

"She doesn't run or use, his girl. She's been headlining at the club. Brings in a lot of business."

"Alright," I tell him as I rise to my feet. I have no problem having a new piece of ass in town. "We'll be in town until tomorrow. Let me know if we can move forward."

"I'll be in touch," he calls after me as we head to the door. I feel confident that all will go according to plan and that we will be doing business in the near future.

Chapter 9

Alana

Stepping off stage, a feeling of dread washes over me. I'm surprised I was been able to concentrate at all as I watched Paul and Hawk in a seemingly heated conversation. I have a bad feeling and need to find out why.

I rush towards the dressing room and quickly throw on a pair of jeans and a sweater before heading towards the front. As I round the corner, I see Paul smiling broadly at Hawk, shaking his hand.

Slowly, I make my way over to them, wondering what I am missing. When Paul sees me approach, his smile broadens. "We'll go over the details some more tomorrow," Hawk tells him before walking past me, nodding as he goes.

"What was that all about?" I ask, trying not to smile. Seeing Paul this happy is contagious and I want to share in his good news.

"You ready to head out?" he asks, not revealing anything.

"Sure," I say, looking at him speculatively. Something has happened and whatever it is, he is ecstatic about it.

Taking my hand in his, he leads me from the club and out onto the street. We walk in silence until we reach the apartment. Opening the door, he ushers me inside, still not letting on as to what is going on but I'm finding myself excited just the same.

Taking a seat on the couch beside him, I look over at him expectantly. "Well? Are you gonna spill the beans or keep me in the dark?"

"What would you say if I told you that our troubles are over?"

"I'd tell you you're full of shit. Seriously, what's going on?" I press.

"Hawk is looking at expanding his business. He's opening a new club in Cedar Falls and wants me to run the place." My heart sinks at his words. If what he's saying is true, then that means he is leaving Langley. Leaving me.

Taking a deep breath, I force myself not to cry. "That's great news," I tell him, plastering a smile on my face. "How soon is he planning on opening it?"

"Everything is in place already. He just needs a manager and staff. Hawk said the club just closed and it's still in good shape." He is beaming, excited at the prospect of not only having a job, but running a club on his own.

I know I can't hide my emotion for long, so I do the most logical thing, burying my head in his chest. "I'm so happy for you," I say, meaning every word, but at the same time hating the fact that I am losing him.

"This is the opportunity we've been waiting for, Lana. Hawk offered me a hefty salary to run the place, plus I'll still get commission on everything I sell. There'll be no more worrying about paying the bills, no more ramen noodles, and best of all, no more private rooms." I lift my head, looking up at him with confusion. "You didn't think I'd leave you behind, did you?" he asks, smiling at me.

"I thought..." I don't finish my sentence because I know what he'll say if I do. "You want me to go with you?"

He laughs, pulling me close to him. "Not only do I want you to come with me, that would've been the deal breaker and Hawk knows it." My heart swells at his words. "You don't give yourself enough credit. I would be just as lost without you as you would be without me. Like you said, we're a team."

He presses his lips to the top of my head as tears stream down my face. My fears were for nothing. He's not leaving me.

"Hawk wants you to headline at the new club. That's completely up to you. We'll probably need your income for a while until the club takes off, but when things kick in, you can find something else or go to school. Hell, you can stay home and sleep all day if you want, just as long as you go with me. Will you?"

I raise my tear filled eyes to meet his, so many emotions rushing through me. Nodding my head, I answer him. "Yes."

His lips crash onto mine as he pulls me astride him. As his hands reach for the hem of my sweater and his warm fingertips grip my hips, his tongue pushes at the seam of my lips, begging for entrance. Slowly, his tongue enters my mouth, tasting me with such gentleness before passion takes hold and he begins devouring me.

He rises to his feet, holding onto me tightly as I wrap my legs around his waist. His lips still on mine, he walks us to the bedroom and only then does he break our kiss. Lowering me to my feet, he pulls the sweater over my head and tosses it to the floor before gripping my jeans and tugging them off.

Reaching around, I unclasp my bra, letting it fall gently to the floor. Tossing me to the bed, he pulls my thong down and buries his face between my legs, his tongue working me into a frenzy quickly. Paul takes oral sex to a new level, capable of bringing me to multiple orgasms even before penetrating me.

I moan loudly as he sucks my hardened nub into his mouth and bites down on it gently. "Make me come hard," I plead with him, raising my hips. He obliges, manipulating my clit just the right way that sends me spiraling. I scream out his name as my orgasm takes hold, gripping his hair and pulling him tighter to me.

Three Weeks Later

"Well, what do you think?" I look around the empty strip club, taking everything in. The furniture looks a little outdated but this *is* a strip club. Overall it's a nice place, better than I had expected. The shiny black floor onstage has me mesmerized, the metallic flecks catching my eye.

I look over at Paul and smile. "It's better than I thought it would be," I admit. I was expecting the place to be in shambles but in fact it looks relatively new and I can't help but wonder why it closed.

"We open for business in exactly one week," he says, his voice filled with excitement. "Can you believe this? One week and I'll be running this place."

Shaking my head, I roll my eyes at him but can't help but smile. This is definitely better than The Lap Room by far. I'm not sure if the clientele will be any better, but at least the atmosphere is. "Please tell me he's not keeping the name," I say, remembering the god awful sign out front. Who names a fuckin' strip club The Lusty Lady?

"The name goes," he chuckles. "The new sign is supposed to be delivered tomorrow. Body Shots."

I nod my head. That isn't too bad, I think to myself.

I spend the next hour familiarizing myself with the layout of the place. The dressing room in back is ten times larger than the one in Langley. There are mirrors lining the far wall in the room, surrounded by bright light bulbs. It reminds me of something you'd see on a set in Hollywood instead of a strip club. It took me months to get Hawk to splurge on one of those tiny vanity mirrors for my old dressing room that looked more like a broom closet in comparison.

The bar is horseshoe shaped and sits at the back of the club, in line with the stage. There are so many stage lights, it reminds me of something you'd see at a concert. Even the restrooms are huge. The booths within the club are all high backs and circular, reminding me of images I've seen in magazines of Vegas shows. But it is the stage that has me convinced moving here was a good choice. This is where I will spend the majority of my time while within these four walls.

Not only is the floor polished to a high shine, the pole is sturdy. No more worrying about the pole collapsing on me in mid act. Obviously, this place wasn't just thrown together. The amount of room on stage is absurd. There is enough room for three or four dancers at once.

"Enjoying yourself?" a voice calls from behind me.

Turning around, my eyes land on one of the most gorgeous men I've ever laid eyes on. He's tall, maybe six three, and has a beautiful shade of sandy blonde hair that is a little long, but suits him. His arms are complete sleeves of tattoos and rock solid. He looks like he's spent his entire life working out and it has definitely paid off. My eyes land on his leather clad chest, even though covered, it is obviously well developed and I can imagine the six pack he has hidden underneath the fabric. But it is his eyes that draw me in. Crystal blue, reminding me of pictures of the oceans in Bermuda.

"I was just checking the place out," I say, tearing my eyes from him.

"You wantin' to be one of the new girl's?" he asks, checking me out. Thinking I was going to be doing nothing but cleaning today, I had chosen a pair of my old shorts and a ratty tank top to wear. I look like a bum, especially with my hair thrown on top of my head.

"New girl?" I ask in confusion.

"You here to apply? If so, I think you're a little overdressed."

"Deuce?" I turn at the familiar sound of Paul's voice. "Didn't expect to see you so soon," he says, approaching the stage.

"Thought I'd drop by and see what you thought of the place. Didn't know you were already doing auditions. I'd be happy to give you my professional opinion."

Paul throws his head back with laughter. "We do have a few lined up today. I see you met my girl."

I smile over at them briefly before rushing from the stage, happy to get out of the way. I don't want to hear about business or anything else for that matter. Making my way to the bar, I see a hallway off to the left and head down it.

Even though I have no plans on partaking in the activities that take place in the private rooms, I still want to see them for the hell of it. I push open the first door and shake my head in disbelief. There is a pole mounted in the left corner of the room, a red leather chair perched in the center. A counter lines the back wall, a very nice iPod station centered on it. *Wow, this place is definitely higher class than what I am used to.*

I make my way down the hall, checking out each of the rooms one by one. Each are laid out similarly, complete with poles and iPod stations in each, but it is when I reach the last room on the left that my jaw drops. The room is three times larger than the others. It contains the same fixtures as the others with a few additions. On the farthest wall is an open shower. Brightly polished brass fixtures come out of the wall and the showerhead is centered in the ceiling above, surrounded by lights.

The leather chair in the center of the room swivels, so the client can turn to whatever position he deems necessary. And it reclines fully, another added bonus. But it is the heart shaped bed to the right that sets this room apart. Mirrors line the ceiling over it, and the purpose of this room is obvious I can only imagine how much a client would have to pay for use of this one.

"Nice, isn't it?" I startle at the sound of Paul's voice behind me.

"Yeah," I breathe, turning around.

"You and I could have a lot of fun in this room," he says, wrapping his arms around me. "That shower, I can think of lots of ways to make you scream my name in there."

"Is that so?" I ask, smirking at him. "And all this time I thought you liked me for my mind."

"There are many things I like about you, Lana. Your mind, your sense of humor and your smart mouth. But what I can't get enough of is that body. The way you work that pussy on my cock. The way you take every inch of me into that luscious mouth, sucking the come right out of me. The way you work your clit when I'm buried deep in that ass. Those are the things dreams are made of, what I love about you. And you're all mine, every fuckin' inch of you."

I step back, looking up at him with a perplexed look. Paul and I have been more intimate recently, but it was just sex, or at least that's what I had thought. We were fulfilling one another's needs physically, not emotionally.

"Don't look at me that way Lana," he warns. "It's just a word," he says, pulling me to him once again. Taking in a deep breath, I begin to calm. It is just a word, a word that holds no meaning.

"So, is this place kick ass or what?" he asks, pulling away.

"It's definitely not what I'm used to." That's an understatement. As far as strip clubs go, this is top of the line.

"We're both gonna be raking in the money here," he says, looking around the room. "Hawk's coming down for opening night. He thinks this place will bring in at least triple what The Lap Room did."

"No doubt. Have you hired any girls yet?"

"A few, but that's what Deuce is here for. We have several auditions lined up though. You want to stick around and help?" he asks, smirking at me.

"No, I think I'll leave that to the two of you. I'm gonna freshen up real quick and head back to the apartment and get to unpacking." It's not like we have a hell of a lot to unpack, but I want to knock it off my list.

"Alright, baby. I'll see you when I get there," he says, kissing me briefly on the lips before leaving me alone in the room.

As I leave the club, I have a good feeling about this place. Things are starting to look up for us and before long, maybe I can stop doing this and get the old Alana back, that is if there is anything left of her inside me.

Chapter 10

I pull into the parking lot of Body Shots, my eyes locked on the tight ass of the girl that has just exited the front door. *Damn, she's got a hot body*, I think to myself as I climb off my Harley and head towards the entrance.

Stepping inside, the music is blaring and a very flexible redhead is working the pole. "Alright, we've seen enough," Deuce calls out, the music dying instantly.

The redhead bounces off the stage and comes to stand at the table where Deuce sits with who I assume is Paul. Hawk has a lot of confidence in this man and I hope he lives up to it.

"Sorry, but you ain't got what it takes," Deuce tells her.

"Excuse me?" she huffs.

"Look darlin', you got good moves, but this ain't no dance recital. Men are coming in here to get their rocks off while you show off the goods."

"But I…" she stops, looking down at the bikini she is wearing.

"This is a full nude club," Paul tells her. "You can't be modest here. You have to be willing to go to extremes to make the customers happy."

She nods her head in understanding and steps back, reaching around and releasing the neat bow she has tied behind her. She tosses the top to the side and begins untying the strings on her bottoms. When she is fully nude, she looks at both men, turning bright red.

"A little small in the tits, but you got a nice ass," Deuce comments, causing me to shake my head. "What are you thinking, Paul?"

"She might do. We'll give you a trial run. Opening night is Friday. We'll see what the audience thinks and go from there," he tells her. She smiles broadly and thanks them, rushing to pick up the remnants of her clothing off the floor, then heading off towards the restrooms.

"You two look like you're having fun," I say, coming up behind them.

"It's a tough job, but someone's gotta do it," Deuce chuckles. "Saw your girl Trix a few minutes ago."

"She's not my girl," I grumble, taking a seat in the empty chair beside Deuce. "I take it you hired her?"

"Yeah. Trix might be a cunt face and have a gaping pussy, but she can work the pole. Speaking of," he turns to Paul. "Might wanna consider making her your headliner."

"Not gonna happen" Paul says. "My girl is the headliner."

"Just because she's your girl, you can't give her special treatment," I interrupt. "Trix was the headliner at The Lusty Lady, so she knows what it takes." I hate that I am giving so much credit to Trix, but when it comes to stripping, she knows what she's doing.

"You haven't seen my girl's moves yet. Trust me, The Lap Room was always packed when she took the stage."

"Alright, we can give her a shot," Deuce says. "But Friday night will be the test. She can't pull it off, then Trix takes lead."

"No problem," Paul shrugs, confident in his girl.

"Now that that's settled, let's talk other business. Got a shipment coming in tomorrow," I say to Paul. "Need you to do your thing."

"Drop off location?"

"Here. Three o'clock." I tell him, not trusting him enough to let him inside the club, at least not yet. Hawk may be confident about his abilities, but I'm not so easily impressed.

"Alright," he says, standing. "I'll be here. In the meantime, I'll leave you two to this. I've got some shit to take care of." Paul nods at us and heads for the door, leaving Deuce and I alone.

"Well, what do you think?" I ask him. If there is one person I trust in this world, it is him and his ability to read people.

"I don't know yet. There's something I can't put my finger on." Meaning he doesn't trust him. Deuce's instincts are always on the mark and he has never let me down.

"We need to keep an eye on him. You puttin' Beast on him?" I ask.

"Already done. Either he'll prove me wrong or we'll have a new ally."

I nod my head in agreement. If Paul crosses The Forgotten Souls, it will be the last thing he ever does.

"Now his girl on the other hand, she's a fuckin' looker."

"Yeah? You already thinking of tappin' that shit?" I ask, amused. Deuce is always looking to bang some chick, although I'm not much better.

"Not sure yet. She's got this whole innocent thing about her but obviously she's gonna work here. Somethin' doesn't add up."

"What's she look like?" I ask, my curiosity piqued.

"Dark hair, bright blue eyes and a rack that makes me want to bury my face between her tits for weeks. And that ass, man! Tight as fuck and boy do I wanna ride that thing all night long."

"So Paul may be losing his girl?" I ask, throwing my head back in a fit of laughter.

"She ain't really his girl. She's his roommate or some shit. Fucker told me he's getting it from her and on the side. If he plays, you know she does too. Well, I'm done here for the day. Let's lock this place up and head back to the club. I need to lighten my load after all the ass and tits today," he says, standing.

Three Weeks Later

I am not just tired, I am downright exhausted. Closing a deal with Los Lobos took more negotiating than I had thought. Two weeks being cooped up with those fuckers was more than just an adventure. I can still smell fuckin' burritos and enchiladas wafting off me. I need a shower and some fuckin' pussy.

Stepping inside the clubhouse, I spot Deuce banging some chick on one of the pool tables while she sucks Blaze's dick. This is exactly why club whores will never become ol' ladies. No one wants a worn out bitch that will take anyone's cock that's willing to give it to her.

"Was wonderin' when you'd show your face again!" Deuce chuckles, unaffected by the fact that he is slamming into some whore and talking to me. "Did you close?"

"Yeah," I call out to him, reaching across the bar for the bottle of whiskey underneath. I don't bother with a glass, popping the top and taking a swig. With the bottle in my hand, I walk over to where he and Blaze are. "How are things here?"

"Well Trix is pissed for starters," he laughs. "But what else is new?"

"What happened now?" I ask, taking a seat in one of the stools against the wall.

"Paul's girl. He wasn't lying about that bitch," he pauses, groaning loudly as he reaches his climax. He pulls out and motions to Beast who steps into the space Deuce just abandoned, slamming his dick into the whore's ass.

Deuce rolls off the condom and tosses it onto the floor, knowing one of the club whore's will take care of it later. "You've gotta see her, man. I kid you not, she knows her way around a pole."

"Oh yeah?" I ask, intrigued. Deuce rarely gets excited about a piece of pussy, but this girl has him acting like a damn teenage boy.

"She takes fully nude to a whole new level."

"I thought you said she has that innocent look to her?" I ask, perplexed. A person can't be both.

"She does and yet she got up on that stage and had my dick standin' at attention in seconds."

"So she's a whore and an actress. What's the big deal?" I've met plenty of them over the years. Women playing the whole innocent thing and when you get them in the bedroom, their pussy is so worn out it's a wonder you can even get off.

"That's the thing, I don't think it's an act." I almost spit the whiskey from my mouth. "I talked to her, man, before and after her set. She doesn't like being up there. I could see it in her eyes, like doing it fucks with her head or something."

"Then why does she do it?"

He shrugs. "Not sure. Maybe she doesn't have a choice. Overheard Paul talkin' to her. Told her he wasn't makin' the money he was expecting. That's bullshit, man. Fucker scored big the last two weeks and I know for a fact his cut was nearly four grand. Fucker's playin' on her sympathies is my guess."

"Why would he do that?"

"Just goin' with my gut here, but I think he does it to make her stay. Paul gets loose lips when he's drunk. Told me he found her sleeping under a tree in the park a few years back. Took her in and got her into the whole strip club thing because they needed money.

Fucker even told me he had her fuckin' for cash. Pissed me the fuck off."

"So he's usin' her," I say, shrugging. "Why's it botherin' you?"

"Because, I feel like I've met her before. I mean, I know that's impossible, but there's something about her that's... familiar."

"I think you're losin' it in your old age," I laugh, but stop when I see the look on his face.

"I had a sister, remember. I'd kill the fucker if he was pullin' that kind of shit with her. For all we know, this girl's someone's sister." At least now I have an explanation for his behavior.

"Tell you what, let's head on over to the club and see what's what," I offer.

"She's off tonight or my ass wouldn't be here."

"Alright. We'll head over tomorrow then. Deal?"

Deuce slowly nods his head. "Deal."

Chapter 11

"This wasn't part of the deal!" I roar, jumping to my feet.

Hawk remains seated, unaffected by my outburst. He raises his brow, silently challenging me. As I take the seat I had just abandoned, he chuckles, finding amusement in this entire situation. "And what deal was that?" he asks as he reclines back into the chair. "Our deal has nothing to do with your little fuck buddy, except when it comes down to cash. In the week I've been here, you've turned down thousands for your little piece of ass."

"Alana doesn't do private shows anymore," I retort, reminding him of our agreement back home.

"Wrong. Alana got a break and now that break is over. This is about business."

"That's bullshit and you know it!" I argue. "Alana kept the doors open at The Lap Room!"

"That she did and then some, but we aren't in Langley anymore. There's more competition here, four other clubs in the vicinity, one of them upscale. Being the only full nude club has its advantages, but not when every girl isn't willing to go the extra mile, either inside the club or on the side. When was the last time you two teamed up outside the club?"

I don't bother to answer because he already knows. Since moving here a few months ago, things have changed. Alana works the stage and that's it. That in itself has her walking out of here with hundreds a night, even after her cut to the club.

"I have no use for her if she's not earning her keep. There's still a market for her outside the club and several potential buyers willing to pay top dollar for her. I've kept my mouth shut, even let you have a little fun, but that comes to an end tonight."

His words infuriate me, making me want to rip his throat out.

"Deuce has been eying your girl and his pockets run deep. All you have to do is set it up."

"No," I say, shaking my head. I made a promise to Alana, and this one I intend to keep. "There's got to be another way."

"I don't know what kind of magical pussy your little friend has, but she ain't worth losing everything you've worked for. The choice is yours." An ultimatum. He says he's giving me a choice, but there isn't an option here and he knows it. It boils down to Alana or me.

"This is fucked up," I tell him as I rise from the chair, feeling totally defeated.

"She still doesn't know, does she?"

I freeze momentarily before lifting my eyes to meet his. "She knows more about me than anyone."

"But she doesn't know the real Paul, does she? She may know about your past, about what they did to you, but she doesn't have a clue who you really are. If she did, she wouldn't be here and you know it." He leans forward in his chair, resting his chin on his clenched fists. "Whatever feelings you think you have for that girl, they aren't worth losing your life for."

Swallowing hard, I look over at the man who I have respected all these years, all reverence now lost. No matter which path I choose, I will lose. Turning towards the door, I accept defeat.

Alana

I am sitting on the couch with a bowl of popcorn watching television for the first time in so many years when the door opens, Paul walking in looking down in the dumps. "Bad night?" I ask, giving him an encouraging smile.

He nods, taking the seat beside me. "Had a meeting with Hawk. There's gonna be a delay in my getting paid," he says, staring at the television screen. "What are you watching?"

"The news. Why can't he pay you?" Right now, we are living off what I am making, and without Paul's income, we are going to be come up short.

"He got in over his head again. The overhead in both clubs is more than he expected." He reaches over and grabs a handful of popcorn, popping a few pieces in his mouth.

"What about the other?" I normally don't ask about him dealing, not outright anyway. I know what he does and I don't like it, but it has kept a roof over our head and food in our stomachs so I can't argue.

"Business is booming, but Hawk's putting every dime into the club."

Taking in a deep breath, I look away. This place was supposed to be different and here we are, doing the exact same thing we did before. I want to curl into a ball and cry, I'm so damn let down. I've been doing my part, doing something I despise, thinking it was going to be temporary. I should have known it was too good to be true.

"I'm sorry, Lana. I'll find a way to make it up to you." He breaks my heart when he says this to me.

"Don't worry about it," I say, pulling myself together. We've gotten through worse and we will get through this. I stand up, deciding I need to be alone. "I'm gonna go to bed," I tell him.

He grabs my wrist, causing me to turn to face him. "Don't hate me," he says, looking up at me with pleading eyes.

"I could never hate you," I tell him honestly. There is nothing Paul could ever do to make me despise him. Myself, that's another story because I hate who I am, who I have become.

"Let me take your mind off things," he says, rising from the couch. Pulling me to him, his lips meet mine. I want to pull away, tell him I'm not in the mood, but I don't. Instead, I part my lips, inviting his tongue inside where it collides with my own. The self-hate I have for myself swells within me. *I don't want to do this. I don't want to be this.* The words replay in my mind over and over as he lifts me in his arms and carries me to the bedroom.

I grab three Xanax and wash them down with a shot of bourbon, preparing myself for this evening. Not only am I going out there and doing the same thing I have been doing for years now, but I will be doing what I hate most. Pinning some random man in the crowd, reeling him in so he will fork over money just to fuck me, and I will give him that because I have no other choice.

"You OK, hun?" Alexis asks, coming up beside me.

She looks at herself in the mirror, admiring her reflection. She and I are completely different. She seems to crave the attention she gets out there, lives for it. I despise it and the person I am when I am out there. I force a smile, nodding my head at her. She'll never understand what it's like to walk in my shoes, but then again, she doesn't have the past I do.

"You nervous?" She looks at me in bewilderment.

"A bit," I admit, although that's not the entire story.

"The way you are out there, I didn't think it was possible. I have something to take the edge off if you want."

I look over at her, contemplating. I know I should say no, but the xannies are having little effect.

"Yeah, that'd be good," I mutter, knowing I don't go on for another hour. Plenty of time for whatever she gives me to get in my system.

She walks over to her bag and moments later, passes me a capsule. Staring at it for only a second, I toss it in my mouth and wash it down with the last of my bourbon. "Thanks," I say, regretting my decision immediately, but there is no other way I am getting through this night, or any other, knowing what must be done.

"Anytime," Alexis calls over her shoulder as she leaves me alone in the dressing room. Sitting back down at my station, I bury my face in my hands, letting my tears fall freely.

Chapter 12

JAX

It's been a while since I've been inside a place like this, at least to watch a show, which is the only reason I'm here tonight. All this talk about Paul's girl has been bothering me since my conversation with Deuce ended last night. Deuce doesn't get rattled easily but whatever is going on with this girl has gotten to him.

Tonight, I plan on getting answers. If Paul is mistreating this girl like Deuce believes, there will be hell to pay. The Forgotten Souls are capable of a lot of things, but we don't mistreat our women, even the club whores.

Deuce and I take a seat at the reserved table by the stage. Lucky for us, being a Forgotten Soul has its perks, even if it is in a place like this. I'll give Paul credit, the place is better than it ever was. The last time I was in here during normal business hours I had to down almost an entire bottle of whiskey before the broads became remotely attractive. Not now.

Even the cocktail waitresses are catching my eye, so I can't wait to see what's in store for me onstage.

I spot Trix out of the corner of my eyes and inwardly cringe as she makes a beeline over to our table. The last thing I need tonight is to deal with her.

"Hey, baby!" The sound of her voice grates on my nerves, worse than fingernails on a fuckin' chalkboard. "Did you come by to see me in action?" she purrs. "We can spend some time in one of the private rooms afterwards. You know, have a little fun."

"Fuck off, Trix! We ain't here to see your fuckin' ass," Deuce says, motioning for one of the waitresses to head over.

"And I wasn't talkin' to you, *Deuce*. I was talkin' to my man," she sneers.

"I ain't your fuckin' man Trix and never will be!" I've tried being nice and even diplomatic, but she is getting out of hand.

"You know you want me. I bet you can't wait until I take that dick of yours and ride it hard. You'd like that, wouldn't you baby?"

"That's it!" I shout, louder than I intended. "I ain't fuckin' you! Made that mistake before and it ain't happenin' again. I'd rather sink my dick in a pile of fuckin' shit before I'd ever stick it into that rank pussy of yours! Now move the fuck on or tonight will be your last night workin' here. You feel me?"

Her bottom lip begins to quiver, her eyes filling with tears. "I hate you," she mutters before storming off.

"Bout fuckin' time," Deuce mutters before roaring with laughter. "You ain't kiddin' about rank pussy. I can smell her from a mile away. Bet that girl has had every STD known to man."

Shaking my head, I begin to laugh. "And you'd have a better chance of gettin' off if you stuck your dick in the Grand Canyon. I've had some gaping pussies in my life, but hers is the worst. And her ass, don't get me fuckin' started."

Our laughter is thunderous, almost drowning out the music playing in the background. The waitress drops off our drinks, looking at us like we've lost our minds but says nothing. Picking up my whiskey, my eyes wander to the stage, a very attractive blonde wrapping her legs around the pole.

"She's got a nice rack," Deuce comments, lifting the highball filled with scotch to his lips. "Too bad they're fake."

I nod my head in agreement. It isn't very often that you see a woman that is well endowed who doesn't have implants, especially in a place like this. Big tits equals big money. "Speaking of tits, what happened to the redhead?" I ask, thinking about the audition I walked in on a few weeks before.

"She didn't make the cut," he says, shrugging. "But she gives decent head."

Shaking my head, my eyes dart towards the stage when Trix is announced. She comes on stage wearing a naughty nurse's uniform. Within minutes, she has shred every bit of clothing and is working the pole like she does best. I'll admit, watching what she can do on stage gets me fuckin' hard, but there is no way I'm tappin' that shit again.

"How's it going, guys?" Paul asks, standing at the edge of our table.

"Not bad," Deuce says, slamming his glass down. "You're girl going on in a few?"

"Yeah, she's on after Alexis," he says, taking the seat across from us. "Just so you know, all the girls are available tonight."

Deuce's eyes narrow, his brow furrowing. "Even your girl?"

He shrugs. "She'll cost you a little more than the others, but trust me, she's worth it."

"Thought she'd be off limits?" Deuce asks, his eyes flaring.

"Everything has a price, you know that. Trust me, she may cost you more but she's worth every penny. Girl can deep throat better than a pro. And nothing is off limits," he says, raising his brow. "Interested?" he asks, looking straight at Deuce.

"How much?" I ask, seeing the look on Deuce's face. He's pissed and about to come across the table at Paul.

"Two hundred for the room. She'll take you both on for six," he says, his gaze finding mine.

I look over at Deuce, who simply nods, before reaching for my wallet and pulling out eight hundred in cash. "She better be worth it," I add for good measure, tossing the bills towards him.

"Like I said, worth every penny and then some. I'll set you up in the VIP room after her set," he says, rising from the chair and disappearing into the crowd.

"He's pimping her," Deuce seethes. "The fucker is fuckin' pimping her out!"

"Calm it down, brother. Maybe you've got it wrong," I tell him, even though I know it's doubtful. One of two things was happening tonight. Paul is either losing his job or Deuce and I are in for the time of our life.

"Understand you booked a room," Trix says, walking over to me with a smug look on her face. "I knew you couldn't resist."

"Shut up Trix," I mutter, my eyes trained on the stage.

"I know you've got a room, and Deuce is in the john so it's just you and me, Jax. Admit it, you want me. You and I are good together."

"You are the last thing I want, Trix. And yeah I've got a room, but you won't be setting foot inside it."

"Who is it?" she demands, looking at me in disgust. "Melanie? Alexis?"

"She's up next," I tell her, hoping she gets the hint that I'm done with her.

"Alana?!" she shouts. "That fuckin' bitch. First she steals my job and now my man. I'm gonna..."

"What did you just say?" I ask, grabbing her by the arm.

"I said she fuckin' stole my position here and now you," she says, looking down at my hand clamped onto her arm.

"Before that. What did you call her?" I must be hearing things.

"You don't even know what you're paying for?" she jerks her arm free. "Alana's a conniving bitch and she's with Paul so you're playin' with fire. Hope he beats the piss out of you!" She storms off, angrier than I've ever seen.

Alana. That name brings back so many memories, both good and bad. I haven't heard that name in so long yet it has the same effect on me it always has.

"Good, she hasn't gone on yet," Deuce says, taking a seat. "I'm telling you man, I hope you're right and I've got this all wrong cause I really want to sink my dick in that sweetness." I nod my head but mind is elsewhere. "You OK?" he asks, his voice filled with concern.

Shaking it off, I look over at my friend and brother. "Just thinkin'," I admit, not going into any detail. A name shouldn't have this kind of effect on me.

"Well stop thinkin'" he says, motioning towards the stage.

Swallowing hard, I turn to see a gorgeous brunette take the stage, dressed as a naughty schoolgirl. Her hair falls in loose waves past her shoulders, in stark contrast to the white button down shirt that fits snugly across her large tits, stopping abruptly underneath them and tied in a makeshift knot. The red and black plaid skirt is short, accentuating her toned legs and tight ass. My cock hardens at the sight of her and she is still fully clothed. She bites her lip as she comes to the edge of the stage, moving her body in a way that makes my cock harden even more.

She removes her shirt first, tossing it to the floor, revealing a black and red lace bra underneath. My eyes are affixed to her tits as she works the pole, wrapping her leg around it and swinging slowly, revealing the matching thong underneath. When she reaches around and unzips her skirt, I involuntarily hold my breath, waiting impatiently for her to lower it. It drops to the floor and she steps out of it, moving to the beat of the music with ease.

The crowd is going wild around us, men hovering around the stage. She makes her way over, dropping to her knees, crawling the remainder of the distance, her eyes glazed over. It is then that I see her face clearly, in all its beauty. She is not only stunning, she is perfect in every single way. My eyes are locked on her, afraid that she is a hallucination and if I blink she will disappear.

When she rises again, she walks back over to the pole, reaching around and releasing the clasp to her bra, letting it glide off her silky skin. When she turns back to the crowd, her arm covers her tits and slowly, she moves it to the side, revealing one and then the other.

I watch her move with precision across the stage, ridding herself of the last piece of clothing until she is completely nude. I stare in awe as she exposes herself, her waxed pussy glistening under the lights. I have dreamed of seeing her this way for so long and now she is here, right in front of me.

When she finally leaves the stage, her image is still burned into my mind. My cock is straining relentlessly against my jeans, begging to be released.

"What'd I tell you?" Deuce says, sounding distant. "Hey, you still with me?"

"Huh?" I ask, turning my attention to him.

"I told you," he says, smirking. "Still can't get over the fact that she looks familiar. I'd never forget a body like that though."

After a long moment of silence, I finally find the words. "You should recognize her," I manage to choke out.

"I should?" he asks, still grinning at me. "How's that? I promise you bro, if I tapped that, I wouldn't forget, no matter how wasted I was."

"She's the reason we went to prison," I mutter, almost under my breath.

His smile disappears as realization sets in. "You fuckin' with me?"

Shaking my head, I look over at him stoically. "I wouldn't fuck with you about something like this."

Deuce looks over his shoulder at the stage she just abandoned and then back at me. "You're sure?"

I nod. There is no way I will ever forget that face. "Alana," I say her name, merely a breath on my lips.

Alana

I am happy. There is no other word to describe what I am feeling. Life is simply amazing in this moment, and nothing can bring me down. Gone is all the self-hate, the misery and discontent I normally feel, being replaced with pure joy. Everything is intensified and pleasurable. And being on stage was beyond exhilarating. The music became a part of me, coming from within. I know the feeling will not last, but I am enjoying the ride while it's there.

The door to the dressing room slams open, Paul entering, red faced and seething with anger. "What was that?" he demands, coming to stand beside me while I dress.

"What was what?" I ask, feigning ignorance. I knew he would see something was off, but I don't care. For the first time, I went on stage without my heart pounding in my chest. There was no sick feeling in my stomach, no reliving my past, only pure joy and amazement.

"What did you take?" His voice is laced with an anger he has never directed towards me before. It should have an effect on me but it doesn't. He grabs hold of my arm, jerking it sharply so that I am facing him.

"Why does it matter? The point is I feel good," I argue.

"God damn it! What'd I tell you? Who gave it to you?!" he demands, his face inches from my own.

Jerking my arm free, I step back. "Just let it go," I tell him.

"I have two men lined up for a private room and you're telling me to let it go? Why would you do this Lana?"

"Because I can't take it!" I finally say, my high dissipating rapidly. "Because every night I go out on that stage and degrade myself a little more. Because I do things that disgust me. Because I hate the person I am and what I am about to do. Alana Jacobs may have been destroyed a long time ago in a basement back in Langley but this... this is slowly killing what little part of her remains. And I do it, because the need to survive should outweigh my feelings, but it doesn't. Do you know how many times I've wanted to end it all? How many times I've contemplated ending my sorry existence? But I don't because I'm a fuckin' coward!"

I am breathing frantically when I am finished with my rant, the look on his face full of torment. When he finally speaks, his voice wavers, barely a whisper. "Why didn't you tell me?"

"Why did I need to tell you? You've been doing the exact same thing I am. I know you hate it as much as I do, and after everything you have done for me, how was I supposed to tell you what it was doing to me? It shouldn't matter how I feel."

He steps back, his face ashen, saying nothing. Without another word, he storms from the room leaving me alone. I stand there for several moments, trying to fight the tears that threaten to fall.

Twenty minutes later, I am still standing in the same spot, my high completely gone and my heart aching. When Alexis enters the room, I don't even notice until I hear her voice. "Hun?"

"Yeah?" I say, blocking out every emotion that has been rising within me.

"Marty said you have two waiting in room one."

I feel the color drain from my face. Words are meaningless as I am faced with the ultimate decision. Do I go in there, do what I've been doing for years and watch another piece of myself disappear or do I walk away from it all? It would be so easy, or at least that's what I try to convince myself.

The pit in my stomach knows the answer. I will do what I always do and bury every one of my emotions. I nod my head, staring at the shell of a human being gazing back at me in the mirror. "I'll be there in a sec," I tell her, surprised my voice doesn't crack.

She gives me a comforting smile, not knowing what this is doing to me inside. This has nothing to do with nerves, but has everything to do with my mental state which is completely shattered.

When I step out of the dressing room and enter the main room, I spot Paul standing at the bar. His eyes meet mine, cold and filled with disappointment. I have let him down in his mind, hiding my true feelings from him. I should have kept my mouth shut, continued on as though it had no effect on me, but I didn't and now he hates me for it.

Lowering my head, I pass him by, making my way towards the hallway. As I approach the last door on the left, I hear him calling out my name from behind. I turn to him, my bottom lip trembling.

"Come here," he says, his eyes searching mine. Rushing towards him, I bury my face in his chest. "I should've seen what this was doing to you and I'm sorry."

"It's OK," I mumble into his chest. "I overreacted," I lie, telling him what I think he wants to hear.

"You're too good for me, Lana. You always have been and I will make this up to you somehow. I promise."

Nodding my head, I pull back. "I'll see you after a while," I tell him, turning towards the door. He nods his head, giving me a shy smile before turning back towards the main room.

As I reach for the handle, my heart lurches and my stomach begins to turn. *It's just mechanics. This shouldn't affect you.* But it does. It always has. I push the door open and step inside, leaving behind my dignity and self-respect.

Chapter 13

JAX

Call it an intervention of sorts or maybe even a reunion. No matter what you label it, this isn't gonna go well, and I know it. My Lana, the precious girl I fell in love with so many years ago will be within my reach in moments and my nerves are going crazy. I don't even know what to say to her. The last thing she remembers of me is the day before I was sent away. She must think that I abandoned her, but that is so far from the truth. I came back for her, wanting to save her like she had done for me.

Deuce and I thought we were purging her life of that monster forever. So many times I have thought about Lana, and I always imagined her life full of happiness and now I know that she replaced one monster with another. She doesn't deserve this. She never did.

And now I sit in this room, having paid for this time with her. She will come in here for one reason only, because Paul has convinced her to do so. I know this with all of my heart. He has a hold on her, one that makes her use her body to his advantage. If it were anyone else, I wouldn't think this way, but it is her. I know her, or at least I used to. And from what Deuce has told me, this is not where she wants to be.

"Maybe she's not coming," Deuce says, pacing the room. With my revelation of who we are dealing with, his anger has escalated. He wants nothing more than to rip Paul's throat out. That may happen in time, but not before I hear the truth from her lips.

Before I can respond, the door opens and she steps inside, her gaze lowered to the floor. She can sense our presence and I watch her instantly transform into something she is not. She lifts her head, her gaze meeting mine. She recognizes me, I can see it in her eyes, but just as quickly as it appears it vanishes.

"You two wanted a private dance?" she asks, her eyes growing vacant as she walks across the room, turning on the iPod station in the corner. She turns, her eyes filled with pain and anger. "Am I taking you both on at once or are you taking turns?" she asks, her tone laced with pure hatred.

"Lana..." I whisper her name, hoping to spark something within her of the girl I knew so long ago.

She says nothing, pretending she did not hear me, but there is no mistaking the flair in her eyes at the mention of my nickname for her. "I guess that means this is a double team," she says nonchalantly, like this is an everyday occurrence. Who knows, maybe it is, but that all ends today.

"No double team," I say, taking a step towards her. "What happened to you, Lana?"

Her eyes reach mine and there is no disguising the pain within them. "Don't call me that. You lost that privilege when you left me."

I close my eyes at her words. Even after all these years she doesn't know the truth. "I didn't walk away from you, Lana. I came back for you."

"Don't lie to me!" she shouts, her eyes filling with tears. "Why are you here?"

"I'm here for you," I tell her as I reach out for her. "Just give me a chance to explain."

"Explain what, Jax? You said it all when you left me in that house without even saying goodbye. You didn't even have a clue, did you?"

"Lana, please…"

"No!" she shouts. "I have waited a long time to tell you what I think of you, and now you're gonna listen!" She pauses for only a second, a single tear escaping her eye. "I loved you, Jax. There was nothing I wouldn't do for you, including handing myself over to that man so that he would never lay a hand on you again. I owed you that much and I would've done anything to keep you safe because you had always protected me. That night... I thought he was going to kill you."

I close my eyes, feeling the same anguish I felt so many years ago. When I open them again, my gaze meets hers and my heart breaks. The damage Phil inflicted on her years ago is still with her today.

A steady stream of salty tears flow down her pale cheeks, releasing the hatred, resentment and sorrow she has kept pent up for so many years. "I begged him to stop and he promised he would, if I gave him what he wanted. So I did. I walked with him into that basement where he... where he..." she cannot say the words and I don't need to hear them. I know what he did to her and am filled with so much regret for not realizing it sooner. "He did things to me that you could never imagine! And I let him, because of you! Because I thought I was protecting you and that we would be together forever. But that was a lie! The moment you had a chance to walk away, you did, without even caring what happened to me! So there is no need to explain anything, Jackson Cade. You said it all the moment you walked out of my life!"

She is openly sobbing, a rawness to it, the pain of her past still an open wound. I reach out to her, engulfing her in my arms, willing the pain to go away. At first she welcomes the comfort I am offering, but suddenly jerks away, the pain in her eyes crushing me.

"I never left you, not in the way you think. I found out what he was doing to you and I tried to stop him the only way I knew how." My eyes are silently begging her to listen to me, hear my words and know I am telling the truth. "I cut school the day before I left. I cut school when you didn't show up and I came home looking for you. I went upstairs and heard him in your room. It killed me to know what he was doing to you and I wasn't strong enough to stop him."

"So you left? You knew and you left me there? It only got worse when you did! He didn't have to hide from anyone anymore. He could do whatever he wanted, whenever he wanted. Janet never stopped him! She would watch him do things to me, calling me a filthy whore the whole time!"

I never knew Janet took part in the abuse. I had always assumed she had stood back, saying nothing like she had done in the past.

The night Deuce and I arrived at the Martin house replays in my mind, and then I remember seeing Janet exit the basement and the shocked look on her face. She had been in there with him, doing God knows what to Alana.

"I didn't leave you! I didn't know what else to do, so I went to school the next day and told the counselor what I overheard. I thought he would help you, get us both out of there, but instead he called Phil and told him I was causing trouble. A social worker picked me up from school and I was moved to another foster home." She has to understand that I tried. All I wanted was to save her, but I had failed, leading me to take matters into my own hands.

She shakes her head, not believing a word I have said.

"It's true," Deuce says, taking a step forward. "That's where Jax and I met."

"I tried calling you, but Phil wouldn't let me talk to you." *Please believe me, Alana. I've never lied to you.*

"And you expect me to believe that?" she asks, still doubting my words.

"Alana," Deuce says, reaching out to her. He grabs her by the elbow, stepping in front of me so that he is face to face with her. "You don't remember me, do you?"

"Deuce," I warn him, not wanting her to hear this way.

Turning towards me, he looks me in the eyes. "She needs to know the truth, man. She thinks she knows what happened back then, but she doesn't." He turns back to her, his voice soft and comforting, unlike the Deuce I know. "Do you know who I am?"

"Of course I know," she jerks her arm free. "And if I knew you were friends with him, I wouldn't have wasted my time talking to you."

"I'm not talking about the last few weeks," he begins, and I know where he is going.

"Deuce!" I shout, bringing his attention to me. "Let it go!" I seethe.

He nods his head, but his expression speaks volumes. He believes I should let it out, tell her the truth all at once, but now is not the time. She already hates me and throwing the truth in the mix will only make things worse.

"I came back for you," I tell her, pushing Deuce aside. "I didn't leave you. I loved you, Alana!"

Her knees give out from under her and she falls to the floor, heart wrenching sobs escaping her throat. Deuce nods at me once more before he heads for the door, giving us this time together. Crouching down in front of her, I reach for her and pull her to me. She doesn't resist this time, holding onto me for dear life. Wrapping my arms around her, I try to comfort her as she trembles against me, letting every bit of emotion she has kept inside for all these years out.

I don't hear the door open and only when I hear Paul's angry voice do I realize we aren't alone. "Get your fuckin' hands off her," he growls. Snatching Alana up and from my arms, he glares at me. "What the fuck did you do to her?" he asks, his cold eyes filled with fury.

"Alana? Baby, are you OK?" he asks, his tone making me sick. When she doesn't respond, his cold gaze returns to me. "I will fuckin' kill you!"

"Don't be makin' threats you can't back up, pretty boy. I didn't hurt her... at least not tonight." I know he sees the look in my eyes. If he's as smart as I think he is, he will back down now or I will fuckin' kill him.

"Stop," Alana mumbles, looking between the two of us. She wipes away the tears that stain her face, "I just want to go home."

He turns her towards him, looking down at her with concern, before turning his cold gaze to me. "I don't know what you did to her, but you come near her again and it'll be the last thing you do."

Holding Alana tightly to him, he turns and leaves the room without another word. I stand there speechless, unable to move as I take in everything that just happened. Alana was here, right in front of me and just like that she is gone.

Chapter 14

Alana

"Lana?" Paul calls out before opening the bathroom door, stepping inside. Taking a seat on the floor beside the bathtub, he looks over at me with worry etching his face. "What happened back at the club?"

I shake my head, not knowing what to say. Seeing Jax again brought out emotions in me that I haven't felt in forever. At first, I thought it was a hallucination, that my mind was playing tricks on me. The moment I heard his voice, I knew it was him and for a brief moment I was overcome with joy, but it was quickly replaced with anger.

"Lana baby, please talk to me," he pleads. Lifting my eyes to meet his, I fight back the tears that threaten to fall. "Did he hurt you?"

"No," I mutter, shaking my head. "Not the way you think."

He creases his brow, a puzzled look on his face. "I don't understand."

"I never thought I'd see him again," I whisper. "I don't know what came over me," I add, taking in a deep breath. I am quite accomplished at pushing my emotions aside, but this time it's different. He still has a hold on me, one that I thought was severed a long time ago.

"Who? Did you know him?"

I nod my head. "It was Jackson," I manage to strangle out. I am trembling, not out of fear of Jax but because seeing him again has uncovered memories that I have kept buried.

"Jackson?" he asks, shaking his head. "Are you sure?"

"I could never forget him," I whisper.

Paul swallows hard, his face etched with pain. He closes his eyes, resting his head on the wall behind him, his sharp intake of breath filling the silent room. "This can't be happening," he mutters as he fists his hands.

"I don't want to see him again," I say, looking down at my submerged hands in the water. "I can't forgive him for abandoning me."

Paul opens his eyes, lowering his gaze to meet mine. "I'll talk to Hawk," he says, smiling at me. "Are you sure you're OK?"

"I'll be fine," I tell him, but more than anything I'm trying to convince myself.

He rises to his knees, looking over at me with sympathetic eyes. "I don't want to lose you, Alana."

Letting out a ragged breath, I smile at him. "You'll never lose me, and Jackson Cade is nothing more than a bad memory, one I don't want to be reminded of. He walked away from me a long time ago. There's no way in hell I'm letting him back into my life to walk away all over again."

"I'm sorry again, about earlier. I just worry about you."

"I know," I whisper, as I rise to my feet. Reaching out, I grab for the towel hanging on the rack behind him. "And I worry about you."

As I start to wrap the towel around me, Paul reaches up, grabbing it from my grasp before tossing it to the floor. His calloused fingers glide up my body as he stands, stopping at my breast. He looks at me with hooded eyes, causing wetness to pool between my legs. I know this look, the meaning behind it and why we both need this more than anything.

Grasping the back of his hand with mine, I pull it towards my heaving chest, silently begging him to make me forget. His fingertips graze against my nipple, the friction causing it to pebble under his touch.

Before I can utter a single word, he lifts me in his arms, stopping only when my rear end is resting on the countertop. He says nothing as he spreads my legs, burying his face between my thighs, the only audible sound is my moans as his tongue lavishes my drenched pussy.

As I exit the stage and head down the hall, my eyes land on Hawk in a heated discussion with Paul and Jax. Clenching my teeth together, I push past them and make my way to the dressing room, slamming the door shut behind me.

"What the fuck is he doing here?" I mutter to myself, unaware that Trix is staring at me like I've grown two heads.

"Sweetheart, you've got some major issues," she says, rolling her eyes at me. "For the life of me, I don't know why Paul insists on keeping you around."

As I pull on my shorts, I glare at her. Trix has hated me since the first night we met. I get it, she's angry because she's not headlining here, but this isn't The Lusty Lady anymore. From what I've heard from the other dancers, The Lusty Lady was doomed when the doors opened. Business was always slow, even on the weekends and the girls were lucky to make fifty dollars on a Friday night. With the opening of Body Shots, not only is the place packed every night, but the clientele is much more desirable. Trix was the star at The Lusty Lady, banking more than any other girl, but her standards were as low as you can get. She didn't care who she had to blow or what she had to do to make twenty bucks, and it doesn't surprise me one bit.

"Maybe he has things for the crazy ones," she smirks, turning away from me.

"You know what your problem is, Trix? You think your shit doesn't stink, that somehow you are better than anyone here."

"Because I am," she says turning towards me. "I'm prettier, have a better body, definitely a better dancer, and let's not forget that I'm a better lay than any one of you. Sooner or later, Paul will realize that and kick you to the curb. In the meantime, I'll play his little game, but I know he wants me. They all do."

"Keep telling yourself that," I say, shaking my head. I grab my tank top and pull it over my head, trying not to let Trix get inside my head. Yanking the door open, I throw my bag over my shoulder and walk out.

"Hey," Paul says rushing towards me. "Are you leaving?"

"Yeah, I think that might be the best idea," I say, looking past him at Jax, his eyes locked on me. "Why is he here? I thought you were gonna talk to Hawk."

"It's out of Hawk's and my control. The Forgotten Souls own the club until Hawk can buy them out, so neither of us have any say."

"I can't believe this," I mutter, closing my eyes. I don't think I can handle seeing Jax on a regular basis. "We could just move back to Langley," I say opening my eyes, inspiration striking me.

Shaking his head, he looks at me with regret. "I wish it were that simple." He pauses, looking over his shoulder at where Jax is standing. When his gaze returns to me, I see the despair in his eyes. "Jax wants you and he'll stop at nothing until you're his."

Sagging my shoulders in defeat, I lower my gaze. The last thing I want is to deal with Jax on a regular basis. I hate him and want him to go far away.

"Here," Paul says, reaching into his pocket and pulling out a baggie. He passes me a bar, watching as I toss it back. "I'll be home in an hour or two."

I nod at him and watch him walk back towards the main room before I make my way to the back exit, trying to avoid running into Jax. As I step out into the cool night air, I breathe a sigh of relief. One down and many more to go, I think to myself as I begin the mile hike home.

Chapter 15

JAX

Standing in the darkness, I watch as Alana comes down the stairs of the apartment building, completely oblivious that I am lurking in the shadows. She's avoiding me at every turn, keeping her distance from me even when we are in the same room. Paul says she wants nothing to do with me, that I am nothing but a horrible memory, but I refuse to give up.

If she would just hear me out, we could put all of this behind us. She means everything to me and if given the chance, we could move forward. Once she learns the truth, she will understand, but first I have to get her alone.

Trailing behind her, I watch as she follows the same path she does every night, until she pushes through the front door of Body Shots. I stand outside, staring up at the sign, still finding it hard to believe that she's really here.

"You know I never saw you as the stalker type," Deuce chuckles as he comes to stand beside me. "Thought I'd find you here."

"What have you found out?" I ask, refusing to look at him.

"Nothing. I can't even track down a lease back in Langley which makes no sense. I've got Beast looking into it, but so far he's coming up empty handed."

My heart sinks at his words. None of this makes any sense and I know Paul is the key. "What about him? He's been working for Hawk for years. No way has that fucker had luck on his side the entire time."

"That's where it gets interesting. At least with Alana, we could pull up the basics. Birth certificate, school records, doctor visits, the norm."

"What are you getting at?" I ask, finally turning to face him.

He shrugs. "There is no record of a Paul Randall ever being born. It's as if he doesn't exist."

It takes me a moment to grasp what he is telling me. No record of his existence is impossible. I know Deuce, and for him to turn up with nothing is something that doesn't happen every day. In fact, it has never happened before now. "What about Hawk? What are the chances he knows about Paul's past?"

"If my gut is right, I'd say the chances of getting him to fess up to anything aren't good unless he has something to gain from it."

"Or lose," I add. I know very little about Hawk, but he's no different than most. He'd spill in a second if it meant saving his own sorry ass.

"Point taken. First things first. Let's see what Beast digs up. If he's still batting zero, we start looking at plan B."

I nod my head in agreement, all the while my mind is reeling. If Alana would just hear me out, I know I could take her away from all of this.

"Don't even think about it," Deuce warns. "I know you want to get her out of there and away from Paul, but until we know what we're up against, you're fighting a losing battle. She thinks you abandoned her and until she's ready to hear the truth, all you're going to do is make her hate you even more." For being such a notorious heartless bastard, what he says makes sense. I just don't like it.

"I can't just sit back and do nothing. I gave up years of my life for her and it was all for nothing. Her situation is no better than the one I left her in," I say, guilt ridden.

"First of all, you didn't leave her. Second, it wasn't for nothing. Ridding this planet of someone like Phil Martin was a necessity and you know it."

"It doesn't change the fact that she's in there doing whatever that fucker tells her to do. He's playing her and she's gonna be the one who gets hurt," I say, running my hands through my hair.

"I get it, but there ain't shit you can do about it, at least not yet. Give me a few days to see what I can come up with and if we're in the same boat, we'll do whatever is necessary. You feel me?"

Nodding my head in agreement, I follow Deuce inside, my heart pounding in my chest. My eyes land on her as she stands by Paul, the smile on her face illuminating the room. As I approach, her gaze lands on me, the smile on her face vanishing.

There was a time when I was the only person who could make her smile, who knew the Alana she was before Phil Martin got his hands on her. The same Alana I want back in my life, scars and all.

PAUL

I follow Alana's gaze as it falls on Jax. She can tell me over and over again how much she despises him, but the look in her eyes isn't one filled with hatred, it is one of longing. She loves him and if I had one shred of decency, I'd let her go.

It wasn't supposed to be this way. I think back to the first moment I set eyes on her. She was a perfect target, just out of jail, no family or friends, and living on the streets. When I approached her that first night, I had one thing in mind, the same as all of my prey. I saw dollar signs, but there was something different about her. Her eyes told me that her past was as tortured as my own. Little did I know how similar our pasts actually were.

The first time she uttered Phil Martin's name, the horror came rushing back to me. It took everything I had not to lose my composure. She had lived the life I had been born into, experiencing the same agony I myself had faced and by the same hand.

To the outside world, Phil and Susan Martin were the perfect parents. They had it all – money, influence and power. What the outside world didn't see was their sick perversion.

I wasn't their first victim, but I had hoped I would be their last. Being an only child, I should have been exempt from their sick games, but instead I became their focus. I was thirteen the first time he brought me into that basement. For three years, I dealt with their brutality, succumbing in every way thinking that one day it would all end - and it did, but not by their choice.

There was not an ounce of guilt when I plunged the knife in my mother's chest. For the first time, I saw remorse in her eyes, and it took years for me to realize that what I had witnessed wasn't repentance. There was no shame in her or my father's actions towards me. It was all about her demise, knowing that she would no longer exist in this world, and that life would go on without her.

My weakness cost me the one chance to eliminate all evil from my life. I did not hear him approach, and he was able to wrench the knife from my hands, turning it on me.

Instinctively, my hand reaches up, halting on the scar that is a permanent reminder of that night. There had been no pain or discomfort. Fleeing from the house, I was finally free, but the damage they had done stayed with me forever, making me the heartless person I am to this day.

I had somehow believed that that night would put an end to Phil Martin. Losing his wife should have had an effect on him. Instead, he remarried another vile woman, not unlike my own mother, and together they tortured Alana.

I am brought back to the present when I feel Alana's nails digging into my arm. Her eyes are wide, a panicked look on her face. Out of the corner of my eye, I see Jax approaching.

"I can't do this," she mutters, and before I can stop her, she disappears down the hallway.

"Still planning on killing me pretty boy?" Jax asks, smirking as he comes to a stop in front of me.

"What do you want, Jax?" I ask, turning my attention towards Becky who passes me a beer.

"Thought I'd drop in and check on my assets."

"You mean you wanted to check up on Alana." I lift the beer to my lips and down half the bottle, slamming it on the bar. "Nothing's changed. She still doesn't want to see you."

He takes the empty seat beside me, nodding at Becky. Seconds later, he has a full glass of whiskey in front of him. "Got that impression by the way she ran out of here. It's a shame you've got her so fucked up in the head, but sooner or later she'll hear me out. When she does, it'll be the last time you see her."

He's not making a threat. This is a promise, one I have no doubt he will try to keep. "Keep telling yourself that. Unlike you, Alana is loyal. She won't leave me," I tell him, not believing the words as they escape my lips.

"You can believe what you want, but I didn't leave Alana. I tried to save her."

I wish I could call him a liar but I know the truth. He served time trying to protect her from a situation I could have prevented if I hadn't run away. "But you didn't. I was the one who found her sleeping in the park, took her in, gave her a place to call home."

"And forced her to use her body to make you money. Don't try to romanticize it. She's nothing but a whore to you, someone you can manipulate. Don't think for a minute I'm not onto you. Do you tell her you love her before you sell her to the highest bidder or do you save that for when she hands over the cash?"

His words are cold and heartless but not undeserved. "We do what we have to do to survive. You wouldn't know anything about that, would you?"

"She may fall for your lies, but I know better. I know how much Hawk is paying you and I'd bet my life Alana has no clue, but she will, and when that happens, I'll be the one who's there for her." He grabs his drink as he stands. "And you'll lose her forever."

As he walks away, my mind is reeling. I cannot risk losing Alana, no matter the cost. I have to get us out of this mess one way or another.

Chapter 16

Alana

"Thanks for staying with me," Alexis says as we step out the front door of the club.

"No problem." When Alexis asked me to stay late until her boyfriend could come pick her up, at first I hesitated. Normally, I prefer to get out of the club the first chance I get, but going home to an empty apartment is far from appealing. It's not so much that I'm afraid as it is that I hate the silence.

"Happy Birthday, by the way."

"It's just another day," I mumble. I haven't celebrated a birthday since... I was thirteen. Ten years later, and I still remember that night like it was yesterday. Why would I want to celebrate the day Phil Martin ruined me?

"Oh, I didn't mean to upset you," Alexis says, giving me a concerned look. "I just..."

"It's OK," I tell her. "I just don't see a need for it. Age is just a number," I laugh, trying to lighten the mood.

"So when's Paul coming back?" she asks, leaning against the brick wall.

"I'm not sure," I admit. Hell, I don't even know where he went, let alone how long he will be gone. Most of the time, Paul gives me some clue, but this time he left without saying much of anything.

"So how does he deal with you... you know?" she asks. "Rick would have a fit if I was still doing that. He was against it long before we got together."

"What do you mean?" I ask, ignoring her question about Paul. No one could possibly understand the relationship we have.

"Rick never liked me working here, but I think he understood why I was doing it." She smiles, no doubt thinking of her son Peyton. He is her pride and joy. I can only imagine how hard it must be to raise a child with Down's syndrome, but she manages. Even after Peyton's father walked out on the two of them, she kept everything together. Luckily, the club had just opened up, giving her an opportunity to work the flexible hours she needed and still make the money necessary to raise a special needs kid. I admire her in every way. "He offered to pay my bills for me, but he finally got the hint. I wasn't going to take any handouts. So instead of giving me hell, he supported me until he found out about the private rooms. Then he flipped out."

"Is that why you quit doing it?"

"No," she says, shaking her head. "I did that for me. I was becoming a different person. I had stopped feeling, was only existing. Now I'm back to my old self, and I made myself a promise that I would never do that to myself again. In a few weeks, all of this will be behind me."

"You're quitting?" I ask, trying to hide my disappointment.

"I never intended to do this for as long as I have. I was just trying to get on my feet after Ben left. So yeah, I'm leaving."

"Wow," I whisper, not knowing what else to say. I am envious, wishing I could walk away from this life too. "What are you gonna do?"

"I got a job at Bar None. You should talk to Deuce about working there. I talked to a couple of the girls and they're making just as much as I am here, and they get to keep their clothes on."

"Really?" I ask, my interest piqued.

"Honest to God. He's starting me out at eight an hour and you're pretty much guaranteed two hundred in tips a night. Beats the hell out of this place."

"I'll talk to him about it," I tell her, even though I have no intention of doing so. I'd like nothing more than to walk away from it all, but that's not an option. Working for Deuce would mean seeing more of Jax, and I want to avoid him as much as possible.

"Good. I like you Alana and I know you hate being here." She doesn't know how true that is.

"Deuce's a good guy even though he comes across as a badass. Did you hear what he did to Trix?" she asks, grinning.

"No, what did he do?"

"Made her clean the employee restroom. Handed her a gallon of bleach and a scrub brush. Told her not to show her face until she got her filth off of every surface," she says, trying to contain her laughter.

"What am I missing?" I ask in confusion.

"Let's just say it's her time of the month and that hasn't deterred her from making a few extra bucks," she says, scrunching her nose in disgust.

I can't help but burst out into fit of laughter. "That bitch is fuckin' nasty,"

"I know, right? And apparently, Deuce isn't gonna tolerate her shit. Wish he was here every night." I nod my head in agreement. Having Deuce around isn't so bad. He looks out for the girls and doesn't take shit from anyone. Too bad he's friends with Jax. "Bet Trix is wishing Paul would come back."

"Yeah," I mutter, my mind preoccupied. I have made more in the few days Deuce has been here than I ever have, and not once have I had to set foot into one of the back rooms. It's not like we've been busy either.

"That bitch hates you, but I don't think she likes anyone but herself," she says.

"I'm not very popular with anyone here, besides you," I say, shrugging. It's not like I'm an unlikeable person, or at least I don't think I am, but most of the girls steer clear of me.

"That's because they're jealous of you. Don't take it personally. It's their loss, not yours."

"I've never given them a reason to be jealous, have I?" I try to recall anything I may have done, but am coming up empty handed.

"Alana, you haven't done anything. It's just you. I mean, look at yourself in the mirror sometime. Not just a quick glance, but a long, hard look. You have what everyone wants. You're gorgeous and you have a body to die for, not to mention that you go home with Paul Randall every fuckin' night. And to top it all off, you have Jax, the VP of the Forgotten Souls pining for you. Hell, even I should be jealous of you, but that's not me."

I shake my head, trying to grasp everything she has said.

"You really don't see it, do you?" she asks, looking at me with a perplexed look. "I mean it's not an act with you, is it?"

"I don't understand."

"That's the beauty of it," she says, smiling at me. "And that's why I consider you my friend." She pauses for a minute when the rumbling sound of a Harley approaches. "That's Rick," she says, grinning.

As if on cue, Rick pulls into the parking lot, stopping a few feet away from us. She makes her way over to him, her lips crashing with his, causing me to turn away.

"I'll see you tomorrow," she says as she climbs on the back of his bike.

Smiling, I nod at her as Rick pulls off and out of the parking lot. *She's happy and in love*, I think to myself as I push off the brick wall and make my way towards the sidewalk for the trek home. *Happy and in love.* Those two words seem foreign to me. I can't remember the last time I was truly happy. I've only loved three people in my life, and all of them left me. It's a hard lesson in life to learn, but I promised myself years ago I would not make the same mistake again. I don't do love.

I try to push aside all my emotions, albeit the negative ones always seem to resurface. Pain, heartache and misery – those are the ones that remind me that I am still alive. Taking in a deep breathe, I begin the long walk towards home.

"Hey!" The sound of Deuce's voice echoes through the otherwise silent night. I turn to see him stalking towards me. "Where are you going?"

"Home," I say, my tone full of annoyance. Don't get me wrong, I like Deuce, but he is Jax's friend. I have to remember that.

"I can give you a lift," he offers, and I am so tempted. It's cold out tonight and I'm tired. All I really want to do is go home a soak in a hot bath and climb into bed.

"I'm fine," I tell him as I turn and resume the trek towards home.

"Come on Alana, don't be stubborn. It's cold, late, you're tired and this isn't the safest part of town. It's on my way anyway."

"How do you know it's on your way?" I ask, turning to face him once again.

"You work for me, remember? I know where all my employees live," he explains, making me feel like a paranoid idiot.

"Thanks, but I can manage."

"You won't give me an inch, will you?" he says, stepping in beside me as I beginning walking away. "Fine. Misery loves company anyway."

Five minutes pass, Deuce matching each of my steps, before his intention becomes apparent. "You do realize that I walk home most nights, so there really isn't a need for you to follow me," I point out.

"That comes to an end tonight. Beautiful girl like you walking down the streets in the middle of the night is an invitation for trouble. You won't take me up on my offer, then I'll just walk you home. It's simple."

"Why are you doing this?" I ask, coming to an abrupt stop.

"Because that's what friends do. Look out for each other."

"You and I aren't friends," I retort.

"Well that ends tonight too," he says in a matter of fact tone. "And since we're friends, I'm walking you home. Period."

I want to argue with him, tell him to fuck off, but I don't. Deep down I like Deuce. "Fine," I mutter, before I begin walking again, ignoring the fact that he is matching each of my strides.

After ten minutes of walking in silence, I start to relax. "How long have you known Jax?" I ask out of curiosity.

"Since we were seventeen." At least Jax had been loyal to someone over the years. "Met in foster care. Been friends ever since."

I bite the inside of my cheek, fighting back the tears that threaten to follow. Deuce was my replacement. It's all perfectly clear now, and makes me hate Jax even more.

"How about you? How do you two know each other?" he asks, glancing over in my direction.

"He was placed in the same group home as me," I tell him, remembering the day I first met Jax. "You mean he didn't tell you?"

"I figured small talk was better than no talk," he shrugs. "Actually, I know a lot about you Alana."

"I'm sure," I mutter, clenching my fists at my side. That asshole knew what Phil was doing to me and not only did he leave me, he reminisced with his newfound friend. *I fuckin' hate him.*

We continue to walk in silence, neither of us saying a word until we are finally standing in front of my apartment building. "You know you could already be inside curled up in bed if you'd let me give you a ride?" he says, smirking at me. "I'll see you tomorrow." He winks at me before turning on his heel and heading back in the direction we just came from.

Shaking my head as I climb the stairs, I take one final glance at Deuce as he walks away, wondering if I should open my heart up to misery once again.

Chapter 17

JAX

One Week Later

As I close the distance between myself and home, my mind is focused on one thing... Alana. She hates me, or at the very least she despises what she believes happened in the past. I never abandoned her even though that is her reality, and never once did I forget about her. How could I? She was and is the most important person in my life, but trying to convince her of that won't be easy.

I've given her the space she wants, but that is coming to an end real soon. She needs to hear me out, and once she knows the truth, we can mend the damage that was caused all those years we were apart. I will make sure of it.

Then there is the real issue. Paul is nothing but trouble. Alana means nothing to him, no matter how hard he tries to convince me otherwise. He is the reason I didn't want to go on this run, but Deuce promised to keep an eye on her, and I know he has done just that.

Pulling into the compound, a feeling of dread washes over me when I spot Doc's car parked near the entrance. It's been a long time since Dr. Jennings has graced us with his presence, meaning only one thing. Something went down while I was away, something Bones couldn't handle.

When I push open the front door, I'm surprised to see nothing out of the ordinary. Red is perched at his normal spot at the bar, a beer in his hand and a club whore at his side. Beast is seated next to him, drowning his sorrows in a fifth of whiskey.

I make my way over to where Bones is seated, his eyes focused on Jazz and Desiree as they go down on one another.

"Where's Deuce?" I ask, causing Bones to tear his eyes away from the action taking place in front of him.

"Jax!" he says, jumping to his feet. "Didn't think you'd be here this soon. Deuce wanted me to bring you to him as soon as you got here," he says, motioning towards the office. "He's waitin' for ya."

I nod at him before making my way towards the office. Grasping the knob tightly in my hand, I pause for a moment before turning it and pushing the door open.

"What the fuck happened?" I ask as I enter the room.

He lifts his head slowly, his eyes meeting my own. "We lost Crow," he says, his voice filled with sorrow. "Heart attack."

Fuck! Crow has been a part of the club since before my time. "I'm sorry, man."

"He and dad were good friends," he says, his eyes reflecting the pain I know he is feeling. With his dad locked away for life and his mother still behind bars for another ten years, Crow was the closest thing to family he had remaining. "Gonna miss that fucker."

Crow's health had been declining for years and we all knew his life was coming to an end, but no one can ever truly prepare for it. "We'll send him off the way he deserves."

He nods his head in agreement, his face solemn. I take that as my cue to give him some time alone. Rising from the chair, I head towards the door, giving him the space he needs.

"She reminds me of Renee," he blurts out, causing me to freeze. Slowly I turn around, narrowing my eyes at him at the mention of his sister. He hasn't mentioned her name in years, his attempt at trying to forget the past. "Beautiful inside and out."

"You've been talking to her?" I ask as I cross the room, taking the seat I had just abandoned.

"She was heading home the other night when I was closing the club. I offered her a ride, but she wouldn't take it, so I walked her home. There's a lot of pain there, not just because of what Phil Martin did to her. It's you. She tries to hide it, but it's there."

"I know," I whisper, wishing things had been different.

"She's still in there, the Alana you used to know, but it's gonna take time for that part of her to reemerge. It can't be forced. It has to happen on its own."

I nod my head in agreement, knowing what he says is true.

"I need you to trust me," he says, as if that was ever a question. Nodding my head, I silently let him know that will never be an issue, but I can't help but feel like this means I am losing her. "Don't look at me that way. I'm not asking you to walk away from her. I'm asking you to trust me to bring her back to you. I know you love her, you always have."

Letting out a ragged breath, my eyes meet the man I would lay down my life for without question, and for the first time since I met him, I doubt Deuce's ability. Ignoring that uneasy feeling, I nod my head, putting my trust in him.

Chapter 18

Inwardly seething, I watch Alana as she smiles up at Deuce. Staring at her from across the room, completely unnoticed, I see her entire focus is solely on him, and I don't like it one bit.

My whole purpose for returning to Langley was to get the dirt I needed to get Jax out of the picture, never once considering that Deuce would be the real issue. In a matter of two weeks' time, he has managed to move in for the kill. The way he is looking at her sends up all sorts of red flags.

"It's pathetic, isn't it?" Trix says, coming to stand beside me.

Trix is not someone I trust. She's never liked Alana and the last thing I need is to believe anything she says. But she is the eyes and ears of this place. "Did you need something, Trix?"

"Just wanted to welcome you back. I missed having you around," she says, smiling up at me.

"Bet you did," I tell her knowing that Deuce has made the last two weeks a living hell. Deuce hates Trix and has never hidden the fact that he wishes she weren't around. "What'd he make you do?" I ask, unable to hide my amusement.

"I'm glad you think it's funny that Deuce tormented your staff while you were away. You know it's not fair that we get treated like shit," she says, her voice laced with annoyance.

"Doesn't look that way to me," I say, my eyes landing on Alana as she laughs at something Deuce has just said. Immediately my amusement is gone and once again my blood is boiling.

"Well Alana's always the exception to the rule, isn't she?"

"What's that supposed to mean?" I ask, becoming defensive.

"Just that Alana always gets special treatment, but you already know that. She must have a magical pussy the way all you men bow down to her. First you and now Deuce," she says looking over in Alana's direction. "Guess if Jax was here, he'd be getting some action too."

"Alana's not like that," I say, coming to her defense. No matter what Trix or anyone else thinks, Alana is no slut. She only does the things she does because of me, and I hate myself for it.

"Yeah, whatever you say," she mutters before walking away, leaving me alone to stew over the possibility that I might be wrong.

For the next several minutes, I do nothing but observe Alana and Deuce, watching the way he touches her, the way they both look at one another and cannot help but wonder if Trix is telling the truth. Without thinking, I stalk across the room, stopping only when I am within Alana's sights.

She turns, looking up at me with those innocent damn eyes and smiles. "You're back," she says, rushing towards me and wrapping her arms around my waist.

All anger dissipates in that moment and contentment washes over me as I engulf her in my arms. "Miss me?" I ask as I force myself to step away from her.

"Always," she grins.

"Well I guess I'll leave the two of you alone," Deuce says, taking the hint he is no longer welcome.

"Oh Deuce?" Alana asks, turning towards him.

"Yeah, darlin'?"

"Thanks for everything," Alana smiles.

"Anytime," Deuce says, smiling back at her before turning his cold gaze towards me. "Good to have you back, Paul."

"Yeah," I mutter, matching his glare until he finally turns and makes his way back to the office.

"I was starting to wonder if you'd decided to skip town," Alana says, bringing my attention back to her.

"I promised I'd never leave you and I meant it." I wish I could say I meant those words when I first said them to her, but that would be a lie. I never intended on her staying with me and now I can't imagine her not being in my life.

"I know, it's just..." her eyes sadden as she speaks, remembering a time long ago when Jax left her.

"Hey," I say, moving towards her. "I will never let you go." She smiles up at me, instantly relaxing, not understanding the depth of my words. "You and me are forever."

We stand in silence for several minutes, staring into one another's eyes. "Well I better get ready to go on," she says, her eyes growing vacant as she speaks.

Without another word, she turns and leaves me standing there watching as she makes her way towards the back of the club, and for the first time I realize how hard it is going to be when she walks away from me for good.

Chapter 19

Two Weeks Later

"What?" I ask, staring at Deuce in disbelief. Of all the scenarios I pictured, this one never crossed my mind.

"It's not confirmed, but I'd say Spyder's right on the money."

Shaking my head, I try to grasp what he is saying, but can't. "We have to get Alana out of there."

"In due time, but not a second before. If Paul had plans for Alana, he wouldn't be keeping her around. We go in guns blazing, who knows what he'll do."

I know he's right, but it doesn't make me feel any better. The sooner Alana is away from Paul, the better. "So I'm supposed to stand by and watch the girl I have loved for as long as I can remember slowly dwindle away at the hands of that fuckin' monster? I can't do it! I won't do it!"

"So what do you suggest? That we just snatch her up one night and bring her here?"

"If that's what we have to do to keep her safe, then yeah!"

"Listen to yourself, man! Alana still fuckin' hates you and you want to drag her away from the guy who, in her eyes, saved her? How you think that's gonna work out?"

I let out an exasperated sigh, hating that he is right. If there is any chance that Alana will allow me back into her life, it will end right then and there. "So what am I supposed to do then? He is destroying her Deuce, and I can't let that happen again."

"I know," he says, looking at me with a pain in his eyes I've never seen. "When you and I met all those years ago, we instantly connected. I knew I had found not just a friend, but a brother. Alana means the world to you, and because of that, I was willing to do whatever it took to help her. That was before I even met her. Now that I've spent some time with her, I can promise you that I would lay down my life for her. She doesn't know it yet, but she's family, and that's what family does."

"So what do we do?" I ask, feeling just as helpless as I did so many years ago when I discovered the truth.

"We take small steps instead of giant leaps. Alana is just starting to trust me and if I blow that, we're through. But in time, she will have complete faith in me, just like you did, and then we'll work on repairing the damage Paul's done to her. You have my word."

His words mean more to me than he could ever realize. There was a time when all I had was Alana, but that has all changed. I am part of a family now, one that will take Alana into the fold and give her what they have given me. For years I have regretted what happened, wishing I could go back and change things. Deuce has always told me that things happen for a reason, and I finally understand what he meant. There is no going back. Nothing about the past can be changed. Alana was brought into my life to give me hope. At my darkest hour, Deuce came into my life and with his help we ended one nightmare. Together we will end another.

Fate has brought Alana and I back together because that is where we belong. No one knows what the future holds, but I know without her, mine will be meaningless.

Chapter 20

Alana

One Month Later

"OK, I take it back," Deuce says, chuckling. "Not everyone can play miniature golf."

With my hands on my hips, I narrow my eyes at him, feigning annoyance. Inside, I am laughing as hard as he has been for the last hour, and it's such a good feeling. "I told you I suck at these things."

"Darlin', suck doesn't even begin to describe what I have just witnessed." He bursts out laughing, something that is becoming a common theme with him.

"Then next time let me choose an activity that I am actually good at instead of just planning these little outings without even consulting me." I roll my eyes at him as he roars with laughter, finding my suggestion even more humorous. "There are things I'm good at, you know?"

"Of that I have no doubt," he says, holding his hands up in surrender. "I'm sorry, darlin'. It's just that I've never seen someone launch a ball quite like that."

Shaking my head, I let out an exasperated sigh. I'll admit, miniature golf turned out to be a huge bust. So did bowling, and I won't even mention our day at the arcade. "At least give me credit for trying," I argue causing his laughter to die down.

"I give you all the credit in the world, Alana and I can't tell you the last time I had so much damn fun," he says, making me smile.

"Thank you," I whisper, blushing. It's been a long time since I've had this much fun too and I hate that it is coming to an end.

When Deuce first asked me to go out, I thought he meant a date. I vehemently refused, wanting no part of it. I can still hear his laughter when I told him I had no interest in dating him or anyone else. My anger quickly turned to embarrassment when he explained what his true intention was.

"You got it all wrong, darlin'. I wasn't asking you on a date. First of all, I don't do the whole dating thing. And trust me, I'm not lacking in

the pussy department," he laughs, causing me to turn a bright shade of red. I start to walk away, completely mortified by my assumption. "Where are you going?" Deuce asks, gripping my arm.

I immediately jerk away from his hold, looking back at him in complete terror. "Don't touch me," I whisper, feeling like the wind has been knocked out of me.

"I'm sorry," he says, holding his hands up in defeat. "I didn't mean to scare you."

"I'm fine," I tell him, even though I'm not. The exact moment his hand grasped my arm, memories of the past flooded me, something hard to erase. I begin to walk away again, wanting to put as much distance between us as possible.

"Wait a minute," Deuce says, following behind me. "I think you misunderstood me completely."

"And how is that?" I ask, turning to face him once again.

"Just because someone asks you out doesn't mean they want in your pants. Don't get me wrong. You're a beautiful girl, and I would love to dote you around town, but not like a piece of ass. I like you Alana and I just wanted to *get to know you outside the club. I think both of us could use a friend."*

I stare up at him in disbelief, not knowing if I should take his words as a compliment or insult. "Friends?" I ask, as if the word is foreign to me.

"Yeah. You know, two people that have something in common enjoying time together. It could be fun."

"What do we have in common other than this place?" I ask, looking at the club that surrounds us.

"I guess I have the advantage here. We have more in common than you might think."

I didn't know how true his words were until I gave him a chance, and he hasn't let me down. He too knows all about loss. I remind him of his sister, an honor I don't take lightly. And he has upheld his promise to me, never making Jax a topic of conversation. I have gained a new friend, one that has never asked for anything in return.

"Let's go grab some lunch," Deuce says, bringing me out of my daydream. "Pizza or burgers?"

"Pizza," I tell him, smiling broadly.

I can't help but laugh as the waitress walks away from our table. "Unbelievable," I giggle, shaking my head at Deuce.

"Told you I wasn't hurtin' when it comes to pussy," he chuckles, his eyes leaving mine for a brief second to stare at the girl's ass as she makes her way into the kitchen.

"I could've been your girlfriend for all she knew," I say as I lean back in the booth, smiling over at him. Deuce is an extremely good looking guy, the problem is that he knows it and so does everyone else.

"Did it bother you?" he smirks. He's an attention whore and makes no bones about it.

"No," I tell him honestly. I like Deuce, but definitely not in that way. "We're just friends, remember?" I say, smiling at him.

He nods his head in agreement. "Damn! And I was hoping you'd fall madly in love with me," he chuckles. He looks over at me and smiles for a brief moment before his face grows serious. "Can I ask you a personal question?"

"Sure," I say, shrugging my shoulders.

"Why do you do it? You're a different person when you are away from the club. I see how that spark in your eyes disappears the moment you walk through the door. You hate being there, so why do it?"

His question is a valid one, but I'm not sure I want to answer it. He wouldn't understand. "It's complicated," I manage to say.

"I've got time. So spill it. Why are you doing something you despise?"

I let out a ragged breath. "There aren't many options," I tell him truthfully.

"There are lots of options for a young, pretty girl like you. What did you do before you started dancing?"

"This is all I've ever done," I admit. "It's all I'm good at." *Except for sex.*

"I don't believe that for one minute. You are one hell of a dancer, and the main reason the club is doing so well, but you don't enjoy it. And yeah, I know you're making the big bucks, but you are capable of making just as much by doing something that doesn't make you hate yourself," he says, his tone filled with sincerity and concern.

He sees it. I never had to say a word and yet he saw it in me. "How?"

"How do I know you hate yourself? Because I've been there. That look in your eyes is a familiar one, the same look I carried around for many years." There is honesty in his voice mixed with pain and I know he is telling me the truth.

"What happened?" I ask, unable to stop myself.

"I told you that I lost my sister, I just didn't tell you how. Her name was Renee. She was three years older than me and had been seeing this guy. He seemed like an alright fellow. Turns out he was one hell of an actor." I can see the pain in his eyes as he speaks. "He raped and then killed her," he says, his voice filled with finality.

"I am so sorry," I tell him as I reach over and cover his hand with my own.

"I blamed myself for not protecting her, for not realizing what a monster he was. I wanted revenge, to make him pay for every ounce of pain he inflicted on her."

I swallow hard as I watch his eyes turn cold. This is a side of Deuce I have never seen before and hope never to again. "Did you...?" my voice trails off. I am unable to say the words that are on the tip of my tongue, afraid of what his answer will be. I can see Deuce as a killer, and although the thought frightens me, I can understand why he would have gone to such lengths.

"No, I didn't kill him. I wasn't given the chance. My father took him out. And you know what happened? They locked him away, my mother too, for doing the right fuckin' thing."

I can't even imagine what he must have felt. Losing his sister and then his mother and father, all because of one heinous act. One man had destroyed an entire family in the blink of an eye.

"My mom and dad were the only family I had besides the club. I felt alone, and because I had no immediate family, I was thrown into foster care and that's when I met..." his voice trails off, refusing to say the name I have forbidden him from speaking.

"Jax?" Maybe I'm a glutton for punishment or maybe I'm just curious, but I sincerely want to know their back story.

"Yeah," he whispers.

"It's OK if you say his name," I reassure him. Out of the corner of my eye, I see the waitress approach. As she places the pizza in between us, neither of us utter a sound.

"Can I get you anything else?" she asks, her eyes solely focused on Deuce.

"No, we're good," he says, reaching for his wallet. He pulls out two twenties and passes them to her. "The rest is yours. Don't bother us again."

As she takes the money from his hand, she looks quickly over at me and then back at Deuce before leaving us alone.

"Jax was my first real friend," he begins, a story that sounds all too familiar. Jax was my first friend too. "When we met, I saw the same pain in his eyes as I did my own. When I discovered the source of it, I knew our meeting each other had a purpose. You were that reason."

I lower my eyes as he speaks, knowing deep down that he knows the truth about me. I am ashamed of my past, and mortified that Jax would reveal it to him. "He told you?" I ask, my voice barely a whisper.

"He loved you Alana. Truly loved you and still does. He never wanted to leave you, he wanted to save you."

I lift my head at his words, narrowing my eyes at him. "How can you honestly believe that?"

"Because I was there, listening to every word he spoke about what that fucker did to you. I saw the pain in his eyes, heard it in his voice whenever he spoke about you." I feel my eyes fill with tears as he speaks. I am unable to speak for fear that the dam will break and I will have a complete meltdown right here. "And I saw the devastation on his face the night he went back for you."

My eyes immediately meet his, my bottom lip trembling. "He never came back for me," I say, shaking my head.

"He did. We both did."

I continue to shake my head, not believing his words. No one came for me or tried to help me except... I lift my head, staring into Deuce's eyes, trying to remember a time I have tried so hard to forget.

"You remember me now, don't you? You never saw my face, but I was there. Jax was there."

My chest tightens and I can't breathe. It can't be. I close my eyes, wanting to remember for the first time ever.

"I've got you, babe. He'll never hurt you again," the guy whispers, holding me in his arms. His voice is soothing, familiar, yet I can't focus on it. My mind is still trying to grasp the horrors I have seen tonight.

"Darlin', can you hear me?" another voice asks. I will myself to look at him but can't, fear gripping me. *"I think she's in shock, but she'll be OK. The threat is gone."*

"Look at her. I can't leave her this way." The conversation around me sounds muffled, like this is nothing but a dream.

"We have to go, man," the unfamiliar voice beckons. *"She'll be safe."*

"You go. I won't leave her."

I lift my eyes at that moment, everything suddenly becoming clear. That voice and the feeling of safety. I have only ever felt that way with one person – Jax.

Looking over at Deuce, I am overcome with emotion. His eyes, the familiarity they contain, it was all right in front of me this entire time.

"You do remember, don't you?" he asks again, this time prompting me to nod my head in agreement. "All these years you have blamed him for abandoning you, for leaving you in that situation. He was forced to leave, but he made the decision to come back for you. He didn't want you to see him that way, to think of him as a killer, but it was the only way to end it."

Tears stream from my eyes, reality hitting me full force.

"I convinced him to leave you that night. He wanted to stay, but I was certain that when the cops arrived, they would see what was really going inside that place and know it had been an act of self-defense. I was wrong, Alana, and I'm sorry. We came forward, admitted what we had done, but even in death, Phil Martin held all the stakes. You were supposed to be living out your dreams, not continuing to live a nightmare. If you have to blame someone, blame me."

This is all too much to take in. I don't know what to believe in this moment. All I know is that everything I have ever thought was true is a lie, and I have hated the one person who truly never let me down. No longer able to contain my emotion, I release it all, not caring that all eyes in the restaurant are on me.

Three a.m. phone calls usually only mean one thing, especially when they come from Deuce. I have no idea what I am about to walk into, but I am prepared. With my .45 tucked into the waistband of my jeans, I mount my bike and peel out of the compound.

Fifteen minutes later, I pull into the parking lot of Body Shots, immediately spotting Deuce's bike parked at the entrance. Scanning the area, I see no sign of anyone in the vicinity, making me feel even more uneasy. I contemplate placing a call to Doc but decide to analyze the situation before I call for reinforcements.

Reaching for the door, I slowly pull it open, half expecting to see Deuce laying in a pool of blood. Instead, I am met with a devoid, dimly lit room. "Deuce!" I call out as I walk towards the hallway leading towards the back of the club.

"Over here," his voice echoes into the otherwise silent room. I turn to see him standing in the hallway, a grim look on his face.

"What the fuck's going on?" I ask as I close the distance between us.

"There's something you need to see," he says before turning, his face remaining solemn. I follow behind him as he leads me to the office, pausing outside the closed door. "I told you that I would lead her back," he says before pushing open the wooden barrier.

Stepping inside behind him, I scan the room, stopping when my eyes land on her. She is curled up on the couch, her eyes reddened from crying. My immediate reaction is to run to her, but I force myself to stay put, not knowing how she will react. When she stands, her tear filled eyes boring into mine, I almost lose it.

"I think you two have some catching up to do." Deuce slaps me on the back before turning towards the door.

"Deuce," Alana whispers. He turns slowly, looking over at her with more emotion than I have ever seen. "Thank you."

"No need to thank me, darlin'. I'd do it all over again." He smiles at her one last time before exiting the room, leaving Alana and I alone.

We stand in silence for several minutes, neither of us moving, unsure of what the other is thinking.

"I'm sorry," she whispers, her eyes filled with pain. "For not believing in you. I hated you for all these years when I should've been thanking you."

"Alana, if anyone should apologize, it's me. I wanted to protect you and I failed."

"You didn't fail," she says, taking a step forward. "You ended something I thought would never end. Deuce told me everything."

"I never wanted you to find out this way," I tell her, closing my eyes. "I should've been the one." Only when I feel her warm hand touch my arm do I open my eyes, looking down into her tear filled ones that shine so impossibly blue.

"And I should've given you a chance to explain. Instead, I treated you like you were a monster, when it was me all along." Her words are filled with pain and despair. "I failed you. You didn't fail me."

"Don't ever say that, Alana. You were never the monster. It was him. It was always him."

Without saying another word, she rushes into my arms, gripping me tightly as she sobs into my chest. Wrapping my arms around her, I close my eyes. I tried so hard to forget her, to move on, but in the end I knew it was impossible. Alana has always been in my heart, ever since the day we first met. No amount of distance could ever change that, and having her in my arms at this very moment is proof. This is where she belongs, where she will stay for as long as I am on this earth.

When she steps back, Alana looks up at me with shimmering eyes. "I never deserved you and I still don't, but I don't want to lose you again."

"Alana, you never lost me babe. You could never lose me. All the years we spent apart, you were always here," I say, placing my hand over my heart, "where you have always been."

"You mean you didn't forget about me?" God I hate that she could ever think that way.

"It's hard to forget someone who gave you so much to remember. Our pasts, the history we shared, what we meant to one another, none of it will ever end. You're stuck with me Alana, no matter what." This is more than a promise, it is my vow not only to her, but to myself. I couldn't let her go now if I tried.

She nods her head, accepting my words as truth. "So where do we go from here?" she asks, her eyes searching my own.

"We can't start the next chapter in our lives if we keep re-reading the last one." My words are just as much for me as they are for her. She has been letting the past control her present and future, and that ends today. The pain and sorrow in her eyes will be replaced with love and happiness, something she deserves more than anyone, and I will be the one to give it to her.

Her eyes fill with tears and for the first time in so very long, I see her smile at me. In that moment, I know we will survive.

Standing in the shadows, I watch as Jax pulls into the parking lot of Body Shots. He scans the parking lot, his eyes landing on the Harley sitting outside the front door, the one belonging to Deuce.

It seems as though I have been standing here for hours, when in fact it has been less than thirty minutes. I had been on my way to the car when I spotted Deuce pulling into the parking lot, the image of Alana holding onto him tightly permanently burned into my mind. Now with Jax's arrival, I am more than a little concerned.

I know what Deuce is capable of and that alone has me feeling like everything is falling apart around me. Add Jax into the mix and I am downright fearful. Both have made it perfectly clear what they want and neither will stop until they get it –Alana. If I had a bit of sense, I would walk away and let them have her, but I can't. She is mine and I won't let her go without a fight.

I slowly make my way to the back door of the club, pulling out my key to unlock it. Cautiously, I open it and step into the darkness, letting my eyes adjust for a moment before I make my way down the hallway, stopping in front of the office door.

As I press my ear to the cold wood, I hear Alana's frail voice.

"You mean you didn't forget about me?" she asks, and I can tell she is crying.

"It's hard to forget someone who gave you so much to remember. Our pasts, the history we shared, what we meant to one another, none of it will ever end. You're stuck with me Alana, no matter what," Jax tells her, causing me to clench my fists at my side.

"So where do we go from here?" I close my eyes at her words. I know she loves him and he loves her. If I were a better person, I would just walk away and give her the happiness she deserves.

"We can't start the next chapter in our lives if we keep re-reading the last one." I step away from the door, my head swimming. I have to end this or I will lose her forever. I just don't know how I am going to accomplish it.

Reluctantly, I push myself away from the door and through the exit, quietly locking it behind me. I move swiftly across the parking lot until I reach the car parked at the curb and climb inside, my mind reeling the entire time. How does one man take down an entire MC? If it were anyone but The Forgotten Souls, I might stand a chance.

My options are limited and with Jax back in the picture, time is running out. Desperate times call for desperate measures and I am willing to do whatever it takes not to lose her.

One Month Later

Standing at the edge of the bar, I watch as Alana enters the room, Jax following close behind. The two of them have been spending a lot of time together the last few weeks, rekindling the friendship they once shared. Alana is happier than I have ever seen her and it is all because of him.

She smiles over at him as they walk side by side further into the club, both of them oblivious to my presence.

"Looks like Jax has moved in on your girl," Hawk snickers from beside me. "Tried warning you about her, but you wouldn't hear it. Now look at you."

"What's that supposed to mean?" I ask, turning towards him.

"You should've had your fun with her and shipped her off like the rest of 'em. Like I told you, pussy is pussy. I'm surprised you haven't gotten your fill," he chuckles.

"Alana's not just another piece of pussy," I tell him defensively.

"What are you saying?" he asks, his tone becoming more serious. He lowers his voice, narrowing his eyes at me. "You can't honestly believe that she is gonna stay with you when the truth comes out, and you know eventually it will."

"It hasn't come out yet," I retort.

"And you're a fool if you think you can keep everything a secret forever. You may have been able to convince Alana you care about her, but Jax and Deuce don't buy it for a second." He pauses, looking around the room before turning back to me. "You need to do yourself a favor and get rid of Alana. Armando is waiting in the wings for me to close the deal. All you have to do is give the OK."

"Alana's not for sale," I seethe. We have been over this more times than I can count, but he just doesn't seem to get it.

"Look, you've had your little fun. It's time to move on to better things. Cut your losses now."

"I'm not letting her go," I tell him firmly.

"Let me put it to you another way. The Forgotten Souls have taken an interest in your girl. They start digging too much, and our cover is blown."

It's never been a secret that if Deuce and his men learn the truth behind our business, they would destroy us. They have already put a stop to Alana's working the back rooms at the club, much to my relief, and Hawk has reluctantly obliged. His only concern is them learning what goes on outside of these four walls. "Alana's non-negotiable. We keep doing what we're doing and I'll think of a way to get The Forgotten Souls off our backs."

Hawk shakes his head, letting out a ragged breath. "I hope you know what you're doing, because if I go down, I'm bringing you down with me." He gives me a knowing look before pushing away from the bar and crossing the room.

My eyes scan the room, landing on Alana immediately as she smiles up at Jax. The image alone infuriates me, but it is the cold gaze of Deuce staring back at me that has me questioning whether I am making the right decision.

Chapter 21

Alana

"You've got to be kidding me," I mumble as I look over at the alarm clock on the nightstand. Rolling over, I pull the covers over my head, trying to ignore the pounding coming from the front door. Pulling a pillow over my head, I try to block out the sound, but instead the noise seems to get louder.

Cursing, I throw the covers off of me as I stumble from the bed and rush towards the door, praying I can silence whoever has made ruining my day their main focus.

I reach for the knob, not bothering to find out who is on the other side, yanking the door open abruptly. "What the fuck...?" my voice trails off as my eyes land on Jax standing on the other side of the threshold.

"Well good morning to you too, sunshine," he says, smirking at me before he pushes he way past me. "You gonna sleep the day away?"

I turn towards him, scrunching my face in disgust. "You do realize it's six-thirty in the morning and I just got home three hours ago?"

"But you have the next two nights off, so you shouldn't be wasting it by sleeping," he says, plopping onto the old couch in the living room. "We still have a lot of time to make up for so you better get your sweet ass in there and get dressed. Unless you prefer traipsing around town in your..." he looks me up and down, "is that Eeyore?"

I look down at the tank top and boy shorts I have on and can't help but smile. "I happen to love Eeyore," I say, grinning at him.

"I remember," he beams. "What ever happened to that huge stuffed Eeyore you used to sleep with?"

The smile on my face vanishes in an instant. "I almost forgot about that," I whisper, looking away. I can still remember the day Jax won it for me at the carnival. One of many happier times that seem like a distant dream.

Mary, our foster parent at the time, had taken all of us to the annual carnival in Langley, the first and last time I ever went to one. It was the most exhilarating experience of my life, a time I vowed never to forget. From the moment Jax passed the oversized stuffed animal over to me, I had fallen in love with it and the boy who won it for me. A distant memory resurfacing, bringing out emotions in me I don't want to feel.

"Hey," Jax whispers, rising to his feet and walking towards me. Gripping my chin, he forces my eyes to meet his. "I didn't mean to upset you."

"You didn't," I say, looking up at him. "It was just a stupid toy." It's a bold faced lie, because for me it was so much more. It was a reminder of a happier time in my life and gave me hope for the future. Losing it meant that had all ended.

"I know what you're doing and it won't work. This is me, Alana. I know you better than anyone."

"At one time that was true. People change," I tell him. It's true that he knows the real Alana, the person I used to be, but she hasn't been around in a very long time.

"People don't change Alana, but eventually their masks fall off," he says, his eyes meeting mine. Swallowing hard, I desperately try to tear my eyes away from his only to find that I can't. In them I find comfort and a sense of security I haven't felt in a very long time. "The real Alana is still in there somewhere. I just have to make her realize that this time, nothing will tear us apart."

I want nothing more than to believe him, but know I need to guard my heart. I can't go through losing him again. "What you see is what you get, take it or leave it," I say, shrugging.

"That's where you're wrong. You might be able to hand Paul that load of bullshit, but not me. You're my Lana. Always have been and always will be."

I try my hardest not to smile at his words but to no avail. Grinning up at him, I shake my head. "You called me Lana."

His hand caresses my cheek, the hard callouses of his hand scraping against my tender flesh. "My Lana," he whispers before pressing his lips to my forehead and pulling me into his arms.

I close my eyes, relishing in the warmth of his arms wrapped around me, a feeling of contentment washing over me. Reminding myself that I am opening myself up to more heartache, I pull away from him. There is no mistaking the pained look in his eyes as I take a step back. "Please don't look at me that way."

He nods his head, the look on his face disappearing. "How about I start the coffee while you get ready?"

"OK... exactly what are we doing today?" I ask, hesitantly.

"It's a surprise," he smirks. "Now go do whatever it is you need to do so we can hit the road."

Shaking my head, I turn towards the bedroom. "Give me twenty minutes," I call over my shoulder before disappearing behind the door. Leaning against the wooden barrier, I try to wrap my head around the fact that Jackson Cade is once again a part of my life.

Three hours later, I'm smiling. Not just any old smile either. This is the kind of smile that makes your cheeks hurt but you couldn't stop it if you tried, and it feels so damn good.

"I take it I did good?" Jax asks, winking at me.

He knows he did good without me saying a word. "I can't believe you brought me to the beach," I say, still amazed that he would remember something so miniscule.

"It's a little cold to go for a swim today, but I still wanted you to see this place. We can come back over the summer and let you get your feet wet if you want."

"I'd like that," I say, still unable to erase the smile that seems to be permanently affixed to my face.

"Come on," he says as he grasps my hand in his. "Let's see if we can find you any seashells."

As I come to a stop outside the apartment door, I bite back the smile that threatens to break free once again and turn towards Jax. "Thank you for today. I had a good time." More than a good time, if I'm completely honest with myself.

"This was just the beginning. We have a lot of time to make up for," he says, smiling at me. "How about tomorrow?"

I stare at him dumbfounded. "Tomorrow?"

"You know the day that follows today. Whataya say? Anything you want to do, I'm game," he says. I want nothing more than to spend as much time with Jax as possible, but by doing so, I'd be hurting the one person who has been there for me over the last few years. I have shunned him for the past few weeks, although not intentionally, and it isn't fair.

"I can't," I say, already regretting the words before they leave my mouth when I see the disappointed look in his eyes. "I really need to spend some time with Paul." His eyes turn cold at the mention of Paul's name. "Please don't be mad at me."

"I could never be mad at you, Lana," he says, his eyes softening. "But I just got you back and I'm not willing to share you just yet." He reaches out, his fingertips grazing my cheek, causing me to instantly melt.

"Jax," I whisper, pulling away from him.

Slowly, he drops his hand at his side. "I'm sorry. I didn't mean to make you feel uncomfortable."

"You didn't," I mutter.

"We'll take this as slow as you want. I've waited a long time to have you back in my life, so time is meaningless. But I'm not going anywhere Lana."

"What?" I ask, my eyes reaching his.

"They say you're lucky to have one best friend in life. I was lucky enough to fall in love with mine," he says, taking a step towards me. "I was in love with you years ago and that hasn't changed Lana. Time may have passed, but my feelings never wavered."

His words make my heart swell yet they cause me fear. I have loved Jackson Cade for as long as I can remember, but I'm afraid. If I open my heart to him again, will he abandon me like everyone else in my life? I have already lost him once, and the thought of losing him again terrifies me. "I have to go," I whisper breathlessly, turning quickly and reaching for the door knob. Pushing the door open, I slip inside without saying another word, shutting it behind me before he has a chance to change my mind.

Leaning against the wooden barrier that separates us, I close my eyes and breathe in rapidly.

"Alana?" I open my eyes at the sound of Paul's voice. "Are you OK?" he asks, looking down at me with concern.

"Yeah," I whisper, trying to regain my composure.

"Hey," he says, taking the few steps necessary until he has his arms wrapped around me. "You look shaken up."

I instantly calm as he engulfs me in his arms where he holds me for several minutes. Taking in a deep breath, I slowly pull away. "I'm OK, I just panicked a little."

"Does this have something to do with Jax?" he asks, narrowing his eyes.

"A little," I confess, "but not in a bad way. He admitted he has feelings for me. It kind of freaked me out," I laugh nervously.

I lift my head when I sense him distancing himself from me to see Paul taking a step away from me, a look of discontent contorting his features. "He told you he loves you? He just came back into your life and now he's devoting himself to you?"

"Jax has always had feelings for me just like I have for him. This didn't happen overnight." Paul already knows this, so why is he acting this way?

"Bullshit," he mumbles, turning away from me. "Don't you think it's kind of strange that he disappeared from your life for so many years and suddenly he's back and in love with you?" He suddenly turns, his gaze meeting mine, filled with such hatred and discontent. "He abandoned you and you're just gonna forgive him?"

"He didn't abandon me!" I retort. "He didn't want to leave me!"

"And you believe him?!" he shouts, causing me to startle. "You are so fuckin' naïve!"

"Jax wouldn't lie to me," I say, defending him.

"And how can you be so stupid to believe that? Everybody lies."

"Real friends don't lie to each other," I say without hesitation.

Paul is silent for several moments, his eyes never leaving mine. "I just don't want you getting hurt," he says in a hushed tone.

"There are very few people in this world I trust implicitly – you and Jax are it. I know in my heart that neither of you would ever lie to me nor hurt me."

He swallows hard, the look on his face full of agony. Reaching out to me, he gently touches my cheek. "You know I care about you, right Alana?"

"Of course, but…"

Pressing a finger to my lips, he silences me. "I can't lose you, not to Jax or anyone else. You have to promise me that no matter what happens, you won't leave me."

"Who said anything about…?"

"Promise me," he says in a sharp tone. "I need to hear the words Alana. Tell me that you will never walk away from me, no matter what."

"Paul," I say his name in complete bewilderment.

"Just say it!" he demands.

"I promise!" I shout out, but before I have a chance to ask him why he is acting this way, he reaches out and grasps my face, crashing his lips onto my own before his tongue infiltrates my mouth with pure need.

Parting my lips, I give him access, my tongue colliding with his, giving into his desires. Suddenly, I am overcome with guilt and for the first time since Paul and I met, I push him away.

"Lana," he breathes, his eyes filled with lust.

When he takes a step towards me again, I place my hand on his chest, stopping him from coming any closer. I don't want this and I am not going to be guilted into doing something I no longer feel comfortable with. "Paul, please," I plead. He stops immediately, the hurt in his eyes speaking volumes making me instantly regret not giving in. "I'm just not feeling well," I lie, hoping he will believe me.

He narrows his eyes at me, saying nothing. When he finally speaks, his voice is laced with concern. "Are you getting sick?"

"I don't think so. I'm probably just tired. I think I just need to get some sleep."

Slowly he nods his head, his eyes softening. "You're probably right," he says, giving me a reassuring smile. "You head to bed and I'll come in and check on you after a while."

Standing on my tip toes, I press a kiss to his cheek, silently telling him what he already knows.

Chapter 22

JAX

One Month Later

"A friend is someone who knows the song in your heart and can sing it back to you when you have forgotten the words."

"What are you talking about?" I ask, turning my attention towards Alana as she takes a seat beside me on the rooftop.

"Just something I read," she says, shaking her head at me. "Tomorrow's the big day. I'm a little nervous."

"Why's that?" I won't admit to her that I am just as scared as she is. This is something we both have dreamed about for a long time. Being a part of a family is something we never thought would become a reality. The fact that the Martins agreed to take in both Alana and myself makes the entire situation perfect.

"I don't know how to explain it. I just have a bad feeling," she whispers, staring out into the dark sky.

"There's nothing to worry about, Lana. The Martins are nice people and they have a huge house. No more sharing a room or wearing hand-me-downs. We are finally going to have a family and the best part is that you and I will be together. What could go wrong?" I already know what she is thinking, but this time will be different. The Martins are not just looking to foster us, they have talked about adoption.

"You're probably right," Alana sighs. "I guess I'm just overthinking it."

"You always do. That's what I'm here for, to make you feel better." I grasp her hand in mine and pull her towards me. Draping my arm over her shoulder, she leans closer, resting her head on my shoulder.

I was wrong. The Martins put us through hell, Alana more so than me. To look at her now, you would never guess the pain and torture she has endured. She wears the mask perfectly, not allowing anyone to see the depths of her anguish, but I am not just anyone.

"Don't tell me your cat died," Deuce chuckles as he comes to sit beside me.

"I hate fuckin' cats," I mumble before nodding at Becky to give me a refill. "Thought you'd be out trolling for pussy. Why the late start?"

"Actually, we've got other plans for this evening," Deuce says, grasping the beer from Becky's extended hand.

"We?" I ask, raising my brow.

"Tonight the truth comes out," he says calmly. "And we shut down Hawk's operation."

We've known about Hawk's little side business for a few months now and could've put an end to it in the beginning, but Deuce's gut told him there was more to it, so we waited. "What changed?"

"Spyder made a little discovery. Seems that Hawk's operation is a lot larger than we first thought. He's got ties we weren't aware of."

"And?" I ask, my patience wearing thin.

"Paul's job is to lure in about twenty or so girls and after a little sex party, they're auctioned off to the highest bidder."

Sex trafficking. A more lucrative form of prostitution than we had believed but it somehow doesn't come as a shock. "Then let Pat shut it down. We've got more important things to worry about." Namely Alana.

Something is off with her. The last few days, she hasn't been herself. I know something is going on and I'm pretty damn sure Paul is behind it.

"Pat's already aware of the situation and will be on standby when shit goes down," he explains.

A bust like this will make Pat's career. He's been vying for lead investigator and taking down a sex trafficking operation will land him the position for sure. Plus, Pat and his men will keep our names out of it completely. The higher ups aren't aware of our affiliation within their ranks, and our involvement may not sit well. "What aren't you telling me?"

Deuce lifts his eyes, worry etching his face. "There's no easy way to tell you this. I got a call this afternoon from Armando Montego wanting to make a deal. He was contacted personally by Hawk inviting him to tonight's festivities. Apparently made him an offer he couldn't refuse. That's when he called me. I'm sorry brother... Alana is on the auction block."

"What?!" I shout, jumping to my feet.

"I need you to keep your head on straight and listen to me. Armando's had his eye on Alana when Paul found her years ago. Offered Hawk top dollar for her, but Hawk turned him down. Said he had other plans for her. When Hawk contacted him, something didn't set well, so he sent out his eyes and ears. Learned that Alana had been spending a lot of time with you. Armando may be a low life son of a bitch, but he's all about covering his own ass. That's why he contacted me. He knows Alana's affiliation with the Forgotten Souls and he's not willing to go to war over one girl. Alana will be safe."

"I don't care what promises that fucker gave you!" I roar. "We have to get her out!"

"You have to trust me!" he counters. "We go in and grab Alana, we don't solve anything. We have to shut this entire operation down."

I know he's right, but it doesn't make it any easier. My thoughts are on Alana's safety and nothing else. "So what? We just waltz in there and Hawk's gonna let Alana leave? You've lost your fuckin' mind!"

"Will you shut the fuck up and listen for once! First of all, you're not going in, I am. Second, Alana will walk out of there safely, you have my word. But most importantly, when she leaves, she will know the truth."

I stare at him for a moment, completely speechless. *The truth.* "What haven't you told me?" I finally ask, knowing that Deuce is keeping me in the dark.

Shaking his head, he looks at me with concern. "Let's discuss all the details later. Like you said, we need to get Alana out of there." He diverts his attention to Becky behind the bar before trying to change the subject. "Spyder rented an SUV. I want you on standby in the alley waiting for us. The moment you see us exit, be ready to hightail it out of there. We won't have much time to get out before Pat and his men move in. I think..."

"Spyder can stay with the car. I'm going in," I say, cutting him off.

"Jax, listen to me. Alana's gonna need your support when we get her out of there. It's best if Spyder goes in with me."

"Not happenin'," I tell him, shaking my head. "I go in with you, but first, put our friendship aside and tell me everything you know." I know he's trying to protect me for some reason, but I am a grown man. I can handle whatever it is.

He stares at me for a moment before finally nodding his head in agreement. "This is against my better judgement," he says before pausing again.

"Spit it out already!"

Taking in a deep breath, he says the words I will remember for the rest of my life. "His real name is Paul Randall Martin. He's Phil Martin's son."

My head is spinning as I try to grasp Deuce's words. How can this be? Phil and Janet Martin had no children, or at least that is what I had been led to believe.

"Spyder thinks Paul was a victim of Phil Martin, just like Alana was. He disappeared around the same time his mother, Susan, died, which prompted Spyder to dig further. All the records indicated that she died of natural causes, but when he dug a little deeper the evidence proved she had been stabbed and we believe Paul was the culprit. There's a hospital record where Paul was admitted for a stab wound to his left shoulder the same night. He claimed he had been robbed. The docs patched him up and called the police, but by the time they arrived, Paul had bolted. From what Spyder uncovered, Paul went to the streets and that's where he met Hawk. If we're completely honest here, Paul was as much of a victim of Hawk's as he was his own father. Hawk manipulated him, making him a pawn in his operation."

"Do not make excuses for him," I choke out, the tightness in my chest increasing. Paul may have fallen victim to Phil Martin and to Hawk, but what he has done, what he continues to do, is inexcusable.

"Paul's job is to find the girls, make them trust him, and then he hands them off to Hawk. Most are runaways or women down on their luck. Many are sold and sent overseas. Others sell drugs or their bodies on the street. A rare few work the clubs. Lucky for us, Alana was one of the few he decided to keep close." Deuce does not try to hide the emotion that is consuming him. He likes Alana, thinks of her as a sister, and to know what could have happened to her is tearing him up.

"I've already briefed Pat on how this is going down. First priority is getting Alana out of there safely. Once that is done, he'll move in. Hawk and Paul will go away for a long time for this, you can count on it."

I shake my head. "Prison's too good for them."

"I agree, but we need Pat on this one. From what we know, there will be at least fifty girls there tonight. They have to make it out safely and that won't happen if we go in guns blazin'. We need numbers and Pat can provide those."

I hate it when he's right, but he makes a valid point. I may be a lot of things, but I am not so cruel that I would endanger the lives of innocent women whose lives hang in the balance. "When do we head out?" I ask, my patience growing thin.

"In ten, but before we head out, I need your word that you won't do anything to jeopardize this. We go in, get Alana out, and let Pat handle the rest. No hero bullshit. For the first time in our lives, we're gonna let the law do their job. You feel me?" he asks, his eyes boring into my own.

"I just want to get Alana out. If she's safe, I don't care what else happens as long as Paul is out of her life for good." Then I can finally have my Lana back.

He nods his head in agreement. "Let's ride," he says, nodding in Spyder's direction before heading towards the door.

Alana

"Where are we going again?" I ask, looking out the passenger side window. I have never been on this side of town and from the looks of it, I hope to never return. Condemned buildings line the streets and only the occasional person walking alongside the road proves there is life out there.

"We'll be there in a few," Paul answers, his eyes glued to the road.

I am feeling uneasy. I've worked many private functions in the past, but something is different about this one. Normally I would have some idea about what I was walking into, but this time Paul has been very secretive. "What kind of function is this again?" I ask, hoping this time he will actually give me an answer.

"Are you nervous?" he asks, turning towards me for the first time since I climbed into the passenger seat.

"Yeah. You haven't told me anything about this gig."

He smiles at me before focusing again on the road. "Here," he says, pulling a bottle from his coat pocket. "Take two of these."

I open the cap, pulling out two oval shaped pills that are greyish-green in color. I toss them back, unconcerned that I have nothing to drink. Passing the bottle back to him, I smile. "Thanks."

"Anytime."

We ride in silence for another five minutes before Paul turns and pulls into a parking lot. "This is the place?" I ask, unmoving. Looking over at the vacant warehouse, I try to find a reason for us to be here. Of all the private parties I have worked, this is undeniably the worst.

"It doesn't look like much from the outside," he says, opening the driver's side door and stepping out. I follow suit, still feeling unsure about the situation.

"And Hawk set this up?" I probe.

"Yep."

Rounding the car, I come to a stop when I am standing beside Paul. "Is there something you aren't telling me?" He turns to face me, a look of regret on his face. The sinking feeling in my stomach suddenly making me feel nauseous.

"I haven't been completely honest with you Alana," he begins. He moves slightly so that he is standing directly in front of me, his hands reaching out to grasp my face. "You know I would never ask this of you if it weren't important."

Shaking my head, I bite back the tears that form in my eyes. "Paul, please..." I plead, without him saying the words.

"It's just one last time, I promise."

"Why?" I ask, my voice breaking. I guess I should feel grateful that I haven't had to do anything like this in a long time, but I don't. "What about the next time we can't pay the rent? You keep making promises but in the end, I'm the one who pays the price. I don't want to live this way anymore."

"And you won't. I know I've asked a lot of you and you've never let me down, but this time will be the last. I'm quitting the club and getting a real job. I start on Monday, but we need the funds to get us by until my first check. No more drugs or dancing. Just you and me living the way we should've been this entire time."

"You're serious?" I ask, wanting so much to believe that this is all coming to an end. He's made the same promise to me before and something always comes up and I am forced to resort back to doing this.

"No matter what, after tonight, neither of us will set foot in the club again. It's history."

"Alright," I agree, putting my faith in Paul once again.

He grips my hand, pulling me into his arms. "I won't let you down again," he whispers. "You mean everything to me."

"We'll get through this," I say, repeating the words I have uttered so many times before. "We always do."

He pulls away, smiling down at me. "There will be a lot of people here tonight, and they are willing to pay top dollar. We just need to make at least a grand."

I say nothing, simply nodding my head in agreement as he leads me to the side door of the building. As he opens the door, I take in a deep breath, trying to tamp down my emotions. I can do this one more time, and then it will all be over. We can finally get away from this life and everything that comes with it, becoming free.

Following behind Paul, he leads me down a dark hallway, pushing forward towards the sound of music. When we emerge, I take in the room in front of me.

The room is filled with women, all varying in age and appearance. Some are completely nude, allowing the random men in the room to touch them. Others are dancing to the dreadful music playing in the background, oblivious to the ogling men surrounding them. My eyes fix on a blonde several feet from me as she pulls her halter over her head, tossing it aside. A man in his late fifties reaches out to her, his hands grasping at her breasts. She smiles at him briefly before lowering herself to her knees, unzipping his pants on descent.

I turn to face Paul whose eyes are affixed on the scene unfolding before us. "I'm not feeling so good," I say, causing him to turn his attention to me as my hand reaches upward to my forehead. A sudden wave of dizziness make me feel as though the room is spinning.

Paul puts his arm around me, supporting me as I begin to wobble. "It's OK, I've got you," he says, pulling me to him.

My knees feel weak, and I am overcome with fatigue making me feel almost detached from my body. Leaning against Paul, I close my eyes, willing the feeling to pass but instead it only intensifies. I feel drunk, for lack of a better word, even though I have not had a drop of alcohol.

As I feel my legs give out from under me, I am suddenly surrounded by warmth as I feel Paul's arms engulf me. "I'm sorry, Alana," he whispers. "It had to be this way."

I open my mouth to speak, but find I can't. I am suddenly helpless, my body refusing to respond to my commands as he lifts me into his arms. "I love you, Alana," he whispers before the darkness consumes me.

PAUL

Carrying Alana in my arms, I weave my way through the people crowding the room, oblivious to the looks sent my way. As I continue to push through the crowd, my eyes land on Hawk who narrows his eyes before crossing the room, headed in my direction.

"What the fuck is this?" he asks, coming to a stop in front of me.

"She must've taken something," I explain. It's no secret that Alana pops pills on occasion, so it shouldn't be a surprise if she took too many. It wouldn't be the first time, but it will be the last. I hate that I have done this to her, but it was the only way this would work.

"Well fuck! Take her into the back and try to sober her up. Armando is here and if I don't deliver the goods, there's gonna be more than just a little hell to pay."

I nod at him before walking away, still holding Alana protectively in my arms. I make my way down the hallway to one of the vacant rooms near the end. Stepping inside, I spot the lone mattress positioned in the center of the room and lay her down gently on top.

Stepping back, I look down at her wishing I could go back in time and do things differently. Treat her the way she deserves to be treated. She never should have had this life, especially after everything she has been through. I knew the moment I laid eyes on her that she had been through hell, but instead of doing the right thing, I did what I had been trained to do. Lured her in, took advantage of her naiveté, and turned her into something she was never meant to be. I have manipulated her, tricked her into doing things she would never have dreamed of doing. And while all of this was taking place, I fell in love with her.

"What have I gotten myself into?" I say aloud, pacing back and forth in the tiny room. This has been my life for so many years, the way I have made my living, and I am throwing it all away for her. When this evening is over, she will be mine the way she was meant to be, and we will have a life together. I just have to pull this off without Alana getting hurt.

Drugging her was a last minute decision. I had a choice to make and I made the one I thought was best. Hawk has been persistent about getting rid of the extra baggage, namely Alana, because she is a liability, especially with the attention she has gained from The Forgotten

Souls. With Jax and Deuce spending so much time looking into my past, I knew I had to make a move, with or without Hawk's ultimatum. I can't – no I won't lose her, no matter the cost.

That is what brought me here today. With Alana unaware of what is going on around her, I can pull this off. I will deal with the consequences when she wakes up and we are far away from this place. She will be upset that we are no longer in Cedar Falls, far away from Jax and Deuce, but once we start our new life, everything will be perfect. She will never have to know the truth and we can live out the remainder of our days together. I can make her happy once we leave this world behind.

With Armando on my side, there is no way I will fail. It took several grand to ensure his cooperation, but it was a small price to pay considering the alternative. He made contact with The Forgotten Souls and filled them in on all the sordid details planned for this evening, leaving Alana out of it completely. I may despise Deuce, but he is a man of conscience and won't be able to sit back and do nothing while this is going down in *his* town. When Deuce and his men make their move, Alana and I will make a run for it. Hawk will go to prison for a long time, and no one will be any the wiser.

I grab a crate from the corner of the room and place it beside the mattress, taking a seat. "I'm sorry for putting you through all of this," I whisper to a sleeping Alana, knowing she will not remember anything that occurs this evening. "But it had to go down this way."

She lays there unmoving, looking peaceful as she sleeps. She is the epitome of beauty, both inside and out, and I had been a fool for not seeing it from the beginning. "We will have our happily ever after, Alana. It will take some time, but you will forget all about Jax. You'll see."

I continue staring at her for what seems like hours, my mind going over the plan that is already underway. I am so consumed with my thoughts, I don't even hear the door open until Hawk's raspy voice alerts me to his presence. "You wanna tell me what the fuck is going on?"

Turning to face him, I see the accusatory look on his face. Hawk is a smart man and he has known me for many years. "She took the wrong pills," I explain, hoping he will buy my excuse. "I had a bottle of Roofies and she must have grabbed it by mistake."

He narrows his eyes at me, looking for any reason to call me out. "So you're telling me you had nothing to do with this?"

"Why would I jeopardize my future?" I ask in a defensive tone. "I don't like the idea of having to choose between that and Alana, but I'd be a fool to walk away from what you and I have built."

Nodding his head, he continues to stare at me, still not believing my words. "Armando is here and I'm sure he wants to sample the goods. I guess that's out of the question."

It takes everything in me not to react. I know he is fucking with me, waiting for me to erupt, but what he doesn't realize is that Armando is working for me and wouldn't dare ask such a thing. "Give her a few hours and the Rohypnol will wear off. She'll be good as new."

"Yeah," he mutters, turning on his heel and exiting the room. When the door slams behind him, I let out an exasperated sigh. He doesn't buy it for one minute, but it doesn't matter. In the end, he will be the one who falls, not me. He will spend the rest of his life behind bars while Alana and I begin our new life together. We just have to get through tonight.

When the door slams open again, I turn expecting to see Hawk. Instead my eyes land the three burly men standing behind him. "I warned you a long time ago not to cross me," he says before nodding to his cohorts who move into the room, coming to a stop beside me. "You know what to do with him," he says, a sadistic smile on his face. "Did you really think a few grand would be enough? I knew you would betray me over that little cunt, I just didn't expect you to be so fuckin' stupid about it. Hope she was worth it because this will be the last time you ever lay eyes on her."

He nods at the three men before turning, leaving my fate in their hands.

Chapter 23

JAX

Pulling up to the warehouse, my heart is pounding in my chest. I have never been more nervous than I am at this very moment. Alana is in there and God only knows what is happening to her. Pushing aside my worries, I put my faith in Deuce who keeps assuring me that she will be safe. I have no doubt we will get her out of there or die trying, but what gives me the most concern is what is undoubtedly happening to her this very moment.

"I need you to focus," Deuce reminds me as he climbs out of the SUV. "Spyder, you already know your assignment. Make it happen," he barks, prompting Spyder to head towards the back of the building.

"What assignment?" I ask, feeling left in the dark.

"When you and I walk in, Hawk's gonna know somethin's up. Spyder's job is to find Hawk, detain him, and then locate Paul before we make our move," he explains. "He has ten minutes."

Taking in a deep breath, I try to maintain my composure. I want nothing more than to barge in, do what I feel is necessary, but by doing so I would be placing Alana in jeopardy and I refuse to do that. No one knows what measures Hawk and Paul will go to in order to protect themselves.

"I go in first," Deuce says abruptly, interrupting my thoughts. "If shit goes south, you get to Alana."

He is willing to sacrifice himself for her, yet another reason I am proud to call him my friend and brother. I nod my head in agreement, not because I want him to risk himself for Alana, but because she is the priority here.

The remainder of the ten minutes is filled with silence as we wait for Spyder to accomplish his task and I find myself counting the seconds until Deuce gives the signal for us to move in.

As we push our way through the door to the warehouse, I immediately begin scanning the room, looking for any sign of Alana. "She's not here," I mutter, my heart sinking at the prospect that we are too late.

Out of the corner of my eye, I spot Spyder moving towards us. "First one down, but no sign of the other," he says as he approaches, the people in the room oblivious to our existence.

Deuce turns towards me. "You find Alana. Spyder and I will take care of Paul." He doesn't give me a chance to argue before disappearing into the crowd.

Letting out the breath I didn't realize I was holding, I push my way through the chaos in front of me, completely ignoring what is going on around me. In another time and place, I might find all of this entertaining if I didn't know the real reason these women are here. Pushing aside those thoughts, I make my way towards the lone hallway to the right, my mind focused on the only thing that matters in this moment.

I go room to room, interrupting several individuals without apology, in hopes that the next door I open will lead me to Alana. As I approach the last room on the right, all hope vanishes when I reach for the handle to find it locked. Taking a step back, I lean against the wall, feeling completely defeated.

At this point, I don't know whether we were too late or if she was ever even here. She could be halfway across the world at this very moment, and there isn't a damn thing I can do about it. My heart feels heavy, completely void of any feeling, at the realization that I have lost Alana for good.

Clenching my teeth, I push myself off the wall and head back towards the main room. After taking a few steps, the sound of gunshots from behind me causes me to reach for the .45 tucked in the waistband of my jeans. As I turn, intent on busting through the door, it opens and Paul steps into the hallway.

Lifting my piece, I aim it directly at his head, my trigger finger itching to take the son of a bitch out. "Where the fuck is she?" I growl, attempting to look over his shoulder into the room he just abandoned.

He lifts his eyes to mine, shaking his head. Taking in his blood splattered clothes, I am filled with a rage I have never before felt. "Jax!" Pat shouts from behind me. I ignore him, my focus solely on the man who has manipulated and destroyed the only woman I have ever loved. "Put the gun down!" he orders.

Staring into the eyes of the enemy, I watch them transform from cold and heartless to being filled with regret. "I never meant to hurt her," he whispers, raising his arms in surrender. "She was the first person who ever truly cared about me. I just wanted to get her away from this life, become the person she believed I was."

His words infuriate me even more. "You mother fucker!" I snarl as I slowly pull back the trigger.

"She would have forgiven me," he continues. "But I don't deserve it." Paul closes his eyes, taking in a ragged breath. When his eyes open again, they are filled with anguish. "Maybe it's better this way."

"What?" I ask, loosening my grip on the gun just as Deuce appears at my side. Grasping it from my hand, he nods prompting Pat and his men to rush forward. In a flash, Paul is tackled to the floor and handcuffed.

Closing my eyes, I bite back the flood of emotions that threatens to consume me. I have not only lost my best friend, but the love of my life. Voices are a mere flurry of chaotic background noise that I can no longer comprehend as the realization of it all finally hits me. Only when I feel Deuce shaking me do I begin to snap out of it.

"Did you hear me?" Deuce asks, looking at me with concern.

I say nothing, staring at him absentmindedly. Losing someone is never easy, but losing someone that was your past, present and future, someone who was a part of your heart and soul, absolutely destroys you. No passage of time will ease my pain.

Gripping my shoulders, Deuce pushes me against the wall as paramedics push their way past us. I watch as Deuce's lips move, unable to hear a word he says, my mind still reeling over my present nightmare.

Only when I see the paramedics begin to exit the room do I move forward, knowing I must face reality. With my eyes locked on the stretcher, I move forward, pushing Deuce out of my way.

Before I can say a word, one of the paramedics stops, looking at me with confusion. "We're taking her to Mercy if you want to follow," he says, looking from me to Deuce.

"We'll meet you there," Deuce nods, pulling me out of their path. "See, she's alright. No signs of any trauma so the chances are she was just drugged. Would've called Doc if Pat wasn't here, but he has to follow protocol."

Shaking my head, it takes me a moment to wrap my head around what I have just witnessed. "She's alright?" I ask, my voice a mere whisper of disbelief. "But the shots, the blood?" There is no mistaking what I heard and saw with my own eyes.

"Looks like Paul took out three goons, all DOA. Don't know what went down, I just know that Alana was out of it the entire time. He didn't hurt her." I breathe a sigh of relief, making a silent vow that from this point forward, Alana will remain safe. "Now let's let Pat do his job and you go take care of your girl."

My girl. My Alana. She's been mine since the day we first met and will be mine until the end of time.

Chapter 24

Alana

TWO DAYS LATER

As I take a seat at the rectangular shaped table, my heart is pounding in my chest. Being in this place brings back memories I would rather forget, but somehow I managed to force myself to come here. I need answers and this is the only place I will I get them.

Jax has been elusive. All he will tell me is that I was drugged. That alone speaks volumes, but doesn't explain much more. Jax knows more than he is letting on, but he refuses to tell me. I want, no I *need* to know the truth.

My nerves getting the best of me, I allow my gaze to wander the room. Several women are seated at tables similar to my own, sitting across from them are various men, all dressed in bright orange jumpsuits. They all seem at ease, comfortable in their surroundings, while I am a nervous mess.

Letting out a rushed breath, I rest my forehead in my hands and close my eyes. *You can do this,* I tell myself, trying to gain some confidence.

"Alana?" I turn at the sound of Paul's voice whispering my name in disbelief.

I rise from my seat, looking up into his tormented eyes. He looks somehow different, his eyes sunken with dark circles surrounding them.

"Ma'am, you need to stay seated," the guard warns, nodding at the seat I just abandoned.

"Sorry," I whisper as I sit back down, the nervousness I was feeling all but gone now that I see Paul is alright.

The guard leads Paul to the chair across from me, and as he takes a seat, I notice the cuffs that bind his wrists and ankles. I hate this, both for him and myself.

"You have thirty minutes," the guard says before walking off.

We sit in silence for several minutes, neither of us saying a word. When Paul finally does speaks, his voice is filled with anguish. "I didn't expect you to come," he begins, his gaze lowered, unwilling to meet my own.

"Why would you think that? We've been through so much together. You getting busted doesn't change anything. I made a promise to you, remember?"

He lifts his eyes until they are meeting my own, immediately softening. "I do remember," he whispers. "But don't make promises you don't intend to keep, Alana. Everything changes. You know that better than anyone."

"One thing that will never change is you and I," I say, smiling over at him, silently telling him we will get through this.

He shakes his head, the lightness of his eyes suddenly turning dark. "There was never a me and you, Alana."

His words are cold and heartless, stinging on impact. "That's not true," I argue. "We are a team." Why is he acting this way?

"No, we were never a team. You were my puppet and you still are. I have to put an end to it. You should just go, Alana."

"I'm not going anywhere, Paul. You aren't making any sense!"

He throws his head back in a fit of laughter, causing all eyes to land on us. "You're a piece of work, you know that?" He continues laughing for what seems like an eternity before finally calming. "I used you Alana. From the beginning I used you."

Shaking my head, I look at him in confusion. "Don't try to chase me away. Let me help you."

"Help me? How are *you* going to help me?" he chuckles.

"We can get you an attorney. Someone who will fight for you," I retort, willing to do whatever is necessary to help him.

"I don't need your help, Alana, and I sure as hell don't want it." His words are laced with pure venom. "You've done enough already."

"What?" I ask in disbelief. Is he blaming me for being in here?

"Quit with the innocent act. You knew what was going on, didn't you? That's the reason you were willing to walk in there without putting up much of a fight. I can't believe I didn't see it."

"I don't understand," I mutter, trying to wrap my head around everything he is saying, none of it making any sense.

"A sex trafficking charge wouldn't hold because I've always protected myself against that. I could have pinned it entirely on Hawk. But murder? There's no coming back from that, is there?" Paul seethes.

Sex trafficking? Murder? I am speechless as he continues his barrage of accusations.

"How did you find out? You couldn't have known all along because you're not that good an actress. It was Jax, wasn't it? He found out what we were doing behind the scenes and pulled you to his side. I knew I should've listened to Hawk and sold you to the highest bidder, but I couldn't," he mumbles, shaking his head. "Jax has wanted me out of the picture since the beginning but he didn't want to bring you down too. So he waited for the opportunity to arise and thanks to Hawk, it did. I'll give the fucker credit, he's smart, but not smart enough. My attorney is already working on a plea bargain, so Jax's plan still failed."

"Sex trafficking?" I ask, finally finding my voice. "You killed somebody?" I have known Paul for a very long time and have never seen this side of him and for the first time ever, I am actually afraid of the man sitting in front of me.

A panicked look crosses his face momentarily, quickly being replaced with one of despair. "Alana," my name escapes his lips as a mere whisper, pleading with me to understand.

Swallowing hard, I fight the tears burning the back of my eyes. "You were going to sell me?" Saying the words aloud makes them sound even worse and suddenly everything begins to make sense. The man I have trusted with everything that I am has been lying to me from the beginning and I was too blind to see it.

"No! That's what Hawk wanted, not me! I fought for you, protected you, and made you mine. That night was about setting you free. Taking you away from this life and us starting over, just you and me. That's why I roofied you, so you would be safe."

I begin to tremble as tears stream down my face, no longer unable to contain my emotions. "So you drugged me?" I ask in disbelief. "I don't know who you are anymore."

"It's still me, Alana. I'm Paul, the guy who took you in when you had no one. The person you confided your deepest, darkest secrets in. The man who risked everything to protect you."

Lifting my eyes to meet his, I finally see him for the person he really is. Using the back of my hand, I roughly wipe the tears from my face, replacing the hurt with anger. "The same man that convinced me to sell myself," I say through clenched teeth. "I always blamed Phil Martin for destroying me, but I was wrong. It was you. At least with Phil, I knew I was

looking into the eyes of the devil. But you...
you disguised yourself, pretended to my friend
so you could have your way. All those years,
you told me what a piece of shit he was for
doing those things to me, but you two are one
in the same."

"I am nothing like my father!" Paul shouts as I
rise from my seat.

My heart stops beating, my legs becoming jelly
as I meet his gaze. His father? I am no longer
trembling, I am shaking with fear, shocked by
his admission. This can't be happening.

"I'm nothing like my father," he whispers, his
eyes filling with tears as he looks up at me
with pleading eyes.

I can no longer bear looking at the man I
thought I could trust. Everything was nothing
but a lie. "I fuckin' hate you," I whisper before
turning on my heel and rushing towards the
exit, wanting to put as much distance between
myself and him as possible.

Stepping out the front door of the detention
center, every single emotion I have been
holding back escapes as I drop to my knees on
the sidewalk. All these years, I put my faith
and trust into Paul and in one brief moment, it
all came crashing down. I cared for him, even
loved him and thought he would never betray
me. I was a fool.

"Lana baby, please don't cry." Just the sound of Jax's voice makes me begin to sob uncontrollably. "I'm so sorry," he whispers as he pulls me into his arms, holding me tightly to him, trying to console me.

I know in this moment that Jax knew everything. He knew and yet he didn't try to warn me. I want to be angry with him, but I can't. He has never hidden the fact that he didn't trust Paul, and now I understand why. Even if he had told me, I would have refused to believe him because I trusted Paul. I never thought he would let me down. "H-how l-long h-have y-you kn-known?" I brokenly ask, barely able to form a coherent sentence.

"Not long," he admits, never releasing his hold on me.

"W-why d-didn't y-you t-tell m-me?" I stammer.

"It's hard to accept the truth when lies are exactly what you want to hear. You had to see it, hear it for yourself to know it was real."

His words couldn't be truer, proving that even after all of these years, Jax still knows me. Even so, it doesn't mean I can trust him. If I have learned anything from this, it's that I am alone in this world. I can only depend on myself and can never rely on anyone else. I can never put my heart on the line again because I won't survive it. I'll never be able to forget the pain Paul has caused me, but I can pretend.

"It only hurts when you start pretending it doesn't," Jax says, clearly reading my mind. "You aren't alone Alana, and never will be again." The words escape his lips with ease, a vow I want so badly to believe, but can't. "To you, they are just words, but to me they are a promise, one that I will never break. I know it's gonna take time for you to trust again, but I'll wait."

"Don't make promises you don't intend to keep," I say, cringing as I repeat the same words Paul uttered moments ago.

He rises to his feet, taking me with him until we are both standing. Turning me to face him, his thumbs brush the remnants of tears that still remain on my cheeks. "After all this time and everything we have been through, do you know why I am still here?" he asks, his eyes boring into my soul. When I shake my head, he smiles warmly at me. "Because when love is true, it waits. And my love for you Lana, is unending."

The pain and sorrow I felt only moments ago is temporarily replaced with the love I have always had for Jackson Cade, his words ringing in my ears. To love someone means losing them and I cannot bear to lose any more in my life.

As the cell door slams shut behind me, I slowly make my way across the tiny room, taking a seat on the wall mounted cot that has become my bed. "What have I done?" I ask aloud, already knowing the answer. I managed to destroy two lives in a matter of seconds, although the process took years to achieve.

She was within arm's reach, right in front of me. If not for the cuffs that bound my wrists, I could have extended my hand and touched her flawless skin. If I close my eyes, I can actually feel her skin beneath my fingertips and smell her scent as it wafts in the air surrounding me.

Opening my eyes, I stare at the concrete wall that confines me to this place, separating me from the future that was within my grasp. *She didn't know.* I saw the confusion in her eyes, followed by the pain. Agony I caused her, never to be forgiven or forgotten.

My mistake was assuming that Jax had told her everything. I was so certain he would, but I underestimated my opponent once again. When I finally realized it, it was too late. I will never be able to erase that image, nor will I be able to forgive myself for everything I have done. If I could go back in time, I would do things differently, but that isn't an option.

Laying back on the cot, I stare at the ceiling, feeling as though my life is over. In fact it is, because without Alana, life has no meaning. Nothing was worth losing her for, yet that is exactly what has happened, and all because of two people - Phil Martin and Hawk. When I escaped my father's reign of terror, I had believed it was for the better. In hindsight, I had walked from one horrendous situation into another. In the beginning, I was nothing more than a pawn of Hawk's, manipulated to go to whatever lengths necessary to survive. When I discovered the truth, instead of walking away, I chose to stay, partnering with a man who was no better than my own father.

"I always blamed Phil Martin for destroying me, but I was wrong. It was you."

I did destroy her, slowly and deliberately, and I took pleasure in doing so.

"At least with Phil, I knew I was looking into the eyes of the devil. But you... you disguised yourself, pretended to my friend all so you could have your way."

Her words cut me to the core. I am nothing like Phil Martin. He was a cruel man, incapable of love. I loved Alana and still do. I should have told her, not just in passing, but truly expressed to her how I felt. Love is a word she has always shied away from because of her past, a word that in her eyes means loss, not gain. I could have changed that by stating three simple words and showing her it could be different.

It would have been easier if Jax had ended my life. I know he wanted to. I was certain I was staring death in the face, was even prepared for it, but instead of following through, he lowered his pistol and allowed the cops to move in. That was his mistake, one that he will soon regret.

I won't let Alana go. She is mine and always will be. All she needs is some time. I know if I can get her alone, explain everything to her, she will forgive me, and then we can have the life we were meant to have, the one we will have.

It won't happen now. It may even take years, but one day, Alana Jacobs will be in my arms again, and when she is, I am never letting her go.

Chapter 25

One Month Later

"Hey stranger," Alexis says, grinning widely as I take a seat at the bar. Turning around, she retrieves a beer from the cooler, sliding it over to me, the smile on her face still present.

"You seem awfully happy for someone who has been on her feet all night," I observe. "What gives?" Alexis is one of the only women aside from Alana that I actually enjoy talking to.

"I think it's cute how you come in here every night to see Alana. Reminds me of Rick in the beginning."

Spyder has been in love with Alexis forever, but he had been her friend first. He wasn't willing to jeopardize their friendship to pursue something more. After Peyton was born and her boyfriend abandoned them, Spyder stepped up and was there for the both of them. It took time, but eventually Alexis realized what everyone around her had been seeing for years. The two of them were destined to be together, and they've been happy ever since.

"I take it Alana's already left for the night," I say before taking a long draw from my beer.

"Left a few minutes ago."

"Where's Spyder?"

"He took Peyton to a baseball game," she smiles, her eyes filled with love for the two most important people in her life. Leaning over the bar, the smile on her face vanishes and she lowers her voice. "Can we talk?"

"Sure," I shrug before downing the remainder of my beer. "What about?"

"Alana," she whispers, looking around the room. "I'm worried about her."

Alexis is one of the few who knows the truth about Paul, mostly because of Spyder's big mouth. She is also very observant and good at reading people. "What have you seen?"

"It's not so much what I've seen as it is what I feel," she says with concern etching her face.

"Explain," I urge, trusting her insight. Unlike most of the women I know, Alexis is genuine and actually cares about Alana, even considers her a friend.

"I found this," she says, laying a folded stack of papers on the bar.

"You went through her things?" I ask in disbelief. I've never known Alexis to be this way and it surprises me that she would even consider it.

"Of course not!" she says, taking offense to my accusation. "She must've dropped it on her way out. I just picked them up and looked to see who it belonged to, but then I saw what it was and…" her voice trails off.

I stare down at the papers, my gut telling me this is wrong on so many levels.

"You need to look at them," Alexis says, sliding the paperwork closer to me.

Hesitantly my hand reaches out, grasping the papers tightly in my hand. Slowly, I unfold the stack, seeing letter after letter from Paul. I read over each one, the first written the day she visited him.

March 5th

Alana,

You left before giving me a chance to explain. I never meant to hurt you - you've got to believe me. What Hawk was doing, I wasn't a part of it, not in the way you think. I did things I'm not proud of, but you were never in jeopardy. I swear on my life that I would never let any harm come to you. After everything we've been through, you should already know that.

Just give me a chance to explain. I promise — no more lies.

Paul

March 9th

Alana,

Why are you ignoring me? You
at least owe me the chance to
explain myself. All I am asking is
for you to come visit, or at
least write me back and let me
know you are alive.

Paul

March 12th

Alana,

Are you really going to hold one mistake over my head for the rest of my life? I fucked up! I know that now. If I could turn back time I would.

I was there for you when no one else was. That has to count for something! I took care of you all these years and you're just going to ignore me?

I should have told you the truth. I've already admitted that, but we had a good thing and we can have it again if you will just hear me out. I am begging you, please come see me.

Paul

March 16th

Alana,

I have never felt more alone in this world than I do at this moment. You were my life and you still are. Why are you doing this to us?

I took care of you for all these years, was a friend to you when you had no one. Now that I need you, you are turning your back on me over mere words. You still don't know the whole truth.

Yes, I made a mistake by not telling you who I was, but the rest was only to keep you safe.

If you really think about it, you
know it's true.

Just ten minutes is all I need. If
after that you never want to
see me again, I will let you go.

Paul

March 20th

Alana,

Obviously promises are one sided with you. How many times did you promise to never leave? We are a team, you said, but it was all a lie. Does it make you feel good to know that I am locked up in here while you are nice and cozy with your new man?

I bet Jax is loving this. He finally turned you against me. That's what he's wanted from the start. I thought we would always stick by one another, or at least that is what you always told me. Guess you meant until something better came along.

I hope he makes you happy
because I am miserable and it is
all because of you.

Paul

March 24th

Alana,

I know I should give up, but for some reason I can't stop trying to get through to you. Maybe it's because I need you as much as you need me.

Do you remember the time you got the flu? You were so sick and there was no way we could afford to take you to the doctor. So I stayed up for three days straight taking care of you until your fever broke.

Every single time you felt bad, were upset or just needed

someone, I was there for you, taking care of you. I want you to think about all those times and tell me that I never cared about you. I want to hear you say those words and actually mean them. I know it will never happen because it would be a lie and you know it.

Please just talk to me Alana. I may be guilty of a lot of things, but I am not the monster you believe me to be. I am the same Paul I have always been - the friend you confided in about your past, the one who consoled you when Jax walked back into your life and the only person to

ever love you unconditionally. You
know why? Because you deserve
it - every bit of it.

What you didn't deserve was
for me to not be completely
honest with you about my past
and my involvement with Hawk.

All you have to do is come talk
to me, and I will tell you
everything. That is a promise.

Paul

March 28th

Alana,

I guess I should be grateful that you showed up at all, but I'm not. What has he done to you? Gone is the sweet girl I adored and in her place is someone I don't even recognize.

You say you never needed me, but we both know that is a lie. You do need me and I will prove it to you one way or another. The only good thing that came out of your visit is knowing you haven't given yourself to him. That means there's still hope for us.

Just walk away from him Alana. He never deserved you. He will use you and when the timing is right, he will leave you again. Do you want to go through that again? We can work through this. Just give us a chance.

Paul

April 2nd

Alana,

Life isn't fair, but you already know that. You've made your decision and you will soon regret it.

I won't make this easy on you. Walking away from me is no longer an option. You and I belong together and I refuse to let you go. You need me and now I'm going to prove it. You have a choice to make and if you're smart, you'll make the right one.

Paul

"He's threatening her," I seethe, finding it difficult to contain my anger.

"That's not all. Look at the last page," Alexis orders. Flipping to the back, I pull out a bank statement showing several cash deposits followed by a transaction the same day the letter is dated of six hundred dollars. "JPay is how you send money to an inmate's account."

This doesn't make sense. There is no way Alana would empty out her account to help him. He did this. Somehow, he got access to a computer and transferred the money. And since Paul is on the account, she can't press charges against him.

"Old habits die hard, Jax. If she feels she has no other option, she might..."

"Don't say it," I warn her. "You said she just left. Was she alone?"

"Yes, but she spent a lot of time with those guys over there," Alexis says, nodding towards the table in the far corner. "I don't know for sure, but I think she's meeting up with them later."

Rising from the barstool, I pull out my phone and quickly punch in Deuce's number. When he answers on the second ring, I breathe a sigh of relief.

"I need you to track down Alana," I bark into the phone.

"Not a problem, since she's already with me. We're heading back to the bar in a few. Wait for us," he says before the line goes dead.

Slamming the phone down on the top of the bar, I look over at Alexis, whose eyes widen with shock. "Everything OK?"

"She's with Deuce" I say, unable to hide the hurt in my voice. She went to Deuce and not me.

"At least she's safe," Alexis says, trying to be comforting but it only angers me more.

"Safe with him, not me," I mutter as I push myself away from the bar and storm out the door, not bothering to look back.

Alana

"Where is he?" Deuce asks the moment we step inside of Bar None, dragging me behind him as he stalks towards the bar.

"He left," Alexis says, giving me a sympathetic smile. "I think you dropped these," she adds, passing me the papers I thought were gone for good.

"Thank you," I say as I take them from her extended hand, feeling relieved that I still have the proof I have been safeguarding.

"Head on into my office and wait for me. I'll see if I can track down Jax," Deuce says before reaching in his pocket and pulling out his cell phone.

Nodding my head, I make my way towards Deuce's office. As soon as I step inside, I take a seat in one of the chairs facing the desk, letting out a ragged breath.

I should have gone to Jax sooner, but I thought I could handle this on my own. The first few letters I received from Paul were relatively harmless, and I thought if I ignored him, he would get the hint. What I didn't expect is for him to try and manipulate me again, but that is exactly what he's trying to do.

Going to see him was stupid, I admit it. Stupid me thought that if I was face to face with him, he would finally understand that I am through. I will never forgive him, nor will I ever trust him. I plainly told him that, but it wasn't enough. Even telling him I hated him did nothing but add fuel to the fire.

In a few short days, my rent is due and I have a whopping three dollars and sixteen cents to my name. I am such an idiot for not taking Paul's name off the account, or at the very least opening a new account, but I never expected him to stoop this low. I should've known better.

Making the decision to go to Jax for help wasn't an easy one, but time is running out. If I can't pay my rent, Mr. Gantt will kick me out without batting an eye.

Finding the Forgotten Souls MC was easier than I had thought. I was literally trembling when I approached the gate, only to find out Jax wasn't there. Feeling defeated, I began the walk home, only to run onto Deuce as I was passing the gas station.

I trust Deuce. It's hard not to when he has gone out of his way to be a friend to me, but then again, he never gave me a choice. He forced his way into my life, and I don't regret for a single moment allowing him in. That being said, Jax was the one who offered to help me out if I needed it, not Deuce.

"Well the fucker didn't answer," Deuce says as he enters the room, startling me. "While we wait for him to call me back, why don't you fill me in. You said Paul was contacting you?"

"Yeah," I mutter. "I really should be talking to Jax about this."

"Alana, stop with the bullshit. You and I are friends, so spill it." To an outsider, Deuce would come across as a complete ass, but I know the other side of him. He's a good guy with a big heart and he has gone out of his way for me.

Hesitantly, I pass the letters Paul has written over to Deuce. I watch as he reads each page, his face remaining solemn. When he reaches the last page, he lifts his eyes to meet mine. "You went to see him?"

"I thought he would leave me alone if I told him face to face, but it only made matters worse." It was a stupid mistake, one I will never make again.

"And he wiped your account clean," he says, stating the obvious. He lays the papers down, shaking his head. "You should have told us he was writing you. We could have put a stop to it. You going to see him was a dumbass move."

"I know," I mumble, feeling like a child being scolded. "I was trying to handle this on my own."

"I know you were," Deuce says, his voice softening. "But you aren't alone anymore, Alana. Friends help each other without asking for anything in return."

"Thanks," I manage to choke out, trying not to let my emotions get the best of me.

"So let's start with the obvious. First thing tomorrow, you head down to the bank and open a new account. Then we get you moved out of that apartment."

"I can't..." I begin, only for Deuce to cut me off.

"You can't afford a new place. I just saw your bank statement, Alana. Three dollars ain't gonna get you much of anything, but you can stay at the club until you get on your feet."

Vehemently, I shake my head. "No!" I shout, my emotions getting the best of me. My brief encounter at the gate of The Forgotten Souls compound was enough for me to know there is no way I am setting foot inside that place.

"I take it you met Beast," Deuce chuckles. "He can be intimidating, but his bark is worse than his bite."

If Beast is any indication of what lies inside the club, I have no desire to meet anyone else. Intimidating is an understatement. "I wouldn't be comfortable there," I say, trying not to be insulting.

"I get it. We'll take it one step at a time," he smiles, making me feel more at ease. "Most of the guys live on the compound, and those who don't have families. Jax has been talking about getting a place outside the club, but he's all talk, no action. Tell you what, you can stay at my place."

My eyes widen at his invitation. There is no way I would consider moving in with Jax, let alone Deuce. No, I want my own place, but at the moment I can't afford it so my options are nonexistent.

"Don't look at me that way," Deuce laughs. "It's nothing fancy, but its four walls and a roof. I'm rarely there, so you'd have the place to yourself most of the time. It's been years since it's had a woman's touch, and the place could sure use it. It'll benefit us both."

His offer is too good to be true, but before I can agree, there is one thing I have to know. "How much?"

"What?" he asks, a confused look on his face.

"How much per month? I'm kind of short on funds at the moment, but I can work extra hours at the bar until I get caught up."

I narrow my eyes at him as he bursts out in a fit of laughter. "You are too much!"

I have no idea what is so damn funny, but his reaction brings a smile to my face.

"I don't want or need your money. Like I said, the place needs a woman's touch. If you take on the upkeep, that's payment enough. I don't have the time to do it myself, and probably should've sold it a long time ago, but can't bring myself to do it." His eyes glaze over as he speaks, his amusement completely gone. "You'd be doing me a favor."

"Alright," I agree, "but only until I can get on my feet. I don't know how to thank you."

"You don't have to thank me, Alana. I should be thanking you." With that, Deuce rises to his feet, the chair scraping the floor as he pushes it back. "Let's get you home so you can start packing your things. Don't worry about furniture or anything like that. Just your personal belongings. Everything else I have covered."

I nod my head in agreement, wondering if I am making the right decision. Pushing aside my worry, I rise to my feet and follow behind

Deuce, a sense of warmth encompassing me. I have friends now, true friends who want nothing more from me than friendship and it is a good feeling, albeit a foreign one.

Downing my seventh shot of whiskey, I slam the empty glass on the bar before lifting the bottle and filling the shot glass once again. Drowning your sorrows always seems like a good idea in the beginning, but by tomorrow morning, I will be regretting my decision.

"You forget how to use one of these things?" Deuce asks, grabbing my phone off the bar and dangling it in front of my face.

"Nope," I reply, lifting the shot glass to my lips and chugging it. "How did things go with Alana?" I ask, my voice dripping with pure venom.

"So that's what this is about," Deuce says, shaking his head as he takes a seat beside me. "Alexis mentioned you storming out. Don't worry though, I didn't tell Alana you were acting like a sulking pussy."

"Fuck you," I mutter as I refill my glass again.

"So you're bailing on her?" Deuce reaches over and slides the now full shot glass towards him, lifting it to his lips.

"I'm stepping aside," I say, gripping the remainder of the whiskey bottle in my hand.

"And why's that?" Deuce asks, raising his brow. "Thought she meant something to you."

"Don't start with me Deuce. She doesn't want me. She's made that perfectly clear." Why I ever thought anything differently is beyond me.

"She has? Because no one gave me the memo, and they sure as hell didn't give it to Alana," Deuce chuckles.

"What the fuck are you going on about?" I grumble, not in the mood for Deuce's sense of humor.

"Well maybe if you'd answered your Goddamn phone, you would know the answer to that question," he says, his tone suddenly serious.

"I'm not in the fuckin' mood for riddles Deuce, so just spit it the fuck out!" I shout, my anger mounting.

"Alright, but you ain't gonna like it. Alana came to the compound tonight," he begins, and a surge of jealousy rushes through me. I rise from my seat, bowing up at the man I consider not only a friend, but a brother. "Sit your fuckin' ass down!" Deuce orders, his eyes and tone turning cold as ice. "You bow up at me again, and it will be the last fuckin' thing you do!"

Taking in a deep breath, it takes every ounce of strength within me not to beat the living shit out of him.

"She was looking for your sorry ass!" he shouts.

"She what?" I ask in disbelief.

"Imagine that!" he says, shaking his head in disgust. "You're a real piece of work, you know that? And you were so worried about her trusting you again. The problem isn't her, it's you!"

I am speechless momentarily, feeling like the biggest ass on the planet. He is right in so many ways. "Man, I don't know what to say."

"I'm your brother, you don't have to say shit to me. Just be glad Alana knows nothing about the way you acted," he says, slapping me on the back. "Now that you're over your little hissy fit, we've got a problem."

I'm just grateful Deuce isn't one to hold a grudge, at least where I'm concerned. "Paul," I say his name with utter disgust.

"Well since you saw the letters, you know he's not gonna stop. The good news is that Pat says the state has a good case against him. The bad news is that he's starting to cooperate with the prosecution and after seeing those letters, I know why."

"I want her out of that apartment." Sooner rather than later.

"Already worked that out. She should be packing as we speak."

"Good," I mutter, feeling a sense of relief. The sooner she is away from that place, the better. "She'll be safe at the compound and there's no way Paul will try to contact her here."

"Yeah, about that. She was against moving into the compound. Let's just say Beast didn't make a lasting impression." When does he? Beast has as much personality as a brick wall. "But I did convince her to move into my place."

"What?!" I can't believe what I am hearing.

"Calm the fuck down. You know I rarely stay there anyway."

That's not the point. Even though I acted like a jealous fool only moments ago, I know Deuce would never cross that line. But if she is living in Deuce's house, I'll rarely have a chance to see her, except for at Bar None.

"And I'm sure she's gonna discover that there's a lot of work that needs to be done to the place. And it just so happens that I know a damn good handyman," he says, as if reading my mind. "I have a feeling you'll be seeing her on a regular basis."

"Thanks man. I owe you one."

"You owe me more than just one. Just name your first born after me and we'll call it even," he smirks before walking off, leaving me alone with my thoughts.

Chapter 26

Alana

Two Months Later

"I'm coming!" I shout as I run towards the door. Through the frosted glass insert on the front door, I see Jax standing on the porch, his fist raised to pound on the wooden barrier once again. Unlatching the dead bolt, I jerk open the door. "You're early."

I stare up at Jax, his eyes wide. "Do you always answer the door like that?" he asks, eying me up and down.

Glancing down, I can't help but smile. Clad in only a towel, Jax is definitely getting an eyeful. "You've seen me in much less," I begin. "And you were banging on the door like the place was on fire."

"Yeah, but... Alana you have to be more careful," he says, looking at me with concern in his eyes. He cares about me, that is apparent, but then again he always has.

"Don't worry, I saw it was you," I say, trying to ease his mind. The fact is that I'm not very careful, but the only two people who ever come here are Deuce and Jax. "Give me a few minutes to finish getting ready," I tell him before heading towards the bedroom.

As soon as I step inside my room, my nerves begin getting the best of me. The time I have spent with Jax over the last few months has been the best of my life. It is as if nothing has changed between us, except there are no monsters lurking in the corners. It is just him and me, the way we always intended. The only difference is we are older, and there is no denying how we feel for one another – just like Deuce planned all along.

Deuce tries to act innocent in all this, but I'm not stupid. Inviting me to live here was his way of letting Jax and I reconnect. My first day in this house, the refrigerator stopped working. The next, it was the dryer. Each day that passed, something new happened requiring the perfect handyman to come in and save the day, and of course that person would be none other than Jax. Mighty convenient that Deuce was unable to fix a single thing. Hell, I wouldn't put it past Deuce to deliberately break each and every item in this house, so long as the outcome was the same. Jax and I rekindled a friendship I had long given up on, and for that I will never be able to repay Deuce.

Jax has told me on more than one occasion how he feels about me and I'd be lying if I said I didn't feel the same. To hear him say he loves me is like a dream come true, and I want so much to say the words in return, but I'm afraid. If I dare utter those words, what will happen? Will I lose him forever? Just thinking about it makes me sick to my stomach, but somehow I manage to swallow the bile that rises in the back of my throat.

I will not let my emotions get the best of me, not now. Tonight is our first official date. What's even more pathetic is that in all honesty, this will be my first date ever. How many people can say that they waited until they were turning twenty-three to begin dating? I could let this bother me, but instead I focus on tonight. I will not ruin it by letting my insecurities get the best of me. I want to enjoy this time, treasure every second with him before it all comes to an end, which ultimately it will.

Rushing over to the dresser, I pull out a pair of denim shorts and a tank top. Jax has assured me that tonight I should dress casually and comfortably. In other words, be myself. After quickly dressing, I decide to put on a touch of makeup. The only time I ever wore makeup was when I went onstage, never seeing the need to use it any other time. Tonight I am making an exception. I want to look and feel pretty for a change.

I take one last look in the mirror, pleased with my appearance. My hair is down, falling in soft waves past my shoulders. The blue tank top I am wearing combined with a touch of eyeliner brings out the blue in my eyes. Reaching down, I grab the lip gloss off the vanity, applying just a dab to complete my look for the evening. Taking in a deep breath, I make my way towards the door.

When I step back into the living room, I find Jax seated on the sofa, flipping through the channels on the television. He turns the moment he hears me enter, his eyes lighting up. "Alana," he whispers, the sound of his voice making me weak in the knees.

"You said I should be comfortable," I say as I come to a stop beside the couch. "Is this alright?"

He nods his head as he rises from his seat. "You're perfect," he says, causing me to blush.

Although I never tire of hearing him utter those words, it still has an effect on me. "Thank you." I look over at him, taking in the sight of him in his ripped blue jeans and a tight black t-shirt, fitting him like a glove. His dark brown hair is mussed, looking like I've been running my fingers through it for hours, a look that suits him. Topped off with his leather cut, he is perfect in every way. "You haven't mentioned where we are going."

"Tonight, I want to give you a glimpse inside my life as it is now. We're going to the club."

I freeze at his words, suddenly feeling uncomfortable. I have only been to The Forgotten Souls compound once and I didn't make it any farther than the front gate. Meeting Beast has left a lasting impression on me, one I have no desire to repeat.

"Don't look that way, Lana. They are my family. You'll be safe there." His words put me somewhat at ease, but I cannot help but feel hesitant. "You already know Deuce and you've met Spyder."

"No I haven't," I reply. If I had met a man named Spyder, I would never forget it.

"You talk to him almost every night," he chuckles. "Although you call him Rick."

"Rick?" I ask in disbelief. "Alexis' Rick?"

"One and the same," he laughs. "And you've met some of the other brothers too. Metal, Bull and Shame... or as you know them, Neil, Mark, and Kenny."

"You're fuckin' with me, right?" I ask, not believing I have been duped. "They are part of the club?"

"Every last one of them, and several you haven't met. That all changes tonight if you're game."

Any trepidation I was feeling completely dissipates. I slowly nod my head in agreement, actually looking forward to meeting all of them.

"Good," he says, extending his hand out to me. "Let's get going."

Being formally introduced to The Forgotten Souls was nothing like I expected. Any preconceived ideas I had completely vanished when we stepped foot inside the compound.

Inside the clubhouse, there were a good fifty to sixty people, bullshitting and having a good time. My assumptions of an MC being filled with nothing but violence couldn't have been more wrong. When Jax refers to them as his brothers, I can fully understand why. They aren't just friends. Each of them share a special bond, one I don't quite understand, but it still warms my heart. Finding the club has given Jax the family he always wanted but I'd be lying if I said I wasn't a little jealous. He wasn't the only one who desired a family, but I am happy he found his.

"So whatcha think?" Deuce asks, coming to sit beside me at the round table seated close to the bar. "Not so bad once you see past the gruff exterior, huh?"

"I'll admit when I'm wrong," I say, smiling over at him. "And I was wrong."

"I know how Beast comes across, but he's a good guy. You two have a lot in common."

"And how's that?" I ask, curious as to how Beast and I are anything but complete opposites. Granted I am a little standoffish, but all in all, I would say I am rather friendly.

"You both put up a front to disguise the real you," Deuce says, raising a brow as if he is challenging me.

"Is it that apparent?"

"Darlin', I knew from the moment you and I met that you weren't the person you pretended to be. I saw the pain in your eyes when you went up on that stage and knew it wasn't by choice. What Paul did to you, the way he manipulated and exploited you, is unforgiveable."

I nod my head in agreement, but I know the truth. Although Paul did coerce me into doing everything I have done, I had the choice to walk away and chose not to. "I'm as much to blame as he is." Perhaps more so.

"That's bullshit and you know it," he says, shaking his head at me. "When are you gonna realize that he was in the wrong, not you?"

"When I don't feel any more guilt," I mutter, looking away. I am ashamed of my past, every single bit of it and nothing will change that.

"You have nothing to feel guilty about, Alana. If anything, you should be proud of being a fighter. With everything you went through, your childhood, Phil Martin and then with Paul, you should be proud you survived. You aren't a cold, heartless person, which by all rights you should be. And not only am I lucky enough to call you my friend, you're like a sister to me." Deuce's words catch me off guard, stirring emotions long forgotten. "You're part of my family now, like it or not."

My heart swells with pride at his words. "Thank you," I whisper, not knowing what else to say.

Deuce reaches over, grasping my hand reassuringly, before looking past me and smiling. "I think someone is getting a little jealous," he says, nodding.

Looking over my shoulder, I see Jax grinning at us as he approaches the table, two beers in hand. "I hope you're done flirting with my girl," he smirks, coming to a stop beside me.

"For now," Deuce chuckles, rising from his seat. As he stands, he looks down at me, a heartwarming smile on his face. Leaning over, he presses a kiss to my cheek. "Don't forget what I said," he says before walking off.

I do not question his statement because it is perfectly clear, and it feels so damn good. It's been so long since I've had a family and to be welcomed like this means more than anyone could ever know, except one person – Jax.

"You look awfully happy," Jax says as he takes the seat beside me.

"I am," I explain, looking over at him. "Deuce just told me I'm a part of his family."

"And I know what that means to you," he smiles. "But I'm not sure you know what that means *for* you." I stare at him, completely dumbfounded, not understanding him. "Deuce's family, *my* family, is this club. You being family means you are under The Forgotten Souls protection."

"Why do I need protection?" I ask in a panicked tone. It's been months since I've received a letter from Paul, so I know he's finally gotten the hint. Hawk was sentenced a few weeks ago and he's looking at forty years on the sex trafficking charges alone. With the drug charges added in, he will live out the remainder of his years in prison, and for that I am thankful.

"I'm not saying you do, but it is one of the benefits to being a member of the family."

I nod my head in understanding even though I do not fully comprehend what he is telling me. "Was it that easy for you, becoming a member?" I ask, more than a little curious as to how Jax found The Forgotten Souls.

"My fate was sealed when I first met Deuce," he whispers, staring straight ahead.

"So Deuce was a member of The Forgotten Souls when you met him?"

"So to speak. Deuce's father was the founder and former President."

Looking around the room, I can blatantly see the loyalty that resides within these four walls and can only imagine what it would feel like to know I had this kind of backing. It is in then that I realize Deuce has given me that gift as well. "I can see why you wanted to be a part of this," I tell him.

"It wasn't really a choice. The Forgotten Souls isn't just an MC. Everyone here has earned their place, long before they stepped inside these four walls. That includes you. Being part of the family means you are part of the club."

"I'm not a biker," I say, my brow creasing. "And I'm definitely not a man."

"Neither was Rachel, Deuce's mother, but she earned her right to be here just as you have," he says, his eyes meeting mine. "When Ace started The Forgotten Souls, it was because he was lacking something in his life. The same thing every single brother inside this club was missing."

"What are you saying?" I ask, finding myself more than a little curious.

"You don't become one of The Forgotten Souls by chance. Every single person you see wearing a patch was destined to belong here. We have all been forgotten in some way, shape or form. Most have a past similar to ours. Ace was the product of an affair, one that his father didn't discover until his wife was on her deathbed. Every bit of anger and resentment he felt for his wife's infidelity was unleashed on Ace. He beat him to within an inch of his life and then mutilated him before leaving him for dead in the field behind their home. It was his neighbor, a biker named Halo, who saved his life and took him in. Ace stayed with him until the state stepped in, but he never forgot the short time he lived among the Satan's Rebels. He saw the brotherhood, the trust and loyalty that came with it, and vowed that one day he would have the same thing. Rachel, Deuce's mother, was forced into prostitution at the age of sixteen by her then boyfriend. He convinced her he loved her and she ran away with him. For three years, she was forced to sell her body to avoid the beatings that would occur if she refused. Renee, her daughter, was a conceived with one of her client's and when her boyfriend discovered she was pregnant, he brutally beat her and left her for dead outside a club. That's where Ace found her. He took her in, cared for her and fell in love with her. He raised Renee as if she were his own. And then there's Deuce. He doesn't talk much about his past, but I know whatever happened to him was bad."

Although all their stories are tragic, ultimately they found the happiness in life they deserved. I am saddened knowing that their family was ripped apart because of one man.

"Spyder, his mother was a prostitute. She started pimping him out at the age of five and it wasn't until Ace found him at the age of thirteen that he was set free. Beast lost his parents when he was two and was sent to live with his uncle. He was locked in a room in a basement for the next ten years, living in his own filth. Ace was doing some electrical work in the house and found him. Beast was twelve years old and weighed a little over sixty pounds."

I can feel tears well in my eyes as he continues to describe the living hell each of these men endured. Suddenly, my past seems insignificant compared to the stories I am hearing.

"Abuse, neglect, pain and loss - all of these things go hand in hand outside these walls, but on the inside, there is only peace. Every single person in this room, aside from a few, has lived a life that no one could possibly imagine. We've experienced pain and torture that regular people read about in books and see on TV, never imagining it happens in real life. We are all forgotten souls, neglected by our peers, abused by the ones who should have protected us, and abandoned by society, and here, we have found everything we always wanted and needed." Jax's eyes never leave mine as he speaks, his words filled with so much emotion, not for his own painful past, but for that of his brothers.

"I'm so sorry," I whisper, not really knowing what I can say to offer him some comfort.

"There's nothing to be sorry for, Lana. Every single thing that happened in our past was out of our control. We can't go back and change a thing, but our future we can dominate. That is what this is and who we are. The Forgotten Souls will be everything you always wanted - friend, family and protector, never to abandon you in your time of need." He turns towards me, leaning forward until I can feel his breath on my lips. "I know I let you down in the past, but I will never fail you again. I love you, Lana. I've said it before but I want you to truly hear me this time. I. Love. You. I always have and always will, until the end of time."

My heart lurches in my chest. There was a time when I doubted Jax's love for me, but I had been a fool. He has never stopped and I truly believe him when he says he will love me forever, just as I will him, but I can't say the words. "I can't do this," I whisper, turning my face away in an attempt to hide the pain I know my eyes will give away. Gripping my chin, Jax forces me to face him.

"I have waited for years to hear those words from you and I will wait the rest of my life if that is how long it takes for you to admit what I already know. You love me Alana, and locking it up inside doesn't change anything. I know you're scared but I promise that you will never lose me." I want to believe him, but fear still grips me.

"I'm not ready," I whisper, praying that he understands.

"I know, but one day soon you will be. Until then, I'll take what I can get," he says, smiling at me, putting my mind at ease, even if only for a moment.

I don't doubt that one day I will utter those three words to him, but I know the moment I do, everything will change. At that moment my life will come crumbling down and I'm not prepared to deal with the aftermath.

Chapter 27

JAX

"What are you doing out here?" I call out as soon as I round the house, relieved to find Alana sitting under the giant oak in the backyard. After knocking on the front door for several minutes and receiving no response, I had been tempting to break down the door. Not only would Alana have been pissed, but Deuce would have killed me.

"Just enjoying the weather," she says as she pushes herself to her feet. She looks beautiful, dressed in a simple gray tank and matching shorts, but then again she always looks gorgeous. "It's so peaceful out here."

Stalking towards her, I cannot hide the smile that erupts on my face. It is always present whenever she is near, something everyone around me has learned to accept. "How long have you been out here?" I ask, coming to a stop in front of her.

"Just a few hours," she replies, a perplexed look on her face. "Why?"

"You're a little pink," I say, brushing my finger along the silken skin of her shoulder, eliciting a moan to escape her lips. She looks up at me with wondrous eyes, nothing but pure happiness emanating from them, something I have dreamt of seeing for so long. "Since you're off tonight, I thought you and I could hit the town. Grab dinner and a movie, or maybe hit a club?"

"A night on the town, huh?" she smirks, taking a step back from me. "I think I'd like that." She walks past me, her scent overpowering me as she heads towards the house, only pausing to look over her shoulder to ensure I am following. "Let me clean up and we can head out," she says before pushing through the back door. "Make yourself comfortable. I won't be too long," she calls out before entering the bedroom, closing the door behind her.

Stepping inside the house is always a shock to me. Each time I am here, something has changed. Alana has gone out of her way at fixing the place up, from repainting the walls to adding personal touches throughout the house to give it a homier feel. Deuce loves having her here, and who could blame him. The place hasn't looked this good in the entire time I have known him. Plus he enjoys Alana's company.

On the few nights a week he spends at home, he and Alana have become extremely close and both have opened up to one another about their pasts. Not so long ago, I would have been jealous of the time they share together, but now I embrace it. The bond they have formed gives me a sense of peace. Alana is filling a void that has existed in his heart since he lost his sister, and Deuce has become the brother Alana always wanted. It is a win-win situation and in no way takes away from what Alana and I have.

She still has not uttered the three words I desperately want to hear, but sometimes words aren't necessary. There is no doubt in my mind that Alana loves me and that we will spend the rest of our lives together, but first she has to overcome her fear.

Watching as her father killed her mother has had a lasting effect on her. Instead of seeing the scenario for the abusive situation it was, she chooses to block it out. Her focus is only on the end result – two people she loved, gone forever.

Deuce was the one to discover the number of calls placed to the police and I have read each of the reports that resulted. Alana's father was a drunk that beat his wife, plain and simple. Her mother was probably too afraid to leave him, so she endured the beatings. Maybe she did it out of fear of losing Alana. No one will ever know.

The police report from that night was an eye opener. Alana's recollection of events was accurate, but there were several details she must have blocked out. The investigator that arrived on the scene was meticulous in his descriptions, down to Alana laying on top of her mother, covered in blood, crying out for her to wake up. Reading it was difficult, but what was even more devastating was seeing her father's intentions.

Investigator Thomas was able to deduce that Mr. Jacobs fired the first shot, killing his wife instantly. He then turned the gun on Alana, although she has blocked that memory out, and fired one shot. Thankfully he missed, unbeknownst to him, before turning the gun on himself, ending his own miserable existence. Investigator Thomas surmised that at the moment he fired that one round, Alana had thrown herself on her mother, and believing he had ended the lives of his wife and daughter, then turned the gun on himself. It is only speculation, but it fits.

Since I have known Alana, she has equated love with loss. First, she lost both of her parents. Her belief was reinforced when Mary, the foster mother we had for some time, passed away. Alana had loved her, as we all did, and it completely devastated her.

I have to get through to her, but I don't know how. Deuce says to give her time, and I have been doing just that, but my patience is running out.

"You could've turned on the TV," Alana says as she enters the room.

I turn, looking over at her and feel my cock begin to harden. Alana's hair is down, falling in loose chocolate waves past her shoulders. The red halter dress she is wearing hugs every curve of her perfect body. Beautiful does not even begin to describe the vision standing before me. She is absolutely perfect. "Wow," I manage to say, my mouth agape.

"I figured I needed to look the part if we're going clubbing," she giggles, walking towards me. "Does it look alright?"

Swallowing hard, I nod my head slowly, unable to say the words that echo in my mind.

"You still want to go, right?" she asks, the smile on her face vanishing.

"Of course," I manage to choke out. "It's just…" I stop myself from saying the first thought that comes to mind. She has made me rock hard in a matter of seconds and I don't want her to misinterpret my raging hard on. I want her, of that there is no doubt, but with

Alana there is more than just a physical attraction. As if she can read my mind, her eyes lower to my crotch, causing me to inwardly cringe.

"We can wait a few minutes until your issue… is rectified," she says, keeping a straight face.

Rolling my eyes, I shake my head. "You sure have a way with words," I mutter.

"Would you have preferred if I told you to go jack off in the bathroom so we can get on with our evening?" she giggles.

"Fuck you," I chuckle, rising to my feet, ignoring the discomfort as my jeans compress my rock hard cock. "Let's go have some fun," I say, reaching my hand out to her. She takes it without hesitation, smiling up at me.

"Don't worry, I won't hold your hard on against you," she says, jabbing my side before turning and heading for the door.

Jerking her back against me, I turn her in my arms, gazing down into her bright blue eyes. "You think you're being funny?" I ask, trying hard to have a serious look on my face, but failing miserably.

"I know I am," she retorts, raising her brow at me. She slowly bites down on her bottom lip in an attempt not to smile, the sight making me even harder.

Taking in a deep breath, I fight the urge to take her right here and now. I know she wants me as much as I want her, but she has to make the first move. With everything that has happened, it has to be this way, but waiting is becoming harder.

"I guess we better get going," Alana whispers, her eyes reflecting that she is fighting her own desires.

"How does Greek sound?" I ask, grasping her hand tightly in mine as we head for the front door.

"I'm game for pretty much anything," she says from behind me.

As she climbs on the back of my bike, pressing her body tightly to mine, all I can imagine is having her legs wrapped around my waist as I pound my stiff cock into her drenched pussy. Even through my cut, I can feel the heat between her thighs, making me want her even more.

Pulling out of the driveway and onto the open road, I push aside my own desires and concentrate on my goal. Alana's happiness is all I have ever wanted and now that she has that, it's time to focus on us spending the rest of our lives together.

Alana

"How many of those are you planning on having?" Jax asks in amusement as I drain the last of my lemon drop.

"That depends," I say, licking my lips. "Am I buying or are you?"

Shaking his head, he waves over at a waitress who quickly rushes over. The club may be packed, but with Jax in the room, we might as well be the only ones here. He has been the center of attention since we walked in. Maybe I should be jealous, but there really is no need because his eyes haven't wandered from me all night.

"What can I get for you, hun?" the over attentive blonde asks, her eyes locked onto Jax.

"Another round for me and my girl," he says with ease. I love when he calls me his girl, because deep down I wish I did belong to him. Jax treats me with respect and showers me with attention. When his arm is around me, I feel safe and wanted, one of the best feelings in the world. And when we kiss, time stands still. There's only one thing missing, and I'm hoping if I play my cards right, that will all change tonight.

The blonde glances over at me, turning up her nose in disgust before turning and giving Jax an award winning smile. As soon as she walks off, I burst into a fit of laughter. "You do realize you're a chick magnet, don't you?"

"Well you're a dick magnet, so I guess we're even," he chuckles.

Fair enough. While Jax has been getting an overabundance of attention from the fairer sex, I've been ogled by nearly every creep in the room. From the looks of things, he is as accustomed to it as I am, but for different reasons. Suddenly I am overwhelmed with thoughts of the past and my chest begins to tighten. "I have to use the restroom," I say, standing abruptly. Quickly I rush from the table, not giving Jax a chance to question me.

Pushing through the restroom door, I stop when I reach the sink. Closing my eyes, I breathe in deeply, trying to calm my nerves.

You can't keep doing this to yourself. I have said the same thing to myself over and over, but it doesn't seem to matter. Whenever I start to forget, everything comes crashing down on me, and I am beginning to think I will never be able to truly move on.

Opening my eyes, I look at my reflection in the mirror, the image staring back me is not the one I have grown accustomed to over the last few weeks. Gone is all happiness. Instead I see the terrified girl crying over her mother's dead body, the young girl begging for mercy as Phil takes her innocence, and the young woman who used her body in unimaginable ways because the man she had befriended had manipulated her into doing so.

"You'll never make him happy," I turn at the sound of an all too familiar voice to find Trix standing in the doorway. "I'll give you credit, you sure know how to pick 'em, but Jax will never love you."

"What do you want, Trix?" I turn my attention back towards the mirror, blocking out all emotion.

"Actually, I saw Jax out in the club and knew you wouldn't be too far from him," she says, letting the door close behind her. "I know you don't like me, Alana. You've never hidden that fact."

"And neither have you," I say, raising my brow.

"Fair enough, but that doesn't mean I can't give you fair warning. Jax is bad news."

I fight the urge to burst out in a fit of laughter. Trix of all people is trying to tell me that Jax is a bad person. "Really?" I say sarcastically.

"He can lay on the charm, make you fall for him, but in the end you'll end up just like the rest of us. Jax is a great lay, the best I've ever had, but he isn't capable of falling in love. He'll hurt you, just like he did me and every other woman who's fallen for his bag of tricks."

This time I am unable to contain my laughter. "Jax wouldn't hurt me." I know this for a fact and he has proven it time and time again.

"He's too hung up on the past to be bothered with someone like you. In fact, I bet you he's out there lining up his next booty call. That's who the real Jax is. He'll give you a taste and then when you're hooked, he'll send you packing. It's always the same story, just with a different lead lady, and I guess you're his next victim."

"Thanks for the warning Trix, but I think I'll be fine," I say, pushing past her as I head for the door.

"Keep telling yourself that Alana, but in the end you will be alone. He will break your heart and you will have no one!" she shouts out from behind me.

Biting back the tears that threaten to fall, I push my way through the doorway and into the hall, her words cutting me to the core. She has vocalized my greatest fear without even knowing the effect it would have on me.

As I round the corner, I spot Jax standing at the bar and my heart breaks at the mere sight of him. Shaking my head, I turn and head for the front door without looking back.

My feet are on fire by the time I reach the house, even though I lost my heels about half a mile into the six mile trek home. As I climb the stairs, I take one last glance over my shoulder to make sure Jax is nowhere in sight and breathe a sigh of relief when I see no sign of him. Pulling my key out of my purse, I slide it into the lock, turning it swiftly before pushing my way inside the darkened house.

Instinctively, I reach over to turn on the lamp, but quickly think twice. If Jax does come by the house, I don't want any indication that I am here. I need to be alone tonight.

"I was wondering how long it would take you to get home." I jump at the sound of Deuce's voice, my heart pounding in my chest. The room is suddenly flooded with bright light as he reaches over and turns on the tableside lamp.

"What are you doing here?" It's a stupid question considering this is his house, but it's all I can come up with.

"I could ask you the same thing," he says, raising his brow at me. "Wanna tell me what the fuck happened?"

"I freaked out," I admit.

"Sit," he orders, nodding towards the couch.

Letting out an exhaustive breath, I walk over and take a seat. Although I'll never admit it, I'm glad Deuce is here. He's easy to talk to, at least for me. "I had to get out of there."

"Because of Trix?"

"How did you...?"

"Jax went looking for you and ran into her. Knew she must've said somethin' so he called me. And in case you were wondering, Beast had your back all the way home. Not sure he's too happy about walking almost six miles, but he knew if you heard his pipes, you'd bail into the woods." He gives me a displeased looks before continuing. "What'd she say that made you bolt?"

"Nothing I haven't been thinking myself," I say, biting my bottom lip in an attempt to control my emotions.

"You have to stop this Alana," Deuce says, rising from his chair and coming to sit beside me. "This fear you have of abandonment has to come to an end."

"I've tried," I say, my voice wavering. "But every time I feel like I'm finally starting to move on, it all comes crashing down on me."

"Because you keep trying to bury it. Everything that happened in your past was real. You can't erase it even though you want to, but you can overcome it." He pulls me close to him, draping his arm across my shoulder as he sits back, trying to comfort me.

"How am I supposed to overcome something like this? I can't even look at myself in the mirror without being reminded of what I've done and who I am."

"What you are Alana is a sweet, beautiful young woman with a fulfilling life ahead of you. What you've done is survive. You were dealt one hell of a shitty hand in life, but it's time to stop living in the past. It's time for you to start living."

Lifting my head, I look over at Deuce with tear filled eyes. "She said he would break my heart. That in the end I would be alone," I whisper.

"That'll never happen," I turn at the sound of Jax's voice. The worry that etches his face disappears when his eyes meet mine. "Now I just have to convince you of that."

Just seeing Jax takes my breath away. I could keep trying to convince myself that I don't love him, but that would be a lie. My heart knows the truth and my mind can no longer fight it.

"I think that's my cue to leave," Deuce says, rising from his seat beside me. He nods in Jax's direction before looking down at me once again. "You deserve happiness, Alana. And it's standing right in front of you." He reaches down and gives my hand a gentle squeeze before heading towards the front door.

"Thanks again," Jax says to him as he passes by.

"Where Alana is concerned, you never have to thank me. She's a special woman and I would do anything to make sure she's safe. That's what family does," he says before exiting the house, leaving Jax and I alone.

I stare up at the man I fell in love with years ago and still love to this day. If there is one person capable of bringing me happiness, it is him. All I have to do is let him into the place he captured so long ago.

JAX

I should feel nothing but anger and a few short moments ago, that is exactly what I was experiencing. Now that I am face to face with Alana, all I feel is relief knowing she is safe.

Staring at her tear stained face affects me in a way I never knew possible, and I've never felt for anyone what I feel for Alana. Love is too weak of a word to describe it.

"You just left," I whisper, hurt that she would walk out without saying a word.

"I'm sorry," she mutters, lowering her gaze from mine.

"Did you believe what Trix said to you?" I ask, unsure if I will like her answer. Trix admitted what she had told Alana, boldly stating that she had "gotten rid of the problem," unaware of the bond Alana and I share. Her selfish attempt did nothing but anger me, something I will deal with in the near future, but for now I want to lay Alana's fears to rest.

"Yes and no," she admits, the look in her eyes filled with regret at her own words. "I know Trix was trying to get to me, and I let her."

"Why? I told you I wasn't going anywhere, and I meant it." She stares up at me, inwardly fighting her own demons and what her heart is telling her.

"Because I'm afraid," Alana confesses. "I'm scared not only of losing you, but losing myself in the process. I'm terrified of what I'm feeling because love means loss," she says, tears running down her cheeks.

"Alana," I whisper, taking a step closer to her. Reaching out, I touch the side of her face. "Don't you think I have the same fears? Losing you would mean losing my best friend, my soul mate, my heart... my *everything*. Where love is concerned, you have to decide you want it more than you are afraid of it. You will lose me one day, just as I will lose you, but that will be after an eternity together because I plan on spending the rest of my life with you, making up for lost time and showing you what life is supposed to be like. You are my love and my destiny. We were meant to be together, Alana. There were a few detours along the way, but we never got lost. I belong to you just as you belong to me, and I won't let anyone or anything come between us ever."

The tears that trail her cheeks are no longer ones of pain but of happiness. "I don't want to be afraid anymore," she whispers.

I know what she is saying, but I need to hear the words. "Tell me," I whisper, taking a step closer so that I am almost flush against her. "Say the words."

"I..." she pauses, looking up at me. "I love you, Jax. I've loved you since I was six years old." She closes her eyes immediately, fearful that when she opens them again, I will have vanished. "But I can't be what you need."

"All I ever need is you," I whisper. Without hesitation, my mouth lowers to hers, my lips ghosting over her own. Her words are ones I have waited a lifetime for and hearing them for the first time consumes me.

Alana gently parts her lips, a guttural moan escaping her throat as my tongue invades her mouth. My breath leaves me in a rush as she deepens the kiss, my body tightening in response as she sucks my lower lip into her mouth. Our tongues work in unison, mirroring each other in perfect harmony, silently revealing the passion she has been harboring for the longest time.

Lifting her in my arms, she wraps her legs around my waist, her mound pressing against my already rigid cock. The nearness of her, what I have been dreaming of for so very long is now within reach, but I know I have to take it slow, not only for Alana but for myself. I want this night to never end, to savor every touch, every taste.

Gently pulling back, she looks at me with a feverish desire. "I want you, Jax. I need you," she whispers, the sweetness of her breath overpowering me. Her eyes meet mine, a sacred tranquility descending upon us at the realization of what is about to occur. From this moment on, we are one.

"You have no idea how long I have waited to make love to you," I groan, my lips grazing the soft skin of her neck. I feel her stiffen as she pulls back from me. Shaking her head, she looks into my eyes, the fear I thought she had overcome resurfacing. "What's wrong, baby?"

"I...," she pauses, swallowing hard. "I don't know how."

"What do you mean?" I ask, gently lowering her to the floor.

She blushes, turning away from me. "I've never... I've only..." her voice trails off as she tries to find the words, but there is no need.

"Neither have I," I tell her honestly. I've had sex more times than I can count but there has never been any meaning behind it. It was mechanical, a means of release, but nothing more. With Alana it will be different. "We can learn together," I say, pulling her to me.

Her eyes meet mine, softening as she realizes this will be the beginning of a lifetime of firsts. "I love you," she murmurs, my heart swelling as the words escape her lips again.

Lifting her in my arms, my lips collide with hers as I make my way to her room, stopping only when we reach her bed. Gently, I lay her on the mattress, pausing before I make my own descent to admire her beauty.

"I want to see all of you," I whisper, my cock becoming even more engorged as she rises on the bed, climbing onto her knees before stepping onto the carpeted floor beside me. Without hesitation she grips my shirt with her fist, turning me slightly, then guiding me back until the backs of my knees are resting against the mattress. With her flattened palm, she pushes me back onto the bed.

Lifting myself onto my elbows, I watch with hooded eyes as she slowly reaches down to the hem of the clingy red dress. With great deliberation, she peels it off, first revealing her lacy red G-string. My cock throbs at the sight, becoming impatient as she takes her time lifting the scarlet fabric until her full breasts are free from their confines. Tossing the dress aside, she stands before me, clad in only a tiny lace G-string.

"My turn," she says, reaching out for the hem of my shirt, prompting me to stand, literally ripping it off in the process, before tossing it to the floor. Alana's tiny fingers reach out to the button on my jeans, releasing it with ease. She takes a step back, her eyes affixed to mine as I release the zipper, lowering them to the floor. Stepping out of my jeans, I kick them aside, standing before her in only my boxer briefs. "More," she whispers, her eyes locking on my bulge as I lower my briefs, releasing my cock from its confines.

Taking a step forward, her lips seek out my own, her tongue passing my lips with ease. A subtle groan escapes my throat as I feel her fingertips grazing my length, causing my cock to twitch with anticipation. I have never wanted someone as much as I want Alana, nor have I ever needed anyone in this way. Sex has always been just sex, nothing more. My desire for Alana far surpasses simple lust and I know that once I am inside her, there will be no going back. She is my addiction, and with one simple taste, I will lose all control.

I trail my fingers down her soft skin, halting when I reach the apex of her thighs only to have her pull away abruptly. Her lust filled eyes meet mine for only a second before she slowly lowers herself to her knees. I open my mouth to speak, to tell her I don't expect her to go down on me, but instead of words, a guttural moan escapes the back of my throat as she slowly licks a trail from the base of my cock to the crown. "God Alana, that feels so damn good," I groan, my fingers entangling in her mane.

As her tongue lavishes the tip of my dick, I can't help but grasp the back of her head, urging her to take my length into her mouth. Slowly, effortlessly, she descends on my hardness taking me deep into her mouth until I feel the head at the back of her throat. She moans before slowly withdrawing until only the tip remains in her mouth, then plunging down again, this time taking me deeper into her throat. Feverishly, she works my cock, sucking hard as her hand and tongue work their magic, bringing me close to the edge.

"Lana baby, I'm gonna come," I warn her, causing her to work me harder until I can hold back no longer. Thrusting forward, she takes every single inch deep into her throat, holding me there as I come harder than I ever have before.

She slowly pulls back, holding my still hardened cock in her hand. Looking up at me she smiles, her eyes silently pleading with me to return the favor. In one swift move, I lift her to her feet. Gripping the sides of her lace thong, I snap the tiny strings, ripping it away from her body. "You are so fuckin' beautiful," I say, taking a step back to admire her perfection.

Reaching out, my fingers trail the sides of her breasts and I smile as I watch her nipples pebble into rigid peaks before cupping each one tenderly with my hands. Leaning down, I softly kiss the delicate skin of her neck, my fingers grazing her sensitive peaks gently before rolling them between my fingertips.

"Oh my God," she says in a throaty voice. "That feels so good," she murmurs, throwing her head back in pure pleasure as I tug on her nipples harder.

"Is your pussy wet for me?" I whisper.

"Mmhmm…"

"Tell me," I murmur, my hands halting their attack.

Alana lift her head, her hooded eyes meeting my own. "Please don't stop," she begs. "I want you, Jax. Show me how it's supposed to be."

They are the only words I need to hear. Placing one hand on her left breast, the other creeps down slowly to the folds of her wet pussy. "You are so fuckin' wet," I say as I dip a finger inside.

"Oh God, that feels so good," she moans.

Taking a step forward, I blindly lead her to the bed, my lips capturing hers once again. Pushing her back onto the mattress, I stare down at pure perfection, my heart swelling at the realization that she is all mine. Lowering myself on top of her, my lips meets hers, passionately claiming her as my own.

With my hands buried in her hair, my tongue plunges into her mouth deeper, mimicking what my cock will be doing to her pussy all too soon. I would like nothing more than to fuck her hard and fast at this very moment, but refuse to give into temptation. This is our first time, and it has to be perfect, the way her first time should've been.

Pulling back, I gaze down at her, loving the whimper that escapes her lips at my absence. "You are mine," I murmur against her warm flesh, licking a trail from her neck to her right breast, then circling around the rigid peak lightly, causing a low moan to escape her lips. Sucking her hardened nipple into my mouth, she groans as I work her other nipple with my fingertips. "Fuck…" she moans, "I need you, Jax."

Moving my fingers to her mouth, I part her lips, sliding one inside as I continue my assault on her nipples, gently nipping them. Alana wantonly devours my finger, sucking it slowly into her mouth as if she is savoring it, the image of my cock in her mouth only moments ago replaying in my mind.

Withdrawing my fingers, I move them slowly down her neck, trailing the wetness from her mouth down to her overly sensitive nipples. "Please…" she cries out as I make my way down to her drenched pussy, flicking out my tongue to taste her for the first time.

Spreading her lips, I run my tongue the length of her pussy, eliciting a soft moan to escape her lips. When I reach her hardened clit, I circle it slowly at first before sucking it into my wanton mouth.

Arching her back, Alana moans with pure pleasure as I continue my assault on her clit, my fingers working her pussy into a frenzy. She cries out as her orgasm takes hold, her taste flooding my mouth as she comes.

Working my way up her body, I halt when I am staring down at her beautiful face. Her eyes are closed, still relishing in the pleasure she has just received. When they flutter open, I smile down at her before slanting my mouth to capture hers again.

"You are so fuckin' perfect, Lana," I whisper as I pull away.

"Please don't make me wait, Jax…" she pleads, our eyes meeting in mutual desire. As good as she made me feel, I want, no I need more.

"Tell me what you want," I say, lining my cock up with her wet entrance.

"I want you to make love to me, Jax," she says, her pleading eyes meeting mine.

Slowly I enter her, taking my time, feeling her pussy stretch as I fill her with my entire length. "Damn, you feel so fuckin' good," I moan as I come to a stop, fully seated inside of her.

"I love you Jax," she whispers, looking up at me with eyes that reflect the words she has just uttered.

"And I love you, Alana. I always have," I reply before lowering my lips to hers, hungrily kissing her as though I am a starved man. Slowly, I begin to pull out, pausing when only the head remains inside her, then driving into her again.

Over and over, I drive into her, my rhythm becoming more vigorous as her pussy clamps down on my rigidness. Sex has never felt so good and although I never want the feeling to end, I feel myself unable to control my impending orgasm. As if on cue, I feel her pussy grip me tightly and my cock swells within her, both of us crying out as we come in unison.

Breathless and feeling sated, I roll from on top of her, pulling her to me as I lay on my back. Life couldn't be more perfect than it is in this moment. Alana is finally mine and nothing will ever stand between us from this point forward.

"What do we do now?" Alana whispers into my chest after several moments of silence.

"What do you mean?" I ask, raising my head slightly off the pillow.

Alana lifts her head, looking over at me with saddened eyes. "This is all new to me," she says as she looks away.

"Hey," I whisper. "Are you having regrets?" I ask, my heart sinking at the thought of my own words.

"No, it's just... I've never done anything like this before. I'm not sure what comes next."

"It's a first for me too," I say, my finger lifting her chin so our eyes meet. "We just take it one day at a time, but we do it together. You will never be alone again, Alana. I will always be with you."

She lays her head back on my chest, breathing in deeply. "I've never felt like this before," she whispers.

"Me either, baby. Only with you," I say, meaning every word.

We lay together in silence, the only sound is that of us breathing. Tonight we have taken a big step. We are no longer two desolate souls living our lives without feeling or meaning. We are now one, never to be two again.

Glancing over at the bedside table, I see that it is nearing two in the morning, and only when I hear Alana's rhythmic breathing do I realize she has fallen asleep in my arms. Pressing my lips to her forehead, I reach down and pull the covers over her naked form, pulling her even closer to me. "Goodnight, Alana," I whisper.

My words are met with silence, but I have never felt less alone. Today begins a new life for us, with tomorrow being the beginning of our forever. As I close my eyes and begin to drift asleep, my thoughts are only of Lana and the future the two of us will forever share.

Chapter 28

Alana

Three Months Later

Happily ever after only happens in fairy tales, or at least that is what I had always believed. Now I know that dreams do come true, even if it takes a long time to become reality. My knight in shining armor may not be what you read in story books or see in the movies, but in my eyes he is absolute perfection, all the way down to his tatted up body sitting astride his Harley.

"You're drooling," Alexis snickers from beside me, causing me to glare in her direction. "Just making an observation," she giggles, her eyes following mine as I stare in Jax's direction.

Just like every other night I am working, he is seated at the far table in the corner, he and Deuce laughing at something Spyder has just said. "I can't help it," I say, wondering where I would be if I hadn't found Jax again. There's no doubt that I still be falling for Paul's tricks, being used and manipulated by someone I thought I could trust. Another hard life lesson to learn.

"Can't say I blame you. Jax is a winner, but I think he lucked out just as much as you did."

I smile over at her, grateful I have a friend like her in my life. In the last few months, I have opened up to her, revealing things about my past that only Jax knows about. In return, she has shared more about her life. Ultimately, we have become as close as sisters. "So have you set a date?" I probe, secretly hoping her and Spyder have finally made a decision.

"No," she groans. "I can't get it through his thick head that all I want is a small wedding, just close friends and family, and nothing extravagant. He seems to think I need some elaborate ceremony, with bells and whistles. Weddings like that are for everyone else. I want ours to be about us."

I smile, liking the sound of that. "He'll come around," I say reassuringly. One thing is for certain, Spyder loves Alexis and he'll do whatever it takes to make her happy.

"What about you and Jax? Any wedding bells in the near future?"

I turn abruptly, unable to hide the shocked look on my face. "We've only been together a few months," I remind her, as if she doesn't know. And these months have been the best of my life. Our first night together will forever be etched in my mind. I can still remember my shock when I awoke to find I had slept soundly in his arms the entire night. Neither of us has spent a night alone since, and if I have anything to say about it, we never will. I love Jax being the first thing I see when I wake up and the last thing before drifting asleep.

"Oh pish posh," she says, fanning her hand at me. "You two have been an item since you were kids. So what if you spent a few years apart. You're together now and nothing's gonna change that."

I wish I had as much faith as she does. It's not like I am worried about Jax leaving me anymore. That thought abandoned my mind long ago. I have only one fear now, and hopefully tomorrow will put an end to it all. I still don't know how he found out where I was staying, but for the last few months I have received a letter from Paul at least twice a week.

"You're nervous, aren't you?" Alexis asks, bringing me back to the present. "Have you told Jax?"

"No," I mutter, trying hard to conceal my concern. "He wouldn't understand. I have to tell Paul goodbye, let him know I have moved on and am finally happy. Maybe then he'll finally let me go."

In two days, Paul will go in front of a judge and learn his fate. When I heard the news that he was foregoing a jury trial, I knew he had given up. After Hawk's sentence made headlines, he probably knew there was no hope. In a way I am sad for him. Deep down I believe Paul is a good man, he just went about everything the wrong way. I could hate him for what he has done to me, but instead I am grateful. If not for him, Jax and I never would have reconnected, nor would I have ever experienced this kind of happiness.

"I mean about the other," she says, nodding at me.

"No," I admit, feeling guilty that Alexis knows and I still haven't mentioned a word to Jax.

"You can't keep hiding it forever. Eventually he's gonna figure it out."

It's not like I'm trying to keep my pregnancy a secret. Hell, I didn't even think I could get pregnant, which is why we never bothered with birth control. I just haven't found the right time to tell him. Hell, I didn't tell Alexis.

Smartass figured it out the first time I turned green at work.

"I'm gonna tell him," I reassure her, making a vow to myself to do so as soon as possible.

"He's gonna be ecstatic," Alexis says, placing her hand on mine. "He loves you Alana, so damn much. When he finds out you're carrying his baby, he's gonna be walking around with a permanent smile on that handsome face."

I hope she is right. We've talked about our future, but children never came up. "I promise, I'll talk to him."

"Good," she says, a broad smile overtaking her face. "Where you going handsome?" she calls out.

I turn to see Jax heading towards the hall beside the bar. "You're such a nosy little bitch, aren't you Alexis?" he smiles, causing Alexis to laugh. "You two continue your little gossip fest and don't mind me," he says as he walks past, winking at me.

"Yep, you are one lucky woman," Alexis purrs, staring at Jax's ass until he disappears down the hallway.

"I know," I say, my eyes locking with Jax's as he reenters the room. He is my past, present and future. The happiest times in my life revolved around him, and now is no different. I'm in love, but then again, I always have been. Denying it didn't change my feelings and never will. In a few months, we will be welcoming a child into the world, our child, created in love and he or she will have everything neither of us had growing up. "Can you cover for me?" I ask, turning towards Alexis abruptly.

"Sure hun," she says, nodding at me in understanding.

Taking in a deep breath, I cross the room to where Jax has just taken a seat.

"Can we talk?" I ask him quickly before I lose my nerve. Deuce looks over at me, concern etching his face.

"Sure babe," Jax says as he stands, his expression mimicking Deuce's. Grasping my hand in his, he leads me towards the hall and into the office, locking the door behind him as soon as we enter. "You OK?"

"Yeah," I mutter, avoiding his gaze. "Something happened." How fuckin' lame is that? *Something happened.* This is Jax. I can be honest with him.

"OK, well are you planning on telling me or am I supposed to guess?" he asks, smirking at me.

I open my mouth to speak, but the words won't come out. *What am I supposed to say? Oh, by the way, you knocked me up.* How do you tell the man you love that you are carrying his child? Will he be happy, upset, or maybe even angry?

"I like guessing games," he chuckles. "Let's see, what could be difficult for you to tell me..." he trails off, a look of amusement on his face. "You decided you were wrong and want to be with Deuce instead?"

"No!" I shout. That has to be the most asinine thing I've heard.

"OK then... you won the lottery?"

"Jax..." *Just spit it out already!*

"You're not who you say you are. The real Alana was abducted by aliens and you are really a Martian impersonating her so you can report back to your superiors."

I cannot help but burst out laughing at his absurdity.

"I give up," he says, grinning at me. "So what gives? Are you pregnant or something?" he snickers, causing my eyes to widen. The smile on his face instantly vanishes. "You're pregnant?"

Slowly I nod my head, taking in a deep breath and holding it, preparing myself for whatever is to come.

"You're having a baby?" Jax asks in disbelief. He closes his eyes, shaking his head as if it is inconceivable.

"I'm sorry," I begin, fighting back the tears that threaten to fall. "I didn't think I could... it didn't cross my mind... I should've..." I can't even find the words.

Taking a step closer to me, Jax drops to his knees and slowly lifts my shirt. He presses a gentle kiss to my belly before looking up at me. "We're having a baby?" His eyes are filled with so much emotion – happiness, excitement, and most of all love. "How far along?"

"Seven weeks," I tell him, finally allowing my tears to fall.

Rising to his feet, he pulls me to him, holding me tightly in his arms. "Why didn't you tell me?"

"I didn't know for sure until last week," I say, trying to soften the blow that is to come. "And I was afraid."

"Of being pregnant or telling me?" he asks, taking a step back.

"Both," I admit, feeling stupid for not coming to him sooner. "Having a baby is a big responsibility and we never discussed it. I didn't want you to think I did this to trap you."

"Alana, you've had me from the moment that six year old girl walked into my life refusing to take no for an answer. Do you remember that night?" he asks, engulfing me into his arms once again. "I remember stepping out on that rooftop and seeing you there. I wanted to walk away, but when I saw your tear filled eyes, I knew I wasn't alone. Someone else was hurting just as much as I was."

"You called me a twerp," I giggle, remembering our first conversation.

"Yeah I did, but that was code word for angel. You see Alana, you saved me that night, made me believe that we would have a happier life one day and you were right. Look at us now. You and me, we're together, happier than we have ever been and so fuckin' much in love. And we're gonna have a baby, one conceived in love, and that is all our child will ever know. He or she is gonna have the life we should've had."

My heart is full at this moment, feeling as though it will explode.

"I know this wasn't planned but I couldn't be happier. There's only one thing that will make this night perfect," he whispers, taking a step back and looking down at me with absolute adoration. "I know you aren't ready yet, but one day soon, you will become my wife and then my life will be complete."

As I open my mouth to speak, Jax lowers his head, his lips meeting mine.

Letting out a ragged breath, I push forward into the visitation room and take a seat at the table in front of me, my nerves starting to get the best of me. I haven't laid eyes on Paul in a very long time and had no intention of ever seeing him again.

The letters seized shortly after my last visit with him, undoubtedly because I had moved into Deuce's place. Naively, I believed it had come to an end up until a few months ago when they resumed. All the letters sit unopened in a shoebox in my closet, where they will remain. That is part of the reason for my being here. It will give him the chance to say what he needs to and will give me some much needed closure. Paul is part of my past and there is no room in my present or future for him.

"You came." I turn at the sound of Paul's voice, caught off guard by his appearance. His face is hard and cold, reminiscent of a serial killer instead of the man at one time I trusted with my life.

The guard leads him to the chair in front of me, ordering him to sit before he stalks off. I look over at him, feeling as though I am in the company of a complete stranger. This is not the Paul I once knew, but I have a feeling he was always there, and I was just too blind to see it.

"I've missed you Alana," he whispers as he leans forward, placing his cuffed wrists on the table between us. "Thank you for coming."

"I didn't come for you," I begin, surprised at the cold tone in my voice. "This is about me."

He nods at me in understanding, but his gaze says otherwise. For the first time, I see the resentment in his eyes, the blame he places on me for him being in this situation. "Then why are you here?"

"To say goodbye," I say in a matter of fact tone. "To ask you to stop with the letters and to let me go."

"So you have gotten my letters?" he asks, already knowing the answer. "And they meant nothing to you?"

"I haven't read them," I admit. When I see the hurt look in his eyes, it tears at my soul. Even after everything he has done to me, I still do care about him.

"Because of Jax," he says, his voice laced with hatred. "I didn't want to believe you would just abandon me, that you would turn to him after everything he has done to you, but I guess you really are a fool."

"Jax never did anything to me," I say, coming to his defense. "He never lied to me. He never betrayed me. Everything I believed about him was wrong. It was you that deceived me, not Jax."

"I tried to protect you and that is exactly what I did. Hawk wanted to see sell you to the highest bidder, but I was the one to stop him. I could've made a killing off you, but I didn't and I was willing to put an end to Hawk to keep you safe. Look where it got me. I'm behind bars because *you* were my priority."

"Are you trying to convince me or yourself? So you put a stop to me being sold on the black market and I'm supposed to be grateful? You convinced me to do things that I never wanted to be a part of. You manipulated me the entire time for your own selfish needs. You are behind bars because of what *you* did, not because of me or Hawk. He's paying the price and so will you."

He stares at me for several moments, the silence between us almost deafening. "You can't honestly believe that. I took care of you, Alana. I made you feel again. I took you out of your little bubble and taught you how to survive. If not for me, you would've been catering to some man's every need instead of making your own rules."

"You used me!" I shout, causing the guard to look over at us in concern. "I was nothing but a fuckin' whore to you," I say, lowering my voice.

"And you're telling me you never used me? How many times did I give you what *you* needed? You didn't even know what pleasure was until I showed you. That made you mine. You will be always be mine, Alana."

"No," I say, defiantly. "I never belonged to you. I was young and naïve, falling for your lies, but no more," I tell him as I rise from my chair. "I'm with Jax now and we are happy. I love him and he loves me."

"Love means loss, Alana. You know that better than anyone."

"You're wrong. Jax has given me more in the time we have been together than anyone. I come first in his life. He would lay down his life for me. He makes me feel for the first time in my life that I deserve the best." And I have never been happier.

"If it's a choice between you and him, he will always come first."

"For years I fell for your lies," I seethe, allowing my anger to overtake me, "but no more. I finally have someone who truly loves me for me, who respects me and will never betray me. You are *nothing*! You never were!" I spit, turning on my heel, walking away from him forever. Coming here was a mistake.

"I won't let you go Alana!" he calls out from behind me. "In the end, you will have to make a choice and I will be the one walking away the victor."

I ignore his words as I continue my escape, never looking back. My only regret is allowing him to still have any effect on me.

My fists are clenched tightly by my side when the cell door slams shut, isolating me from the outside world again. This isn't over and never will be.

Alana thinks she has the perfect life now. I'm sure Jax has promised her the world and she believes every lie he tells her. He doesn't love her, at least not like I do. What we shared was real. Jax thinks he knows Alana. That they share an unbreakable bond, but he couldn't be more wrong. My parting words to Alana were a promise. She will choose me, I will make sure of it.

I don't have much on the inside, but I still have my connections. Trix has been extremely helpful, although her motives are completely selfish. She wants Jax and Alana is standing in her way. Seems that Jax is still standing in mine. Working together, we both can get what we want.

It was Trix who let me know where Alana was staying and for that I will always be grateful. I

know when she works, when she sleeps –
every single detail about her life. Keeping tabs
on Alana will make my plans go smoothly.

Letting out an accomplished sigh, I sit back on
the bunk and start plotting. If all goes well,
tomorrow my plan will go into effect, and in a
few weeks my life will be perfect, one way or
another.

"How does the defendant plead?" The sound of
the judge's voice brings me back to reality.

Giving a sideways glance at the prosecution, I
return my focus my attention on the man who
ultimately holds my fate in his hands, or at
least that is what everyone present believes.

"No contest," my attorney replies. There is
more than enough evidence to prove my guilt
in this case, and a jury would have found me
guilty in a heartbeat. My best chance was to
plea, and when I heard Judge Mitchell was on
the roster this week, I agreed to throw myself
on the mercy of the court.

I tune out the attorneys as they discuss the
facts of the case, already familiar with what
both parties will say. The prosecution wants to
see me rot in prison and the defense is hoping

for a lighter sentence, twenty years max. They both are wrong. I will walk out of this place a free man, thanks to Judge Mitchell and his extracurricular activities. He may not have recognized my name on this morning's court roster, but there is no doubt in my mind that he remembers me. I keep my eyes focused on him the entire time as both attorney's speak, silently reminding him that if I go down, so does he.

"Mr. Martin, do you have anything to add?" Judge Mitchell asks, his gaze meeting mine.

"No your honor," I say, raising my brow at him. If he's smart, he will see things my way.

"Alright," he says, looking anywhere but at me. A lifetime seems to pass as he recites law, talks about the appalling nature of my crimes, and what sentence he could impose on me. "That being said Mr. Martin, I believe you too were a victim of this entire operation. I cannot imagine what horrors you have seen in your years involved with Mr. Daniels and I commend you for stepping forward to bring him to justice."

It's like taking candy from a baby. It's not who you know, it's what you know and in this case, I know the prosecutor and Judge Mitchell quite well. It didn't take much to convince Dale Baker to offer me one hell of a plea bargain. With Trix's help, I was able to pass along my message, which he heard loud and clear. Judge Frank Mitchell will be just as easy. What I know about these two men will not only ruin their marriages and reputation, but their careers as well. Unlike Hawk, I wasn't hiding in the background. I was out front, negotiating with each of these men firsthand when they had needs to be fulfilled. They know what I have on them and that I will use it to my advantage. The best part is that neither knows of the other, making my plan even more devious.

"It's my understanding that the original charges in this case were sex trafficking and three counts of murder, and that Mr. Martin has agreed to plead no contest to the charges of facilitating prostitution and three counts of involuntary manslaughter."

"Yes your honor," the Dale says, nodding his head, an arrogant look on his plump face. He looks over at me, an accomplished look on his face. He thinks I am going down, and I can't wait to see that smug look turn into astonishment when my sentence is passed down. He thinks he has the upper hand here and that the judge isn't in my pocket. He is dead wrong. "The state would ask for the maximum sentence on all three charges." *Sixteen years. Good luck with that fucker.*

"Understood counselor, but I cannot consciously impose such a harsh sentence on someone who was a victim of circumstance. Mr. Martin was forced into this operation at a young age and it is the only life he has really known. As for the charges of involuntary manslaughter, I think it has been established that if Mr. Martin had not reacted, he would not be standing here today."

I fight back the urge to smile as Dale turns beet red. He knows he's lost, he just doesn't know how badly.

Judge Mitchell returns his focus to me. "After careful consideration of the facts in this case, I accept your plea in this matter." He pauses for only a moment before continuing. "On the charge of facilitating prostitution, I sentence you to six months in prison. As for the charges of involuntary manslaughter, I also sentence you to nine months in prison for each charge, all sentences to run concurrent with credit for time served."

As the courtroom erupts in chaos, I continue staring straight ahead, planning my next move. *It won't be long now, Alana. In just a few short weeks, you and I will be together again.*

Chapter 29

JAX

My eyes open instinctively when I feel her absence. Rolling over, I can still feel her warmth on the sheets and realize she has just left my side. Throwing the covers off me, I climb out of bed and pull on my boxers before going in search of her.

Stepping into the living room, I smile at the sound of pots clanging, undoubtedly Alana is attempting to make breakfast. Stalking towards the kitchen, I stand back and admire the view of Alana clad in her tiny tank top and boy shorts, oblivious to my presence. Yesterday marked her fourth month of pregnancy and her body is just as amazing as ever. She is barely showing, only a small bump visible, but in her eyes she's as big as a whale— at least those are her words. To me she is perfect. I can't wait until her stomach is round with my child, evidence of the love the two of us share.

Alana turns to open the refrigerator, her enlarged breasts straining against the thin fabric of her tank top, making me instantly hard. Thank God pregnancy agrees with her or I'd be suffering from an extremely painful case of blue balls. Alana has been insatiable, wanting sex two to three times a day and far be it from me to complain.

Sneaking up behind her as she approaches the stove, I wrap my arms around her and press my lips to her neck. "Good morning," I moan against her silken skin.

"Did I wake you?" she asks, taking in a deep breath when I nip her shoulder lightly.

"No babe," I smile, not wanting to admit I can't sleep without her beside me. "Whatcha makin'?"

"Waffles," she says, turning in my arms. "Unless you had something else in mind?" she asks, suggestively.

God how I love this woman. "Oh, I can think of a few things," I murmur before lowering my lips to hers.

Pulling back, she looks up at me scowling. "Is that all you ever think about?" she asks, putting her hands on her hips. Narrowing my eyes at her, I try to figure out if she's joking or not, but can't tell until she bursts out laughing.

"Did you really think I was being serious?" she giggles.

"Hey, how am I supposed to know if you're getting all hormonal on me or not?" I say, chuckling.

"You're so fuckin' easy," she says, pointing to the stool behind me. "The waffles are almost ready."

"Yes dear," I say, pretending to sulk as I take a seat, my eyes glued to her ass as she continues making breakfast.

Quickly, she plates two waffles with a side of sausage, placing it on the counter in front of me before sliding a coffee mug my way. "I need to go into town today," she says, grabbing her glass of orange juice.

"I can take you after church," I offer around a mouthful of food.

"You sure you don't mind? I need to buy some bigger bras," she says, looking down at her ever growing chest. "Is it possible to carry a baby in your boobs?"

"What?" I choke out.

"I've got to get some bras. I'm wondering how big they're gonna get." She places her hands over her breasts, lifting them slightly.

"I…" my voice trails off, unable to finish my thought, let alone respond.

Shaking her head, she smirks at me. "Finish your breakfast and I'm gonna get dressed," she says, leaving me alone. My appetite, at least for food, has vanished. Shoveling the remainder of food in my mouth, I stand, rushing towards the sink with my plate, desperately needing to curb my sexual appetite.

Just as I turn to head towards the bedroom, Alana emerges, already dressed and ready to go. *So much for that idea,* I think to myself. "Give me five and we can head out," I say as I walk towards the bedroom.

"What do you think about this one?" Alana asks, holding yet another bra up for my opinion.

"They all look the same to me," I say, shrugging. "It's an over the shoulder boulder holder no matter what color you pick out."

"This one is a demi," she retorts, rolling her eyes at me. "Regretting bringing me to the mall?" she asks, giggling at me.

"Not at all," I say, although at this moment I am. I had no clue that buying bras would be an all day ordeal.

"Yeah right," she smirks, adding the bra to the growing collection in her arms. "I'll be right back," she adds before stalking towards the dressing room.

I look around the almost abandoned store, my eyes landing on several pieces of lingerie on display, letting my mind picture Alana in each one of them. Closing my eyes, I try to push those thoughts aside. Last thing I need is to walk around the mall with a raging hard on.

"Jax!" I turn towards the dressing room at the sound of Alana's voice calling out to me. "Can you help me for a minute?"

I glance over my shoulder towards the clerk who is perched behind the counter, intrigued by whatever she is looking at on her iPhone. "Sure," I mumble, walking towards the dressing area to find Alana's head peering from around the corner of the doorway.

"I'm having a little problem," she says, disappearing behind the door, holding it open so that I can enter.

Stepping inside, I see the room is larger than I had imagined, even boasting a chair in the corner. I turn at the sound of the door shutting, my eyes widening at the sight of Alana dressed in a white lace bra, her hardened nipples forming peaks in the barely there fabric, and a matching thong. My cock instantly becomes rigid, straining against the harsh denim of my jeans. Swallowing hard, I force my gaze to meet her eyes. "You said you were having a problem?"

Biting her lower lip, Alana takes the few steps necessary to close the distance between us. Without saying a word, she rises on her tip toes, her tongue darting between my parted lips. Breathing her in, I relish in the taste that is Alana, memorizing the feel of her body pressed to mine.

She pulls back, panting hard, her eyes meeting mine filled with a need reminiscent of my own. Without a word she reaches behind her, releasing the clasps of her bra, letting it fall silently to the floor. As she takes a step closer to me, I reach out, wanting to feel her hardened nipples between my fingertips, only for her to push me back onto the metal chair perched in the corner.

"Hey!" I mutter, only for her to silence me with a single finger pressed to my lips.

"Shhh," she whispers as she takes a step back. Slowly, with precise purpose, she lowers her thong, tossing it towards me. My eyes are torn between her engorged tits and the sweetness between her thighs, my mouth watering at the thought of eating her sweet pussy until she begs me to fuck her.

Closing the expanse between us, she drops to her knees, swiftly releasing my throbbing cock from my jeans, her eyes never leaving mine as her fingers wrap around my girth, caressing it gently. "I want you," she mouths before lowering her lips to the crown, her tongue snaking out to lavish the pearly droplet on the tip. She moans ever so slightly, before taking my entire length into her mouth, ravishing my rod with her tongue as she glides up and down.

I want to touch her, make her feel the same pleasure she is giving me, but as soon as my fingertips brush against the swell of her breast, she pulls back. "I'm in control," she whispers, rising to her feet.

Spreading her legs ever so slightly, she reaches down, giving me a glimpse of her hardened clit before slowly encircling it with her fingertips. Throwing her head back, she continues working herself, her free hand caressing her left breast. Without taking my eyes off of her, I reach down and firmly grasp my cock, stroking it rhythmically, matching her pace. Her eyes lower to my staff, the want in her eyes increasing.

Taking in a ragged breath, her hands drop to her side before she walks towards me. Straddling the chair, she looks down at me with heated eyes. "You are mine," she whispers as she lowers herself onto my raging cock until I am buried deep inside.

It takes everything I have to remain silent as she rides me hard, bringing me closer to release. Just when I think I can hold back no longer, she slows, rising up until only the head remains inside, and then slamming herself down again. Gripping her hips tightly, I thrust up into her over and over again until I feel her pussy clamping down on me like a vice. Leaning down, she buries her face in my neck, biting down as she finds her release at the same time I find my own.

We both are panting as we come down from the pinnacle of ecstasy. No matter how many times I have her, each time seems like the first and I can't help but wonder if it will always be this way with us. Then I look into her eyes, and know it will never change because love like ours will only get stronger with each passing day.

Alana

Stepping out of the store with my bag in hand, I look over my shoulder at the store clerk blushing. I don't know what came over me, but I have no regrets. I never have any when it involves Jax, at least not anymore. I have found my forever and I am never letting him go.

"That was... unexpected," Jax says, grinning over at me.

"Guess you'll never complain about going shopping with me again," I shrug, trying hard to conceal the smile that threatens to surface.

"I think I might want to start going more often," he smirks. "I can't wait to see what you can do in the frozen foods section at the supermarket," he chuckles, causing me to elbow him in the ribs.

"Smartass," I say, narrowing my eyes at him. The bad thing is that now I can't get the image of him taking me in the middle of the grocery store out of my mind.

"So where to next?" he asks as he drapes his arm across my shoulders.

"That's up to you," I say, walking alongside him. "I got what I came for."

"Is that all you think about?" he winks, a smile forming on his lips.

"Shut up," I tell him, rolling my eyes in frustration.

"Make me," he says, stopping abruptly.

Dropping my bag on the tiled floor, I stand on my tip toes and press my lips to his. "There. Now feed me," I add, bending over to retrieve my bag.

"My pleasure," he says, gripping me around the waist and guiding me towards the food court.

As he steps up to the pizza counter to order, I feel eyes trained on me. This isn't the first time I've felt like someone was watching me, but before now I hadn't give it much thought. With a sinking feeling in my gut, I allow my gaze to fall on the floods of people that surround me but see nothing. Not a single person stands out or even appears to be looking in my direction.

Shaking my head, I inwardly laugh at myself for being so paranoid. I am nobody and here I am acting as though I have my own personal stalker.

"You OK, babe?" Jax asks, walking towards me.

"Yeah," I nod, feeling ridiculous. "Just thinking."

"Well stop before you set off the smoke alarms," he snickers, obviously finding much amusement in making me the brunt of his joke.

"Ha ha," I say, crossing my arms defensively.

"You know I'm just giving you a hard time. Come on, let's eat." Holding the tray in one hand, he grasps mine with his free one, leading me towards a vacant table.

As we enjoy our pizza, I still can't shake the feeling someone is watching me. And then it dawns on me – maybe it's not me they are watching.

Chapter 30

Two Weeks Later

Staring out the window, I watch as Jax walks hand in hand with Alana towards the SUV in the tiny parking lot, pausing when they reach the passenger side door. I seethe as I watch him pin her against the vehicle, claiming her mouth with his own.

"Why do you keep doing this to yourself?" Trix asks from beside me. "We've been following them for almost a week and it's always the same thing. You could at least show a little consideration for me."

"Shut the fuck up," I grumble, my gaze still affixed on Jax and Alana. How could she move on like this? Pretend that what we had was meaningless?

"I'm just saying that watching the two of them like this isn't solving either of our problems. They're still together and judging by the look of things, that isn't changing anytime soon."

My blood begins to boil as he places his hand on her belly, guarding the tiny life growing inside. I didn't want to believe it was true, but there is no denying it now. She is carrying *his* child, not mine and it isn't fair. This was supposed to be my life, not his. "Are you giving up?"

"Of course not, but I don't see how spying on the two of them is accomplishing anything."

"Trust me," I say, turning my attention towards Trix. "Do you think I want to watch the two of them like this? Because I don't. I despise it, but also know if we screw this up, there's no going back and I'm not about to lose Alana because you can't be patient." I had planned to make a move long before now, but things don't always go according to plan. Soon, this will all be over.

"I still don't know what you see in her. She has you and Jax both fooled," Trix snarls, saying the same thing she has a million times before. "She isn't that fuckin' special."

She doesn't get it and never will. I shouldn't be surprised. Women like Trix think no one can compare to them. If she were honest with herself, she'd see that Alana is everything she is not. It's not that Trix is unattractive. She's a beautiful woman, but her personality and cockiness takes away from her outer beauty.

I turn in the direction of Jax and Alana, watching as he helps her into the vehicle before climbing into the driver's seat and taking off, completely oblivious to our presence.

Enjoy her while you can Jax, because soon she will be walking out of your life and back into mine and there won't be a damn thing you can do about it.

Standing in the shadows outside Alana's bedroom window, I watch as she enters the room. Walking over to the bed, she sits down and slowly removes her shoes, tossing them into a corner. The look on Alana's face is one of complete exhaustion.

She rises to her feet, stalking across the room. With her back to me, she slips off her jeans, tossing them into the nearby hamper. I hold my breath as she removes her teal colored tank top, balling it with her fists before flinging it across the room. When she turns to the side, only then do I get a clear view of the baby bump she is sporting.

That should be my baby she's carrying. Taking in a deep breath I watch as she reaches around and unclasps her bra, releasing her breasts from their confines. She is even more beautiful than I remember. Staring at her like this makes me rock hard in an instant, but when she lowers her panties, I almost lose it.

Taking in a deep breath, I fight the urge to barge into the house and take her right now. I've waited long enough to claim what is rightfully mine and my patience is running thin.

When she disappears into the bathroom, I'm finally able to make my move. I know I have only minutes before Jax will show up and if I am going to make this work, I have to do it now. Making my way towards the back door, I find it unlocked, making my job all the easier.

With stealth, I make my way to the kitchen. Alana's scent still mingling in the air, causing me to pause and breathe in deeply. This is what I miss – her smell, the way her smile always made everything better, her lips crashing against mine and the feel of her warm body pressed tightly against me as I take her again and again. I will not allow her to become a distant memory.

I rush towards the kitchen and pull out the carton of orange juice, setting it on the counter. Quickly I remove the vial of crushed Mifepristone from my pocket, courtesy of Trix, and as I am about to pour the contents into the container, I find myself unable to go through with it. No matter how much I resent that she is carrying Jax's baby, I can't do this to her.

Shoving the vial back into my pocket, I quickly place the juice back in the refrigerator. As I retreat out the back door, I pause for a moment, taking one last look around before rushing into the darkness, barely making it in time before Jax pulls into the driveway. Crouching down, I watch as he climbs off his bike, thinking how easy it would be to take him out right here, right now, but that's not how this is going down. I want to see the pain on his face when he loses Alana forever, a day that is coming very soon.

Peering through the bedroom window, I watch as Alana reenters the room, a garnet colored towel wrapped tightly around her. Her hair is wet from her recent shower and I can almost smell the scent of her shampoo in the night air. My fists instinctively clench at my side when I see Jax enter the room, stalking towards her as if she belongs to him. Bile rises in my throat when he takes her in his arms, his lips claiming hers.

I know I should walk away, forego torturing myself any further, but I can't. Instead I stand there, gritting my teeth, as he slowly releases her towel, letting it drift to the carpet.

She is mine! I silently roar, reaching for my revolver instinctively before I think twice about it. I want him to feel the pain I am experiencing, know what it is like to watch the woman you love be with someone else.

Taking one last look through the window, my heart crumbles into a million pieces as I watch him enter her, claiming her like I once did. As I turn to walk away from the scene unfolding before me, I am filled with a hatred I have never before experienced, and it is all aimed at one man. Jackson Cade.

Chapter 31

JAX

"Are you gonna stand here all night staring at her?" Deuce chuckles from behind me. My eyes are locked on Alana as she stands beside Alexis,

"Maybe," I admit as I glance over my shoulder at him. It's surreal having Alana back in my life. I always dreamed that this is how life would be, but this isn't a fantasy. This is real.

"I'm glad things finally worked out," Deuce says, coming to stand beside me. "Not too many people are that lucky."

This has nothing to do with luck. Fate intervened and brought Alana back to me and I'm never letting her go. "I'm not going on the next run."

"Figured as much," he says, grinning at me. "Already gotcha covered."

"If it weren't for you…" I pause, trying to come up with the right words. "You had a hand in all this, even from the beginning. Thank you."

"No need to thank me, brother," he says, shaking his head. "Wish I could take credit, but this was all you and Alana."

"You know what I'm talking about." There's no need to say the words.

"Yeah well, that's what family does," he says, lifting his head. "A wise man once told me that blood makes you related, but loyalty makes you family. I think we've proven that theory a time or two."

"Yeah, we have." I think back to the time when we first met and the years that followed filled with loyalty, honor, friendship and trust. The true meaning of family and brotherhood.

"Looks like Alana's drawing some attention," he says, nodding towards the woman of my dreams.

I watch as Beast drops to his knees in front of her and presses his ear tightly to her stomach. "What the fuck is he doing?"

"He's been reading fuckin' baby books, so God only knows. He probably thinks he can hear the baby talk or some shit," Deuce says, rolling his eyes. "I think Beast is vying for favorite uncle. Too bad that title's already taken."

Doubling over, I burst into a fit of laughter. "Favorite uncle?" I chuckle. "He hasn't even been born yet."

"You making fun of me?" Deuce bows up, narrowing his eyes at me.

"Not at all," I hold my hands up in defeat.

"Yeah, that's what I thought," he says, his lips stretching into a smile. Shrugging, he breaks into a full-fledged grin. "What can I say? I like the idea of having a little one running around here and I think I'll make one hell of an uncle."

"The best," I tell him, slapping him on the back before returning my focus to Alana.

"She's gonna say yes."

Shaking my head, I cut my eyes at Deuce who stares straight ahead, his face expressionless. "How did you know?"

"I saw you go into Miller's the other day. Figured there's only one reason you'd be going into a jewelry store," he chuckles. "I'm happy for you, Jax. For both of you."

"She hasn't said yes yet," I remind him, my nerves getting the best of me.

"She will," he says, his expression growing serious. "You belong together. You've belonged together since the beginning. Your souls are intertwined. Two hearts beating as one. Without one another, neither of you is complete. You know this and so does she."

"Are you turning into a romantic?" I ask, raising my brow. This is a side of Deuce I have never witnessed before.

"Fat chance," he snickers, shaking his head. "I'll stick to what I do best."

"Fuck 'em and chuck 'em?" I ask, rolling my eyes.

"What can I say?" he says, shrugging. "If it ain't broke, don't try to..." his voice trails off, his brow creasing.

Following his line of sight, my eyes land on Trix as she heads straight towards Alana. "Fuck!" I shout, storming across the yard, reaching Trix's position before Alana has a chance to notice her.

"What the fuck are you doing here?!" I demand, gripping her arm tightly.

"Actually I came to see you," she smiles up at me. "It's been awhile since you and I had some fun."

Glancing over my shoulder, I breathe a sigh of relief when I see Deuce talking to Alana. Knowing I only have a few minutes to rectify the situation before it gets out of hand. Grasping her arm even tighter, I drag her towards the main building, only stopping when we reach the main room. "What part of stay the fuck away don't you get?"

"Because I love you, Jax. What part of that don't you understand?"

"Trix, we've been over this a million times and nothing has changed. There was never anything between us. You knew that from the beginning."

Trix lifts her tear filled eyes to mine, her bottom lip trembling. "You don't mean that," she whispers. "We had something special."

"We fucked, Trix! A few times, yes, but there was never anything more to it than that! You were just another whore!"

Shaking her head, she takes a step back. "How's it different with her? She's no better than me."

"Alana was never some girl I just fucked," I say through clenched teeth. "I never meant to hurt you Trix, but it is what it is," I tell her, my tone softening. "You need to get that through your head."

"I won't," she says defiantly. "Because it's a lie. You have feelings for me. I see it in your eyes."

"What you see is what you want to see. I never lied to you Trix, and I'm not about to start now. I love Alana, not you."

"Why are you doing this?" Trix shouts. "It's not fair! I won't let her have you!"

"You don't have much of a choice." I turn at the sound of Alana's voice and immediately all tension leaves my body. "Because I'm not giving him up."

"Tell her!" Trix demands, turning her attention towards me. "Why don't you tell her all the lies you told me and every other girl you fucked over? Tell her how you used us and threw us all to the curb!"

"Trix..."

"No! Explain to her why she's fuckin' different from the rest of us. How you'll never break her heart like you did mine!" She quickly turns her focus to Alana, the rage in her eyes nothing like I have seen from her before. "Do you know how many times he has used me? Made me believe we had something and the moment you walked into the picture it all changed. You don't deserve him!"

Without warning, Trix lunges towards Alana and I immediately rush forward, stopping only when the sound of Alana's hand impacting Trix's cheek echoes through the otherwise silent building. "Don't you fuckin' tell me what I do or don't deserve!" Alana shouts. "Jax loves me and I love him! I will be damned if I let you or anyone else come between us!"

I take a step back filled with pride not just by Alana's actions but her words as well. She wants this as much as I do.

"This isn't over," Trix mutters before rushing towards the entrance, disappearing quickly through the front door.

Letting out a ragged breath, I turn my attention towards Alana, overwhelmed by the need to apologize for Trix's actions. "I'm…"

"Don't," Alana says, cutting me off. "You can't change your past any more than I can, so don't say you're sorry."

Pulling her into my arms, I hold her tightly to me, relishing in the feel of her body so close to mine. "You're the best. You know that, right?"

"Yeah, you've told me a time or two," she whispers before pressing her lips to mine. "I meant what I said. I won't let her or anyone else come between us. You're stuck with me forever now."

"Forever's not long enough," I say as I look down into the sapphire gems she calls eyes. "But it's a start," I tell her before claiming her mouth with my own.

Chapter 32

Alana

With every step I take, the sand shifts beneath my feet as I make my way towards the lapping waves below. This is paradise, or at least my version of it.

Placing my towel on the warm sand, I take in my surroundings in all its perfection. I have loved the beach since I first saw a picture of it as a child. When Jax brought me here nearly six months ago, it had been perfect, but being here like this is... there are no words to describe it.

"You gonna stand there all day or finally get your feet wet?" Jax calls from behind me.

I turn to see him walking towards me, wetness pooling between my thighs at the sight of him without his shirt on. "I thought I'd admire the view," I retort, my eyes affixed on him.

"That makes two of us," he says as he stops in front of me, his arms encircling my waist.

As he reaches for the tie keeping my sarong in place, I brush his hand away, looking around the almost vacant beach. There are only a handful of people present, but the last thing I want is for any of them to see me in the far too revealing bikini Jax picked up for me. "I'm five months pregnant," I remind him. In reality I'm barely showing, but I feel like a giant fat ass nonetheless.

"You look fuckin' gorgeous," he says as he slips his fingers inside the knot, pulling it free in one swift movement. As the fabric cascades in a pool around my feet, my eyes lock with his. It is just him and I in this very moment. "And you're all mine."

Without thought, he grabs me by the hips, pulling me to him as my hands reach for his hair, his mouth claiming mine. I groan as he pulls tightly against him, his tongue finding my own, his hands drifting upwards and grazing my enlarged breasts before moving into my hair as he devours my mouth. Reaching down between us, I grasp his already swollen cock through the fabric of his swim trunks, wanting nothing more than to impale myself on him.

When he pulls back, we are both breathless, staring into each other's eyes with unbridled desire. "I think we've gained some attention," he murmurs as he looks into the distance behind me.

Taking in a deep breath, I force my gaze over my shoulder. Three men, probably all in their early thirties, lift their beer bottles in salute of the show they just witnessed.

"Oh my God," I mumble, looking up at Jax in utter humiliation.

"Don't be embarrassed," he says, obviously finding this more amusing than I do.

"It's not that," I explain, my face turning bright red. "It's just…" My voice trails off, the words escaping me.

"It reminds you of the past?" Jax asks, pulling me into his arms.

Nodding my head, I rest my cheek against his bare chiseled chest. "I'm not that person anymore."

"No you're not and you never will be again. That doesn't mean guys will stop gawking at you. It's human nature for men to ogle a beautiful woman and just to set the record straight, I don't mind it one bit."

"Really?" I ask, looking up at him in disbelief.

"Really," he chuckles. "Call me crazy, but I find it kinda hot knowing they want you as much as I do. Sad for them that you're all mine." His lips brush gently against mine, causing my legs to suddenly feel like jelly. "Now are we gonna stand around here all day or do what we came here to do?"

Without waiting for my response, Jax scoops me up effortlessly in his arms and races towards the water.

Cracking open my eyes, I look out at Jax as he dives into the waves. When he emerges, droplets of salt water cling to his chiseled chest. His eyes meet mine, reflecting the same desire I am feeling.

As he turns his back and plunges into the waters again, I let out a ragged breath. "Asshole," I mutter under my breath. He's teasing me, much like he has been all day and its working. I want him now more than ever.

Sighing deeply, I sit upright on the beach towel. An orange haze looms over the water, reflecting off of every wave. The beach is all but abandoned as the sun begins to set in the sky, only a few people scattered in the distance.

Biting my lower lip, I close my eyes and imagine Jax making love to me on the warm sand. Instinctively, I reach around and release the strap on my bikini, tossing it aside before opening my eyes and rising to my feet. Slowly I undo the ties on my bottom, my eyes locking with Jax's as he closes the distance between us.

"What are you doing?" Jax asks, looking around the nearly vacant beach.

"Making a point," I say taking a step towards him, my fingertips gently tracing the droplets of salt water clinging to his chiseled chest.

"And what point would that be?" he asks, his eyes ravaging my now exposed body.

"That two can play the same game," I say before pushing past him. As I wade out into the water, I glance over my shoulder to see Jax behind me and inwardly smile.

"I think I like this game," he murmurs as his arms encircle my waist, the warmth of his body pressing against my back. Turning around in his arms, I stare into his hungry eyes, wanting nothing more than to have him take me right here but not willing to give in so easy. He made me wait and I want him to suffer just as I have.

Reaching out, his fingertips graze my hardening nipples, causing them to form turgid peaks. Drawing in a deep breath, it takes everything I have to push his hand away. "Nuh-uh," I say, taking a step back from him. "You had your fun, now it's time for mine."

"Fun, huh? I can think of a few fun things we could be doing right now," he, grabs me around my waist to pul me back towards him. My mind tells me to resist, make him wait, but my body belongs completely to him. As I turn around in his arms, I press my body tightly to his, the heat of his skin searing my own. "Tell me what you want," he whispers, his lips grazing my own.

"You know what I want," I murmur before enveloping his neck in my arms. "And I'm not taking no for an answer."

Lifting me in his arms, I wrap my legs tightly around his waist, his lips crashing onto mine. Without hesitation, I allow his tongue access, moaning as it sweeps against my own. Our kiss is slow, deliberate and full of passion, want and need. Gripping my ass tightly, he pulls me even closer, his hardness pressing against my mound, the friction alone almost sending me over the edge.

When he pulls away, I am left breathless, wanting more. Just as I open my mouth in protest, he moves in, his mouth consuming mine once again as we begin to move slowly and effortlessly towards the sand above, stopping only when I am lying on my back atop the beach towel.

Pulling back, he stares down at me, a look of pure hunger in his eyes. "Tell me what you want," he whispers against my lips.

"I want you to touch me." The words escape my mouth a mere breath.

Gently, he drags one finger along my slit, a growl erupting from his lips. "You're so fuckin' wet," he says in a low voice.

As he runs his fingers across my wetness again, my mouth falling open as a moan escapes from deep within my throat as his lips make their descent down my body. Gripping my hips, he spreads my legs wide before burying his face between my thighs, causing me to cry out in pure ecstasy at the first flick of his tongue.

"Oh, God!" I groan as he begins lapping up my juices, working me up and down with his skilled tongue before driving it inside of me. Grabbing hold of his hair, I yank hard, pulling him closer to me as I rock my hips against his face, my pussy rubbing against the stubble of his jaw. I begin to move faster, my breathing becoming erratic as my release closes in.

Thrusting a single finger inside me, he crooks it, hitting the perfect spot. My moans suddenly become screams of pure pleasure as my orgasm takes hold, my legs quivering as he lavishes my swollen clit.

My chest heaving, Jax lifts his eyes to mine, his lips glistening with my arousal. Slowly, he moves over my body, licking a trail from my pubic bone up to my left breast, circling it slowly before sucking the hardened peak into his mouth.

"My turn," I whisper as I lift myself into a seated position, reaching down to release his cock from its confines. As I wrap my eager hand around his thickness, he draws in a sharp breath, his eyes rolling back in his head as I begin to stroke him.

Rising onto my knees, I lean down, my tongue savoring the taste of the pearly white droplet clinging to his crown. "No, baby," he murmurs as he lifts my head away from his throbbing cock. "I need to be inside you."

Clutching my ass, he pulls me to him until I am hovering over his hardness. Slowly, I lower myself, my mouth falling open as he fills me with his thick, long cock. Using my hands to brace myself against his wide chest, I slowly rise, relishing in the feel of him buried deep inside me, before dropping down hard onto his rigidness again. His strong hands grip my flesh, his fingers digging into my hips as I continue to move, my mind reveling in this moment.

His fingers entangling in my hair, he leans up and place his lips over mine, slipping his tongue into my willing mouth. Grabbing each side of my face, he moans into my mouth as he rolls me onto my back. "I love you, Alana," he whispers before slamming into me, his cock rubbing against my clit and filling me at the same time. "I want to hear you scream my name, feel you grip my cock as you come hard," he groans.

As if on command, I feel my belly tighten. "Oh God!" I cry out.

"That's it, baby. Come so fuckin' hard for me," he growls, pounding into me as we both come undone together.

"What are you thinking?" Jax whispers into my ear, his arms wrapped around me from behind.

"That it's beautiful," I say as I turn in his arms.

"Just like you," he murmurs before his lips gently descend onto mine. A wave of warmth fills me, rushing to every corner of my body.

As he pulls away, I see nothing but love in his eyes.

Allowing my gaze to stray from his, I take in all the beauty that surrounds me. Waves crash over the iridescent sand that glitters in the moonlight. The stars in the night sky seem to float in the distance, yet the moon appears to be at arm's reach. At this very moment, my eyes catch every corner of the landscape below, memorizing every beautiful detail - the breeze blowing from the tide, the waves as they crash into one another, and the fragrance of the salty ocean. It is the perfect end to the perfect week only because he was here with me.

"Eighteen years ago this very night, I met my destiny on a rooftop back in Langley. We lay there for hours, staring up at the stars. I knew that night that I would never be alone as long you were a part of my life."

I remember that night so vividly, the array of emotions I felt seeming more like a distant memory than reality. I no longer feel alone and afraid. For the first time in my life, my world is complete. "And every year we were apart," I begin as I look up into his eyes, "I would always look into the night sky and find the brightest star and it would remind me of you."

"But you weren't just a star to me, Alana. You were the whole damn sky. The darkness and the light," he whispers as he pulls me to him, holding on to me so tightly as if he thinks I will suddenly disappear.

Taking in a deep breath I reluctantly pull away, smiling up at him. "This wasn't just a getaway, was it?"

"No. This was to celebrate the beginning of a new chapter in our lives, the way it should have been written all along. Look at where we've come. We both believed that we were two desolate souls, destined to live out our lives alone and without feeling. We are no longer alone."

"And so much in love," I say, my eyes filling with tears.

"I never knew what love was until you, Alana. I didn't just choose you. I took one look at you and there was no turning back. You were my forever from the beginning. Love is when two desolate souls meet and accept both the dark and the light within each other. They give each other the strength and courage to grow until they are no longer two, they become one."

"Jax..." his name is a subtle whisper in the night air. "We've only been together a few months."

"Don't hand me that bullshit, Alana. You've have eighteen years to prepare for this moment." Dropping to one knee, Jax looks up at me with pure adoration and if there was ever a shred of doubt as to his love for me, it vanishes in this very moment. "I wished for love and I was given you. Please don't take that away from me," he whispers. "I love you Alana Jacobs, with every breath that I breathe and every single beat of my heart. I promise to be your everything if you'll give me the chance. Will you make me the happiest man in the world by becoming my wife?"

Drawing in a deep, ragged breath, I look into his eyes. Within their depths, I see everything I have ever wanted in life and I never want to let it go. "Yes," I whisper, without hesitation or regret. Jackson Cade gave me hope in the past, today he has brought me peace, and now I see nothing but happiness in my future – the future I will share with only him.

Rising to his feet, Jax lifts me in his arms, his lips crashing onto mine. Slowly he lowers me to my feet, reluctantly pulling away from me. Reaching into his pocket, he pulls out a red velvet box and opens it, and in one fluid movement places the ring on my finger.

Through tear filled eyes I gaze down at this symbol of love and my heart swells. A single solitaire set in a black gold band. "The light shining from within the darkness," he murmurs before his lips claim mine again.

Chapter 33

JAX

Stepping inside the hushed room, all eyes fall on me as I take a seat beside Deuce, all of us unsure why we are all here. Deuce rarely calls a meeting outside of church, and this one has me feeling more than a little uneasy.

"Where's Alana?" he asks, his hardened eyes locked on me.

"Out in the main room. Why?"

Deuce visibly relaxes, but his features are still etched with concern. Something has happened, and I have a feeling I'm not gonna like what he is about to tell me. "We've got a problem," he says, nodding towards Spyder.

"Paul." Spyder says his name with finality, but I know this is just the beginning.

I stare at Spyder expectantly, waiting for him to continue, needing to know what he has found out, but instead I am met with utter silence.

Shaking his head, Deuce begins to speak. "He got out a week ago and we all know what that means. Everyone here knows what this man is capable of," he says, looking around the room until his eyes meet mine. "And he's willing to go to great lengths to get what he wants."

"Alana," I say, swallowing hard.

"Only her," he says, his voice wavering. Turning his attention to Spyder, he nods, passing the floor to him.

"I did a security sweep of the house the moment we found out and I found this," he says, placing a vial on the table. "I had one of Pat's men run an analysis on the contents. It's Mifepristone, better known as RU-486."

Slamming my fist into the table, I am filled with intense rage. "So he was there?" I ask, already knowing the question.

"Yes," Spyder nods. "The vial was full when I located it, but I wasn't taking any chances. I cleaned out the kitchen and disposed of any items that could possibly have been contaminated."

Spyder's words should set my mind at ease, but they don't. He's not telling me something. "What else?"

Looking away, Spyder's gaze falls on Deuce who nods at him. "He needs to know."

Nodding, Spyder rises from the table and stalks across the room to retrieve a box. Setting it in front of me, he lets out a ragged breath. "I found these."

Narrowing my eyes, I look between the box and Spyder. "They were in the closet, unopened," he mumbles as he steps away.

Lifting the lid, I pull out letter after letter, all of them showing the same return address. *He didn't stop.*

"I'll save you the trouble of reading all of 'em," Deuce begins. "Most are just him pleading with her to hear him out. A lot of apologies and promises." Reaching inside his cut, he pulls out a letter and slides it towards me. "But this one... Alana's not safe until we bring him down."

Unfolding the letter, I take in a deep breath. I feel everyone's eyes on me as my gaze falls on the single piece of paper, six simple words scream back at me.

I will never let you go.

For the first time in a very long time, I feel fear. Not for myself, but for Alana and our unborn son. But I also feel anger. Why didn't she tell me and what else is she hiding from me?

"With Paul's whereabouts unknown, I'm putting at least two men on Alana at all times, whether you're there or not. We're not taking any chances here." Deuce's words echo in the otherwise silent room.

Locking his gaze with mine, Deuce continues. "Beast will become a permanent fixture in the house until Paul's located. Me and the other guys will rotate shifts. Ruger, I want you to head on over there and be on the lookout. Under no circumstances is Alana to be left alone. Understood?" Deuce looks around the room knowing full well no one will argue. Alana is well liked and any of my brother's would lay down their life for her. "Everyone else, I want Paul Martin found. The law failed again, but I won't."

"Then what?" Red asks the question everyone in the room is thinking.

Deuce is silent for only a moment. "He will die."

Chapter 34

Alana

"You daydreaming again?" Deuce asks, sneaking up on me.

"Why do you keep doing that to me?!" I shout, nearly jumping out of my skin.

"Not tryin' to sneak up on you, but you make it so damn easy," he chuckles, earning him an elbow to the ribs.

"You're such an ass," I say, but can't help the smile that begins to form on my lips.

"An ass, huh? Guess I've been called worse." Deuce shrugs, grinning widely at me, showing off those dimples people rarely get a chance to see. "Why are you so gloomy?"

"Jax is still mad at me," I admit. He hasn't come right out and said the words, but he doesn't have to. In his eyes I lied to him by not mentioning the letters or my final visit to see

Paul, but an omission of the facts isn't a lie –
or is it?

"It's not so much that he's mad at you. He's
hurt. Why didn't you tell him, Alana?"

"What was there to tell?" I ask honestly. "He
wrote a few pleading letters trying to convince
me to give him another chance. He probably
even made a few empty threats like he did
before."

"And the last time, he wiped your account
clean," he reminds me, as if I could forget.
"Why did you go see him?"

The million dollar question, one I expected
from Jax, but he refuses to talk to me. "To say
goodbye. Even after everything he did to me, I
felt I owed him that much. I wanted him to
know that I was happy, see it for himself, so
he could move on too."

"And how did that work out?"

"Not too good," I admit.

"And even then, you didn't go to Jax. You need
to look at this through his eyes. That man
loves you more than life itself and would do
anything for you. Do you really think he
would've stopped you? He may have tried to
convince you it wasn't a good idea, which it
wasn't, but he wouldn't have stopped you."

"I know," I whisper, lowering my eyes. I could've saved myself a lot of heartache if I'd just come to him, but I can't go back and change the past. "I just wanted to handle it myself."

"That's your problem, Alana. It's not just you anymore. You've got to stop trying to protect everyone else and start protecting yourself."

Nodding my head in agreement, I look up into Deuce's piercing blue eyes, grateful to have found a friend like him. "I need to talk to him, tell him I'm sorry."

As if on cue, the front door opens and Jax steps inside, his eyes locking with mine.

"Guess you're in luck," Deuce says, winking at me. Turning abruptly, he crosses the room towards the entrance. "Beast and Ruger are on watch," he adds before walking through the door, leaving Jax and I alone.

He stands there motionless for several moments, his gaze never wavering from mine. Taking in a deep breath, I march towards him, wanting to put this all behind us. "I'm sorry, Jax."

Closing his eyes, he lets out a rushed breath. "I am too," he whispers. When he opens his eyes again, I see the pain within them and know I am the cause. "Why didn't you tell me?"

"I don't have a good answer," I shrug. "In my mind it wasn't a big deal, but looking at it from a different perspective, I see that it was. There shouldn't be any secrets between us and I'm sorry I let you down."

"Alana," he whispers, pulling me into his arms. "You didn't let me down, you didn't let me in. I want you to trust me completely. The letters, you going to see him, I wouldn't have had a problem with it if it was anyone but him, especially after what he's done to you."

Pulling back, I look up at him and finally understand. All the anger and frustration was over my safety, but I wouldn't jeopardize myself or the life of our son. "Paul may be a lot of things but he'd never physically hurt me," I tell him, hoping to ease his worry.

"I know you want to believe that Lana, but Paul's not sane," he says hesitantly. "Those letters were warnings Alana, and the last one was a promise."

"You read them?"

"Yes. In his sick mind, he does love you and he would do anything to get you back… no matter the cost."

"Is that why Beast has been staying here?" I ask, hoping to finally get an answer.

"Yes."

"So he's out?" I ask, already knowing the answer.

"Yes."

"What else?" I know there's more to it than he is telling me.

"We were at the beach when Deuce got word of his release, he sent Spyder to do a sweep of the house. He found a vial outside our bedroom window that was filled with crushed Mifepristone, the abortion pill. It didn't look like any was missing, but Spyder covered all bases and cleaned out the kitchen."

I am literally trembling, not just out of fear but also anger. This baby means everything to me. Without warning, tears begin to fall from my eyes.

"Don't cry baby," Jax murmurs, pulling me into his arms. As his arms tighten around me, I begin to openly sob. "I won't let anything happen Alana, to you or our son. I promise." He says nothing more, continuing to hold me until my tears finally cease.

"He's sadistic," I finally mutter, lifting my tear stained face. And not so long ago, I trusted Paul with my life.

"He's desperate Lana, and sick, but you're safe. Deuce has two men on you at all times, so if Paul makes a move, we'll bring him down."

Nodding my head, I bury my face in his chest, relishing in the feel of my body pressed tightly to his. As he wraps his arms around me protectively, I feel safer than I have ever felt in my life. I know Jax will do everything in his power to protect me, but I can't seem to shake the feeling that something bad is going to happen.

Chapter 35

Alana

Allowing my gaze to fall on the frosted cake on the counter, I can't help but smile at my accomplishment. My first attempt at making one from scratch and it's perfect, down to the Happy Birthday Jax written in red frosting on top.

"Shit!" I mutter when I catch a glimpse of the time. I make a mad dash towards the bedroom, cursing myself for not keeping better track of the time. Jax will be home in less than forty-five minutes and I'm nowhere close to being ready.

With Paul's location still unknown, I never have a moment to myself so today has been a blessing. Even though I am seemingly home alone, I know Beast, Spyder or someone else is lurking in the shadows outside, watching my every move. It was unsettling at first, more because I know what is at stake – my life and that of my unborn child. Now it has become more of an annoyance.

Even knowing that Paul is out there somewhere doesn't change the fact that I need tonight. Some alone time with Jax is something I have been craving. Thankfully, Deuce agreed to a four hour reprieve. Beast will still be standing guard outside, but I've been assured he will keep his distance so that I can make this night perfect.

Entering the bedroom, I head straight for the closet door, wanting to find something more alluring to wear than the shorts and t-shirt I'm sporting, before stopping myself. Looking down at my growing belly, I am reminded that nothing I own fits quite the same way anymore.

Releasing my hold on the doorknob, I opt for plan B. I may not be able to dress up for Jax, but I can at least make myself more presentable. Making my way into the bathroom, I decide to apply just a little makeup and let my hair down, something I've been slack about lately.

I have just applied a little mascara when I hear the door close. Slapping the tube on the counter, I shut off the bathroom light. "You're early," I call out as I reach for the bedroom door.

"Actually, I'm right on time."

I freeze at the sound of that voice, one I had hoped never to hear again. Holding my breath, I slowly turn around, my eyes widening at the sight of Paul standing there, the gun in his hand trained on me.

"Don't look so shocked to see me," Paul says, stalking towards me, a crazed look on his face.

Swallowing hard, I try to remain calm but inside I am falling apart. "I told you I never wanted to see you again," I say, proud that my voice doesn't portray the fear I am feeling.

"How have you been, Lana?" he asks, taking another step towards me.

"Don't call me that," I manage to choke out as he reaches out to me, his fingertips grazing my cheek as he lowers the gun to his side. "Why are you here?" I ask, already knowing the answer.

"For you, sweet Lana. I told you I'd never let you go." Closing my eyes, I pray that this is just a bad dream. That I will wake up and Paul will be gone. "You are so beautiful," he whispers, his warm breath closing in on me. "You and I can pick up where we left off," he whispers, his lips lightly grazing my ear as his hand comes to rest on my stomach.

With every bit of strength I can muster, I push him off of me, my hands protectively guarding my swollen belly. "Don't touch me," I say through clenched teeth.

"You don't mean that," he says, his eyes boring into my own as he closes the distance between us again, the gun still at his side. "Remember how good I make you feel, the things I can do for you. We can have all of that again."

His lips crash onto mine, his tongue probing the tight seam of my lips. Unwillingly I whimper, trembling in his grasp, as he presses his body against mine. "Don't fight it, Lana. You know we belong together," he murmurs, before trying to claim my mouth once again.

Mustering all of strength, I manage to push him off of me just enough so that I can turn, scrambling to open the door. Yanking it open, I take off at full speed, running towards the front door.

Just as I unlatch the dead bolt, I am slammed from behind. Wrenching my arm behind my back, he drags me from the door. "Don't make me hurt you!" he seethes, pulling me farther away from the entrance.

"Why are you doing this?" I cry out, fighting against his hold on me.

He releases his hold on my arm, roughly turning me around to face him. "Because you're mine. You will always belong to me, not him!" he screams before rearing his fist back.

As his clenched fist connects with my cheek, I lose my balance, falling back onto the hardwood floor, crying out as my head collides with the unforgiving surface. I stare up at the man I once considered my best friend almost in a dreamlike haze. I can now see him for who he truly is – a cold, heartless monster incapable of caring for anyone but himself.

His lips are moving as he drops to his knees, reaching down to me, lifting my head in his hands. I try to push him away but my arms lay lifeless by my side, not responding to my commands.

As the darkness closes in on me, I see him pull his blood covered hand away from me as he reaches for something on the floor beside him. He lifts the gun in his hand, turning in slow motion as the door swings open and for a brief moment a sense of relief washes over me when I see Jax standing in the doorway.

Then it all vanishes as I watch Paul's finger pull the trigger, a flash of light escaping the barrel right before the deafening sound echoes in the room.

I try to scream, but nothing comes out as I watch the only man I have ever loved fall to the floor gripping his chest, his eyes locking with mine.

As the darkness consumes me, I am left with an image that will forever haunt me: Jax's eyes closing for the very last time.

Chapter 36

"You should head home. Be with Alexis and Peyton," I say, finally breaking the silence that is consuming me. The last few days have affected me in a way I can't describe. Alana is missing and my best friend is lying on death's door.

"Let me know if anything changes. In the meantime, I still have some favors I can call in. We'll find her." I don't bother turning my head as I hear the chair scrape against the floor. "You saved his life, Deuce. He'll understand."

"No, he won't. I fucked up. I can't forgive myself, let alone expect him to forgive me. I let them both down." My voice is filled with agony and torment. Beast lost his life tonight. I may not have pulled the trigger, but I am at fault. I left him there alone, and nothing will change that. Alana is still missing and my best friend had a close call with death. "Give me a few minutes and then send her in."

There is a brief moment of silence before I hear the door close. Taking in a deep breath, I slowly release it. "I take full responsibility," I begin. "She just wanted to celebrate your birthday. What was the harm in that? Beast was there and... I fucked up man. I shouldn't have left. I'm sorry, Jax."

I don't deserve his forgiveness, but I want it more than anything. I've known how much Alana means to him since the day we first met. In his eyes this is the worst thing I could've done. "If that doesn't make you hate me and you somehow find it in your heart to forgive me, know that I will make this right. I will bring her back to you," I say, stopping abruptly at the sound of the door opening.

"Spyder said I should come in?"

The sound of Trix's voice grates on my nerves. I've always hated her, but now I completely despise her. "Yeah," I mutter, not bothering to turn my head.

"How is he?" Trix asks, her voice increasing in volume as she approaches.

"He may not make it," I say, contradicting what I know is fact. Jax will make it, of that I have no doubt.

"No," Trix whispers, her voice barely audible. "How did this happen?"

"I was hoping you would tell me," I say, training my glare on Trix.

"I don't know what you're talking about," Trix says, lowering her eyes. She's lying.

"You can stop with the fuckin' games Trix, because I know you're behind this. Did you think Jax would come running to you if Alana wasn't in the picture? Because if that's the case, you're even dumber than I thought." My words are direct and brash, but not unwarranted. She is as heartless as they come, only concerned with herself, or at least that's what she wants everyone to believe.

"I..."

"Before you say another word, let me lay it on the line for you. I want Alana home safely, no matter the cost. You scratch my back and I'll scratch yours." Trix says nothing for several moments, letting my words sink in.

"Are you trying to negotiate with me?" she smirks, looking far too confident.

"I think you got it backwards. You're gonna negotiate with me." I'm not gonna spell it out for her, at least not just yet. Uncovering Trix's affiliation with Paul came too late, but the intel

I discovered may give me the pull I need to bring Alana home again.

"I think I'm the one holding the upper hand here, not you."

Keep telling yourself that. "Is that so? Because the way I see it, there's no way your four of a kind can beat my royal flush. Now that I've raised the ante, you have a choice to make. You can either fold or call. What's it gonna be?" Once I have her admission, only then will I offer my assistance.

Letting out an exasperated sigh, Trix narrows her eyes at me. "I don't have time for your games. I came to see Jax."

"You're not even curious enough to want to see my hand? And here I thought you were a high roller. Guess I was wrong." *Come on, Trix. Don't let me down now.*

"I don't know where Paul is and I definitely don't know where he took Alana," Trix says, shaking her head.

Turning towards her, I can't help but smile. "Is that so?"

One Week Later

Downing the last of my scotch, I slam the empty glass on the bar top before rising to my feet. Biding my time has been hard, but in order to gain Trix's cooperation, I had to put the fear of God in her. I have to hand it to her, she's a lot tougher than I gave her credit for, but in the end she did cave.

Methodically, I make my way towards the basement, pausing at the bottom of the stairs when I see Red seated on an empty crate staring in my direction. His arms are crossed, the look on his face one of pure disgust.

"Got a problem, old man?" I ask, closing the distance between us.

He says nothing for several minutes, but his posture speaks volumes. "You think your ol' man would be proud of what you're doin' in there? 'Cause I'm here to tell you you're wrong," he says, breaking the silence.

"And why's that, old man?"

"You know better than anyone why Ace created this club. Just because he's not here doesn't give you the right to disrespect everything he stood for."

As I shake my head, I can't help the chuckle that erupts from within. Red thinks he knows what's going on, believes I am a monster, but he couldn't be farther from the truth. My methods may be somewhat unorthodox, but they work. "Glad to see you still think so highly of me." Red has never hidden the fact that he doesn't think I deserve my newfound role within the club. In fact, he was the only member to oppose me.

"I was there the night Ace brought you in," Red speaks as he rises from his seat. "I know why he did what he did, but I warned him he was making a mistake. The weak don't have what it takes to survive."

"And you fault me for giving up." It's not a question, but a factual statement, one he vocalized to my father on more than one occasion. "Because I had accepted my fate, you believed I didn't belong here."

"You never did belong here. The Forgotten Souls was created for the strong. For people like me who never gave up hope, who fought to stay alive. But Ace didn't agree with me, so he dismissed my concerns. If he could see you now, he'd realize what a mistake he made. We help people, not hurt them!"

"But some people aren't worth helping," I retort. He has all but said that my father should've abandoned me, never saved my life and allowed me to die alone and afraid.

"You're right," he says, his words full of venom and aimed directly at me.

I say nothing, pushing past him. Reaching for the handle, I pull the door open and stalk inside, knowing Red is following close behind. As I enter the room, Trix lifts her tear filled eyes to meet mine, giving me a pleading look.

"Now that you know the truth, what are you gonna do with me?" she whispers.

"What I promised I'd do," I say as I close the distance between us. "I've got Spyder looking into it. We'll find her."

She nods her head, accepting my words as gospel. I never make a promise I don't intend to keep and even Trix knows that. "I want to help," she says abruptly. "I need to help. I think I know where they could be."

"Alright," I agree hesitantly. Trix is not in the right mindset to truly help, but I'll give this to her. She needs to make amends and this is the only way she knows how. "We can head out now."

"No," she says defiantly. "I have to do this alone. If he sees you, who knows what he'll do. Besides, I owe Alana this."

I'm reluctant to agree, but she has a point. Paul is unstable, all about self-preservation.

One wrong move could cost Alana her life. Slowly I nod my head in agreement, hoping I'm making the right decision.

"Thank you," Trix whispers as she stands. "For everything."

"All you ever had to do was ask."

"I know that now." Taking in a deep breath, Trix heads for the door. "Will you tell Jax?" she asks, turning back towards me. "Just in case I don't make it back."

"You'll make it back and then you can tell him yourself."

She smiles, the first genuine smile I've ever seen from her before she turns once again and exits the room.

"What the fuck was that?" Red asks, breaking the silence.

"That was someone coming to terms with their actions. Putting the good of others before themselves. A change of heart you could say."

Reaching into my pocket, I pull out my buzzing cellphone, smirking when I see the text from Alexis.

Better hurry up or Jax's breaking out of the joint.

Chuckling aloud, I make my way towards the exit.

"That's it?" Red asks, stepping in behind me. "After all that, that's all you got to say?"

"What do you want me to say?" I turn abruptly, my anger-filled gaze falling on him. "Guess my torture techniques far exceeded your expectations," I snarl.

"I admit when I'm wrong," he retorts, holding his hands up in defeat.

"It's not about you being right or wrong, it's about you making assumptions that are way off base. You want to know what all that was about? It was about uncovering the truth. Did I lock her in this room and make her believe I was gonna harm her? I sure as fuck did and I'd do it all over again if it meant bringing my family home! Did Trix finally admit her involvement with Paul because of that? Fuck yeah! She pleaded with me to hear her out, and then... then I learned the goddamn truth!"

"So you know where Alana is?" Red asks, his tone filled with regret.

"Trix believes she knows where Paul is staying."

"And you trust that she's telling you the truth? She could be fuckin' playing you!"

"She's not playing me," I say definitively. "There's too much at stake." Her sister's life hangs in the balance, and Trix is willing to do anything to ensure her return home safely.

Shaking his head, he looks at me with disdain. "You're a goddamn fool."

"For once in your life, you're right. I am a fool, or at least I was, but no more," I say as I exit the room. Pausing for a moment at the base of the staircase, I look over my shoulder at the man I had hoped to one day gain his respect. "Leave your cut with Spyder on your way out. The Forgotten Souls has no use for you any longer."

As I climb the stairs, a weight has been lifted off my shoulders. I no longer doubt my abilities to lead this club the way my father once did.

Chapter 37

Alana

Two Days Later

"Are you hungry?"

Closing my eyes, I turn my head, refusing to look at Paul as he enters the room. Nine very long days have passed since my world crumbled, the future I knew changed forever, and it is all because of him. Biting the inside of my cheek, I force myself not to cry.

"Why do you have to be so stubborn?" he asks, the cot I am seated on dipping as he sits down beside me. "Turning away every time I come into the room and refusing to talk at me accomplishes nothing. You're only making this harder on yourself."

"What would you like for me to say?" I ask through clenched teeth, still looking away.

"She speaks!" he chuckles. "At least that's a start. Maybe we're finally getting somewhere."

Opening my eyes, I turn to face him. "Fuck. You."

"My dear, sweet Alana. What has Jax done to you?"

Just the mention of Jax's name brings tears to my eyes, ripping at my soul.

"You're pathetic." His tone is filled with discontent. "You'll shed a tear for the man who abandoned you when you needed him most, but turn your back on the only man who stood by you through thick and thin."

I remain silent, denying him a response. That is what he wants and I refuse to give it to him.

"Fine," he says as he stands. "Have it your way, but sooner or later, you'll come around."

I say nothing as he storms from the room, jumping at the sound of the door slamming shut behind him. Drawing in a ragged breath, I allow my emotions to surface.

There is nowhere to run. Nowhere to hide. I am trapped in this prison. Alone. Afraid. I have only memories of the love I shared with a man who tried to save me and lost his life in the process.

"I never knew what love was until you." My mind continues to replay the night Jax asked me to be his wife. The sound of his voice, the feeling of his lips pressed to mine - all of it is gone, only the memory remaining.

"How am I supposed to go on without you?" I look around the abandoned room, half expecting to hear his voice telling me I am not alone, but am greeted with only silence.

Instinctively, my hand goes to my belly, a reminder that I will never be alone. Jax will forever live in my heart and in the eyes of the son we created. As long as I have him, I will get through this.

"Fuck!" I roar, tossing my plate across the room, feeling little satisfaction as it shatters into hundreds of pieces.

What the fuck did you expect? Did you think she was gonna be happy that you ruined her life? The rational part of my conscious mocks my decision to bring Alana here, but what is done is done. There is no turning back.

With my head in my hands, I try to devise some plan to make her understand. I am all she has left in this world now that Jax is gone.

Jax. Killing him wasn't part of my plan, but neither was Alana's resistance. She may have forgotten about the love we shared, but I have not. It'll take time, but she will move on, eventually forgetting all about Jax again.

Who are you kidding? Alana has always been in love with Jax. You ridding him from this earth won't change a thing. She will always remember him. Always love him. And don't forget about that little reminder she's carrying around with her.

The baby.

Yeah, the baby. You know, the life Jax and Alana created. You don't stand a chance at winning her back. You've lost, Paul. The only good thing you've ever had in your life and you fucked it up.

"Shut up!" I shout, clamping my head in my hands. "She will love me," I whisper, trying to convince myself. "She has to."

Sinking back into the worn couch, I close my eyes, trying to regain control. This will work. I will make sure of it.

As I begin to calm, I hear a faint knock on the door. Pulling my revolver out instinctively, I rise from the couch, slowly making my way towards the door. Peering out the side window, I see Trix standing on the porch, her eyes reddened and puffy.

Letting out a ragged sigh, I prepare myself for her tirade. "What are you doing here?" I ask as I open the door.

Pushing her way past me, she enters the house. "Why?" she asks, her torment filled eyes meeting mine. There's no need for her to elaborate because I know exactly what she wants to know.

"I didn't have a choice," I explain. "He was early. Came barging into the house. It was either him or me."

"That's not what we agreed on! Jax almost died because of you!"

"He's alive?" I ask, swallowing hard.

"Barely."

"You were the one who propositioned me, not the other way around," I remind her. "I never made any promises."

"So you get what you want and I'm left with nothing?"

"Not nothing, unless Ember's no longer a concern." My one ace in the hole. I knew Trix would never win Jax's heart no matter how hard she tried, but I could guarantee her one thing – the safe return of her one and only sister.

"Where is she?"

"All in good time. Now that I know Jax is still in the picture, we have to get as far away from this place as possible." Staying in an abandoned farmhouse was safe for the time being, but that was before I knew Jax had survived. "We're gonna need new identities. License, birth certificate, passports – the works. You'll have to be the middle man. I have a few favors still owed me. Once you get everything we need to start over, you'll book us a flight out of the country. As soon as we touchdown, all it'll take is one phone call. You'll have your sister back and maybe even a chance with Jax if you're lucky."

"Not good enough. How do I know you'll keep your word?"

"You don't, but if you choose not to help me, I can promise you you'll never see your dear Ember again. It's quite sad, really. Knowing your sister is some sadistic bastard's sex slave, catering to his every whim just so he doesn't beat her senseless. If it were me, I'd do whatever it takes, but what do I know."

Her bottom lip begins to quiver, her eyes filling with tears and I know I have her right where I want her. "Fine," she mutters.

"Good. I'm glad we could reach an agreement that benefits us both. Give me a few minutes and I'll get all the contact information you need. It shouldn't take you more than a few hours to accomplish everything, and by this time tomorrow, you can be reunited with your sister," I tell her before heading towards the back bedroom to retrieve my cell phone.

Stepping into the room, I feel a sense of accomplishment. This will work out, even better than I originally planned. Gripping my cell phone in my hand, I make my way back into the living room area to find it abandoned.

Scanning the room, I spot Trix's purse lying on the floor, her illuminated cell phone falling to the ground. My eyes landing on the screen, I am filled with sudden rage.

You stupid son of a bitch! She set your ass up!

Barreling towards the basement door, I find it slightly ajar. Taking two steps at a time, I rush down the narrow staircase, pulling my gun out in the process. When I reach the bottom of the stairs, my eyes lock on Alana's just as Trix speaks.

"You have to trust me, Alana. Jax..."

There is no hesitation as I pull the trigger, the bullet hitting my mark. Trix falls to the ground in a loud thud, blood immediately pooling around her head.

Instead of chaos, there is only stillness. Alana remains silent, her eyes widened with shock and fear as I lower my weapon, shoving it into the back of my jeans. Clenching my jaw tightly, I say nothing as I reach down and lift Trix in my arms before turning on my heel, leaving Alana alone to absorb everything she has just seen.

Chapter 38

JAX

"Did you get a lock on her position?" I ask, my chest tightening. Leaving the hospital against doctor's orders wasn't a smart move, but one I had to make.

"Not a precise one," Deuce says, his face looking grim. "The tracker on her phone isn't very sophisticated. We've narrowed it down to within a twenty mile radius."

My heart sinks. Twenty miles might as well be a thousand. It's like looking for a needle in a haystack, but I refuse to give up.

"Spyder's trying to narrow the search field. Getting a list of all abandoned and vacant properties. That's where we'll start."

"So no word from Trix?" I'm still taken aback at Deuce's discovery. It didn't surprise me to learn of her involvement with Paul, but finding out about her sister was more than a little shocking.

"She's off the radar," he says, shaking his head.

"And you're sure this wasn't some elaborate scheme of hers?"

"I confirmed everything about her sister myself. Once I told Trix about your and Alana's past, it was game over. She admitted everything and I believed her."

I nod my head in understanding, trusting his instincts. "So what's the game plan? Because I can't just sit here and wait for some miracle."

"I know," he mutters. He still feels guilty and until Alana is home safe, he will continue to blame himself. No words from me will make a difference. "We just got confirmation of where Paul was staying. Hook did a sweep, but I'd feel more confident if one of us checked behind him. He's still a little green. Maybe even check out Trix's place and see what we can uncover."

Rising to my feet, I nod in agreement. "I'll take Paul's place."

"Alright, and I'll tackle Trix. Keep the lines of communication open on this one, Jax. No playing the hero. If you find something, I want you to call me and we'll go in together. Understood?"

I know what he's saying and reluctantly I give in. "That goes both ways," I remind him before I head towards the door.

Five Days Later

Alana stares straight ahead, her eyes honing in on the blood splatter staining the wall, a reminder of what she witnessed nearly a week ago. "Are you gonna talk to me?" I finally ask, breaking the silence.

"What's there to say?" she says, her tone lacking any feeling. She is still in denial, but that will soon change.

"I was protecting you, Alana. Just like I always have." Had I not intervened, Trix would've revealed the truth to Alana, something I couldn't let happen.

"You never protected me," she says through clenched teeth. "You sentenced me to a life of misery."

"That's not true," I mutter. I can make Alana happy again, if she will just give me a chance. "We're a team, remember?" I ask, using her own words against her.

"We. Are. Nothing!" she shouts, her eyes flaring with intense anger.

"Don't say that!" I snap. "Everything I did was for you. Every lie I told was to protect you, keep you safe."

"Safe? To protect me?" she says, turning her nose up in disgust. "How were you keeping me safe or protecting me by making me whore myself out? How was trying to kill my unborn son a benefit to me? How was killing the only man I ever loved helping me in any way? It wasn't! Nothing you did was for me! It was all about you! It was always about you!" she screams, her face turning bright red as she unleashes an anger I have never seen from her before and it only fuels my own fury.

"Shut up!" I shout as I rear back my fist, slamming it into her cheek before I can stop myself.

She doesn't even flinch as she reaches up and covers her already swelling cheek with her tiny hand. "I hate you," she whispers, her cold gaze never leaving mine. "Like father like son."

Her words gut me, cutting me to the core. Clenching my teeth tightly, I close my eyes, attempting to keep the demons at bay. Every image of my childhood, the brutality and torture I endured and kept buried for years resurfaces in that moment.

Opening my eyes, I see only him hovering over me with a menacing look. My father, the man I feared and loathed for so many years, is standing before me and this time I will not let him win.

Alana

"Like father like son." My words are cold and heartless, meant to inflict the exact same pain he has imposed on me. A feeling of satisfaction swells within me when I see Paul's eyes close as he absorbs the meaning of what I have said. He and Phil are not unalike. They are one

in the same, each using different means to torture their victims.

"Can't stand hearing the truth?" I ask, adding fuel to the fire. I am not the same Alana I once was. I have become a survivor instead of a victim, something Deuce and Jax helped me become.

Jax. My heart feels heavy at just the thought of his name. There are so many things I wanted to tell him, to show him, and now I will never have the chance. I try to remind myself that his memory will live on, in my heart and in our son. Daniel Jackson Cade will grow up to be the man his father was – honorable, loyal and trustworthy, with so much love to give.

I am so lost in thought, I don't see Paul lunge towards me, his large hand encompassing my throat as he slams me against the wall. "How does it feel?!" he shouts as he slowly squeezes, cutting off my supply of air.

I begin to panic as I struggle to wrench myself free, when he suddenly releases his hold and steps back, a crazed look is in his eyes. I am gasping for air, my hands instinctively rising up as he rushes towards me, his weight crashing into me as we fall onto the concrete floor. Curling into a fetal position, I draw my knees tightly to my chest in a vain attempt to protect myself as his fists drive into me over and over.

I cry out in pain with each strike, pleading with him to stop as he continues his relentless assault. He's going to kill me and there is nothing I can do to stop him.

Lying on the concrete floor, I come to terms with my impending demise. This is how it all will end. Beaten to death by a man who I once trusted with my life. There is no future, no happily ever after. Only pain and misery until he delivers the final blow that ends it all.

I can no longer scream, no longer breathe, as I close my eyes and await the inevitable. And then it ends, just as quickly as it began, one pain being replaced by another.

Chapter 39

"I'm sorry Alana," I say again as I kneel down in front of her. I am riddled with guilt as I watch tears stream relentlessly down her swollen and bruised cheeks as she stares down at the tiny form cradled in her arms. I did this – to her and an innocent child. "Please let me help you."

"H-haven't y-you d-done e-enough?" She lifts her sorrow filled eyes to meet mine. "W-what d-did I d-do t-to d-deserve th-this?"

She is looking to me for answers I am unable to give. Alana did nothing to deserve the fury I unleashed upon her, nor the pain she is suffering over losing her child. "I never meant for this to happen," I say in a pleading voice.

She shakes her head but says nothing, her eyes lowering to the baby she holds in her arms. I want to take it all away, rewind today's events and erase them from existence but it's too late. I can't undo the damage I have caused and for that I can never forgive myself.

"Do you remember the night I found you in the park?" I ask, breaking the silence. She lifts her eyes briefly to mine but refuses to speak. "I had been following you for weeks, plotting how I was going to approach you. That speech I gave you, I'd given it a hundred times before. You were just one of the countless number of girls I lured in."

She remains silent but I know she hears every word I speak. "That first night, I knew you were different. It was your eyes. They told a story that I didn't quite understand, and that's what first drew me in. The more we talked, the more of a connection I felt. It wasn't until you revealed your past that I discovered why."

Alana finally lifts her head, her tear stained face breaking my heart. "I fell in love with you Alana," I whisper. "But I knew you didn't feel the same way and you never would."

It's hard to speak the truth when you have convinced yourself that the woman you love will one day love you in return. Deep down I knew Alana would never love anyone but Jackson Cade, the boy who stole her heart years before I laid eyes on her, but I refused to give up. "I wanted to believe that I could make you love me."

She remains silent, but I know she is listening to me as I lay my heart on the line. "I lied to you, coerced you into doing things that I knew were destroying you to try and break you down. And when you hit rock bottom, I was gonna swoop in and make it all better. Everything I told you when we moved to Cedar Falls was the truth. I had it all planned out, down to the very last detail but then he showed up. The moment I discovered who Jax really was I should've run. We could've have left town and started over somewhere else, just you and me. But you were so angry at him for abandoning you that I let it go thinking you were still mine. I had to sit back and watch him move in on you and I was helpless to do anything but let him win. But he didn't win, did he? Because you were always his and I never stood a chance."

Closing my eyes, I continue to pour my heart out to her. "I knew that night in the VIP room that he loved you and that you never stopped loving him. Do you know how many times I told myself I should walk away and let you be happy? I knew he was better for you, but I couldn't let him win because I'm not the better man," I whisper, opening my eyes once again.

"I was selfish. I wanted you to be with me and I was willing to do anything to force your hand, even if it meant trying to kill your unborn child. I'm a sick bastard Alana, for even considering it." My voice cracks as I speak.

I should've set Alana free a long time ago but I was too selfish. Only concerned with my own happiness, I continued to do to Alana what I had done from the beginning. Manipulate her to the point that I lost her forever.

Taking in a deep breath, I rise to my feet, my gaze never leaving hers. "We never would've made it. You can't make someone fall in love with you just like you can't fall out of love with someone that is your world." Smiling down at her, I slowly reach behind me and feel for my revolver.

"I always wanted your happiness. I just thought I was the one who would be giving it to you."

Slowly, Alana lifts her eyes to meet mine. "You were my friend Paul and I did love you, just not in the way I did Jax," Alana says, a single tear sliding from her bright blue eyes.

"I know," I whisper as I pull the gun from the back of my warn jeans, letting it dangle from my fingertips at my side. I stare down at the woman who stole my heart and unwillingly claimed it as her own. She has suffered enough in this lifetime and I have only added to her misery. Because of me, she has lost the son she had fallen in love with from the moment she learned of his existence. I stole that from her, ripped her dream right out from under her. There is no consoling her and I cannot bear to ask for her forgiveness because I am undeserving of it.

I could just walk away, but that was never an option. It always came down to this moment. Some people are meant to be together, and others are not. Love means loss, and losing her is something I cannot bear.

Slow desolate tears run from her unblinking eyes and drip steadily onto her shirt as she stares up at me, the pain I am responsible for etching her face.

"I will never forget the moment I realized I loved you," I say as I take in another deep breath. "I'm more broken than you think, Alana. Before you, I never knew what love could be and my heart never knew loneliness until you walked away."

"Paul, please..." her bottom lips trembles, unbridled fear emanating from every pore of her body as I lift the gun in my hand.

"You and Jax belong together," I whisper. This is how it was supposed to end.

Smiling down at her one last time, I close my eyes and take in a deep breath. This is my final gift to her. Now she will finally be free.

Chapter 40

JAX

As I stare down at Alana's sleeping form, a sense of relief washes over me. *She's going to be fine.* The doctor's words replay in my mind over and over again, but it's not enough. I need to see those big beautiful eyes of hers to know for sure.

The past few weeks have been the hardest of my life. Getting shot and almost losing my life pales in comparison to thinking I would never see Alana again. She is my lifeline, my reason for existence, and for a short time, I almost gave up hope.

My mind continues to replay the events of that first night, the beginning of my real life nightmare, just like scenes from a movie. The moment I walked into the house and saw Alana lying there, the blood on Paul's hands, and the intense rage I felt are all still fresh in my mind. The guilt still weighs heavily on my shoulders for not being the knight in shining armor she deserves. I failed her again, only this time she lost so much more and I don't know if she will ever recover. I'm not even sure I will.

After ransacking Paul's apartment, I discovered he had recently purchased some land fifty miles outside of Cedar Falls. I took a leap of faith and made it to the location in record time, praying that I would somehow find Alana there, safe and sound.

The moment I found the shallow grave outside the house, my heart sunk. I stood there, unable to move, for several minutes before dropping to my knees. With tear filled eyes, I began to dig until my fingertips brushed against cold flesh. Holding my breath, I continued to uncover the body, praying that my worst fear was not a reality.

I was overcome with relief to discover Trix's body in the first stages of decomposition, but also filled with despair. Any doubt I had in Trix disappeared in that moment. She lost her life to not only save her sister, but right her wrongs where Alana was concerned. She did not die in vain and her sacrifice will not go unnoticed.

But it is what I witnessed when I entered that basement will forever haunt me.

"Alana!" I call out as I slowly descend the narrow staircase, gripping my pistol tightly in my hand, the only response is faint whimpering in the distance.

As I emerge into the musty room, I am unprepared for the scene in front of me. Paul lies on the concrete floor, a pool of blood encircling his head. Taking no chances, I approach him cautiously, kicking the gun lying on the floor beside him out of reach before pushing him over to confirm my belief, the oozing wound at the back of his head the only proof I need. He is gone and will never be able to harm my family again.

Letting out a relieved sigh, I look to my left and my heart stops beating. Seated on the floor against the far wall, her back to me, I see Alana rocking back and forth, her arms in a cradling position.

"Alana?" Her name is a mere whisper escaping my lips.

My world came crashing down within seconds.

As I round the cot, my eyes land on her tear stained face. Fresh bruises cover her normally flawless complexion, dried blood encrusting the corners of her mouth.

When I take a step closer, only then does she become aware she isn't alone. Lifting her eyes *to mine, there is no relief emanating from them, only pain as an endless flow of tears trail down her cheeks.*

My legs give out from under me, forcing me to my knees as my eyes land on the tiny form she embraces in her arms.

"You should head home and try to get some sleep." Deuce's voice brings me back to the present. Looking over my shoulder, I see him leaning against the wall, his arms crossed in front of him.

"How long have you been standing there?" I ask, turning my attention back to Alana.

"Long enough," he says as he crosses the room, taking a seat in the empty chair beside me. "She's gonna be alright. You know that, right?"

"But will she be the same?" I ask, verbalizing my worst fears.

"Alana is strong. She will overcome this too," he says reassuringly.

I am overwhelmed with emotion. There's no doubt that she will recover physically, the doctor has assured me of that, but mentally I'm not so sure. "Will she?" I ask, turning towards him. "She's lost so much in her life, but this... this is more than anyone can bear. Some wounds run too deep to heal."

"In time, all wounds heal and you're left with a ridged scar. Sometimes it takes weeks, months, even years, but when that scar forms, it means the hurt is over." Deuce pauses, looking over at Alana and smiling. "Alana will heal, one day at a time."

Nodding my head, I turn back towards Alana. She looks peaceful, almost serene, as she sleeps, her mind giving her a much needed break from all the events that have taken place over the last several weeks. When she awakes, it will all become reality again.

"I almost lost her," I whisper, feeling tears well in my eyes. "We did lose our son. I never got a chance to hold him, see him smile or hear him cry," I manage to choke out.

When I feel Deuce's hand on my shoulder, I almost lose it. "Until you can hold him in your arms, hold him in your heart," he whispers, pausing for a brief second. "I had a little brother, Michael. I was almost ten when he was born and I can remember making all these plans. Teaching him to build a fort, stuff like that. We never got the chance. I didn't quite understand it at the time, but he came too early, three months. The doctors couldn't save him and my mom was devastated. I remember my dad saying those exact words to her, trying to ease the pain but it was too much for her. One night, I woke up in the middle of the night and heard her crying in their room. I didn't have to ask why. No one did. I sat outside their bedroom door and listened to my father tell her that an angel in the book of life wrote down Michael's name and then whispered as she closed the book, too beautiful for this earth. Somehow, those words comforted her. The next day, we held a memorial for my brother and it was last day I saw her tears."

I absorb every single word he speaks and somehow it brings me a sense of peace.

"You would've made a great father, just as Alana would've been an exceptional mother. You both have so much to give despite your pasts. Your son was loved from the moment he was conceived and that love will never die. It will live on in both of your hearts forever. Letting go of the guilt won't erase the heartache, but it will begin the grieving process."

I look over at my friend who is wise beyond his years and take everything he says to heart. Casting blame will not bring our son back. Dwelling on his demise will change nothing. Remembering him will immortalize him forever.

"Thank you," I whisper.

"That's what friends are for. I'm here for you and Alana. Together, we will all heal."

Chapter 41

Two Days Later

"I don't know you!" Alana shouts, backing into the corner. "I just want to be left alone!"

"Alana please," I plead as I reach out to her.

"Jax!" I turn to see Doc standing there, a horrified look on his face. "Can I have a word with you?"

Looking back at Alana, seeing the alarmed look on her face, I nod my head in agreement. Doc holds the door open, ushering me outside quickly. "I wish I'd caught you before you went in there," he mutters, as he quickly leads the way to the private waiting room.

Stepping inside the small room, he motions towards the couch against the wall, prompting me to sit. "What the fuck is going on?"

"We've had a little setback," he says, taking the seat across from me. "Alana's suffering from what we call Dissociative Amnesia. I've consulted Dr. Krieger on this case because, to be quite honest, this is out of my realm of expertise."

"I don't understand what you're saying," I say, looking to Doc for answers.

"Dissociative Amnesia. It's a form of memory loss caused by a traumatic event. It would seem Alana is suffering from it."

"So you're saying she can't remember anything?"

"Not exactly. This is a selective form of amnesia where the patient can recall certain events in their life, but the traumatic ones are erased."
"Dumb it down for me, Doc."

"In Alana's case, her first memory is one from early childhood. She can specifically recall helping her mother plant flowers in the garden outside of their home while her father mowed the lawn. She also remembers events from her time in foster care, although nothing of substance. They are random events, such as going to the movies, a slumber party with friends from school, or making cookies with her foster mom. Alana's time with Mary seems to be the most uninterrupted, up until the point where Mary dies. It would seem her next memory is after her release from jail," Doc explains.

"Wait a minute, she doesn't remember me. I was there with her, from the beginning. I've known Alana since she was six years old."

Shaking his head, Doc gives me a sympathetic look. "Your arrival in Alana's life occurred shortly after the death of her parents, when the murder/suicide she witnessed was still fresh in her mind. In fact, Alana doesn't seem to recall much from the first few years or so she was in foster care. You yourself told me that it was during your time with the Martins that the two of you became inseparable. Alana suffered a tremendous amount of abuse from the beginning, and her mind has deemed those memories to be detrimental. Unfortunately, you were a part of those of traumatic events and her mind has locked your existence away as well."

"But it wasn't all traumatic," I argue. "We found each other again, fell in love and conceived a child together. She was happy and so was I."

"I'm not disputing that fact. What I'm saying is that you reemerged in her life during a time that she was being manipulated and used by Paul. The mind is a complex thing. Traumatic events overwhelm the mind's ability to cope.

When it becomes overloaded, a switch is thrown in an attempt to survive the ordeal intact. In Alana's case, much of her past is filled with agony, but it was the loss of your child combined with Paul's suicide that was the catalyst for her mental breakdown. Her mind shut down and when it restarted, everything surrounding those events was eradicated."

"Won't this be worse for her in the long run? When she does start to remember, won't it affect her twice as hard?"

"We won't know until that time comes. Some people start recalling events little by little. Others wake up one day and remember every single event. It can take weeks, months or even years for the memories to resurface but I need to prepare you for the possibility that Alana may never recover."

"That doesn't seem so bad," I say, breathing a sigh of relief. This could be a blessing in disguise.

"I don't think you're fully understanding me, Jax." He pauses for a moment, looking at me hesitantly before he continues. "There's a chance that Alana may never remember you."

The moment the words escape his lips, time stands still. My heart stops beating. My breathing halts. I cannot speak. It is as if the world has come to an end.

"I've asked Dr. Krieger to take her case as a personal favor. He practically wrote the book on Dissociative Amnesia and if anyone can help Alana, it's him."

"What are her chances?" I manage to choke out.

"The prognosis for recovery is generally good, but there are several factors that come into play. Dr. Krieger met with her this morning and her initial reaction wasn't what he was hoping for. At this point, we have to wait and see how she responds to treatment. I know this is hard for you to take in, and you're probably not going to like what I have to say, but the best thing you can do for her right now is to back off. Let Dr. Krieger work with her and when she's ready, he'll bring you in."

"And what if she's never ready?" I ask, drawing in a deep breath.

"Then the Alana you know and love will cease to exist."

As the rush of air escapes my lungs, my heart shatters into a million pieces.

Alana

Six Months Later

They say starting over is never easy. That's an understatement. When you have no past, starting over is your only option.

Leaving Cedar Falls was simple. There was nothing there for me anyway, at least nothing I could remember. A four hour bus ride landed me in Fairview where I would begin my new life. It sounded easy enough, yet here I am, staring down at my half empty glass, tears brimming my eyes.

Maybe Dr. Krieger was right and moving away was a mistake. I just couldn't bring myself to stay in a town where people knew my past and I didn't.

The fact is that I didn't want to remember what happened to me. I read every bit of literature Dr. Krieger handed me on the subject and every single instance of Dissociative Amnesia was triggered by a traumatic or stressful experience that the person endured or witnessed. *Physical or sexual abuse, rape, combat, abandonment, or death of a loved one.* What it boiled down to is that something bad happened in my past and I had no desire to remember any of it.

That doesn't mean it doesn't have an effect on me just the same. Not knowing was eating me alive and I needed answers. So I did the only thing I knew to do.

"You can't let this eat you alive."

Drawing in a deep breath, I look over at Danny – my friend, confidant, and the only person who knows the truth. "I know."

"You aren't alone," he reminds me, his hand reaching out and covering my own.

If it weren't for Danny, I don't know what I'd do. "I keep wondering if I'm making a huge mistake."

"You can't keep second guessing yourself. We all have parts of our past we wish we could forget, but they make us the person we are. They give us strength. You may not remember what happened to you, but at least it's no longer a mystery."

I nod my head in agreement, but it does nothing to alleviate the pain. I have forgotten more than most people ever experience in their lifetime, yet I can't remember a single detail. I know the facts and that alone is enough to torment me forever.

"Thank you," I whisper, laying my head on Danny's shoulder, smiling as he pulls me tighter to him.

"No need to thank me, Alana. I love you and together we'll get through this, one step at a time."

Chapter 42

JAX

Five Years Later

Darkness – the absence of light. Within its depths lies fear of the unknown. It can consume you, making you go crazy. I embrace the darkness because without it, one can never know light. But within the darkness also lies pain.

Losing someone you love alters your life forever, leaving a gap in your heart that feels like it will never close. Alana Jacobs stole my heart the moment she looked at me with those beautiful blue eyes on a rooftop so many years ago and to this day she still owns it. She always will.

Willing my eyes open, I stare into the empty basement - my shrine, as Deuce likes to call it. This room housed all the memories Alana and I shared from the time we met until the day she disappeared from my life.

My gaze falls on the photo album in my hands, Alana's goofy grin staring back at me. At six years of age, she captured my heart and never released it. She always said I helped her heal, but it was her that healed me. She taught me about love and life, making me believe that there was more out there than misery and pain. Page after page of photographs remind me of the times we shared, from our time in the group home to our time with Miss Mary.

Turning the page, my eyes land on Phil and Janet Martin, the picture taken outside the group home the day we left with them. I should've seen the menacing look in his eyes back then, but I had been so blinded by dreams of having a real family that I didn't see it.

Slowly, with each turn of the page, I watch the glimmer in Alana's eyes vanish, being replaced with a torment I did not notice at the time. Landing on the last picture I have from that time, I draw in a deep breath - a simple photograph that depicts the pain she kept bottled inside of herself for years. Taken as we waited at the bus stop on the last day of our school year, I am looking down at Alana in admiration while she stares straight into the camera, her eyes devoid of all emotion except for fear. How did I not see what she was going through until it was too late?

Taking in a deep breath, I turn the page. Staring back at me is an image I will never forget. Her hands places gently on her barely noticeable stomach, Alana smiles broadly at the camera, her eyes alive and shining with happiness – because of me and the child we created.

Not more than a month after that picture was taken, Alana was ripped from me. To this day, I still do not know entirely what happened during her time with Paul and possibly never will.

That first night, I kept vigil at her bedside and prayed for the impossible, but Alana never recovered. The combination of everything in her past mixed with the horror of watching Paul put a gun to his own head was more than most people could take. Delivering your own flesh and blood and having them die in your arms was irreparable. In that moment, the Alana Jacobs I loved with all of my heart vanished.

When Alana awoke the following day, my world crumbled. She had no recollection of what had occurred. In a way, it was a blessing in disguise. Forgotten was all the pain and agony I knew she would be feeling, but Alana didn't just forget the past few days – her mind erased everything. Her parents, the abuse at the hands of the Martin's, Paul's betrayal and suicide, and the death of our son.

Dissociative Amnesia, the doctor called it. A form of selective memory loss where Alana's mind eliminated all recollection of traumatic events in her life. She knew who she was, could remember happy times in her past, but everything surrounding the trauma in her life had simply vanished – including me.

I held out hope, believing that Alana would one day remember me, but that day never came. Our love, all the passion and trust was gone. I was nothing more than a stranger to her, a person of no significance, and five years later, it still breaks my heart.

"Daddy?" Closing the photo album, I place it on the table and look up just as Ava begins her descent down the staircase. "Unc Doo says I can't hab anymo crookies."

Rising to my feet, I scoop my daughter into my arms and smile down at her precious face. "He did, did he? And how many cookies did you eat?"

"Fibe," she giggles, holding up her hand and making my heart sing.

"I think Uncle Deuce is right. Your mama won't be happy with any of us if she comes home and sees all the cookies are gone."

"But I need 'em..." she whines, giving me that sad face that is so hard to say no to.

"Is that so? How about I make you a deal? You go clean your room," I begin, setting her on her feet, "and when you're finished, I'll let you have one more cookie."

"Yay!" she shouts, jumping up and down in excitement. Within seconds, she is climbing the stairs in a hurry to get to her room.

As she disappears up the stairs, I let out a ragged breath. Walking over to the table, I pick up the photo album and place it in the box beside it and close the lid, locking away the last piece of Alana's and my history. Looking around the now barren room, my heart feels heavy. Saying goodbye is never easy, but it's time to finally close this chapter of my life.

Epilogue

Alana

"Once upon a time there was this little boy who looked up into the night sky and made a wish. He didn't ask for money or a shiny new toy. He wanted to know what love felt like and for a long time, he never thought he would experience it firsthand. And then you walked into my life. I took one look at you and there was no turning back. In you, I found everything I never thought I deserved."

A single tear escapes my eye as replay his vows in my mind, each of them heartfelt and true. There is no doubt in my mind that he loves me and would do anything for me, even start over.

"So on this day, I give you my heart and my promise that I will walk hand in hand with you wherever our journey leads us. Sometimes in the middle of life, love enters and gives us a fairy tale. Fate

brought us together and destiny is
providing our happily ever after."

Saying I do was easy. I feel like I have known him my entire life, yet we've only been together five years – at least that's my take on it.

When I awoke in the hospital a little over six years ago, I was surrounded by complete strangers. Terrified doesn't even begin to describe how I felt, but what was even more horrifying was learning what I had forgotten. Not just a few random events, but the majority of my existence. Only bits and pieces remained. How does someone move forward from such a thing?

The answer wasn't so simple. Remembering meant reliving the events that had traumatized me to the point that my mind shut down. I didn't want to remember, I wanted to escape, and that's exactly what I did, which lead me to Danny.

As I look out into the darkened sky, I think about where my life is today and wonder if it would be the same for the old Alana. I am now happily married to a wonderful man and together we created a child that I love more than life itself. Would life had been the same for her or would she be reliving the trauma in her life on a daily basis?

"I thought I'd find you out here." Turning around, my eyes land on the man who stole my heart from the moment we met.

"I just needed some fresh air," I smile up at him.

"Is that all?" he asks, taking the seat beside me.

"I was doing some thinking too," I admit. "About the old me. Would she be as happy as I am today?"

"I'd like to think so," he says as he drapes his arm across my shoulder, pulling me to him. "What's really bothering you, Lana?"

"What if it all comes back one day and I can't take it? What if I lose even more of myself than I already have?" The thought weighs heavily on me every single day.

"If that ever happens, I'll be there holding your hand through it all."

"Like you've done since the beginning," I say as I rest my head on his shoulder.

"If you ever fall Alana, I'll be right there to catch you and if I can't, I will lay down beside you. We're in this together."

I know he will because he would do anything for me. "Did Deuce tell you I was out here?"

"So you're finally starting to call him Deuce now," he chuckles.

"Yeah, it's kind of grown on me," I smile. If not for Deuce, or as I called him for so long, Danny, wouldn't know what true happiness is. "You miss her, don't you?"

Slowly, Jax lifts my chin until my eyes meet his. "How can I miss someone who never left my heart?"

"But I'm not the same Alana I used to be. You said so yourself."

"You're right. But you are the Alana you were always meant to be. Free of pain and misery. I was just lucky enough to have you fall in love with me twice in this lifetime. It's a gift I'll never take for granted," he whispers, his lips lowering to my own.

"I love you Jax," I say as he pulls away.

"And I love you Alana, forever…"

COMING SOON

DESOLATE HEARTS

FORGOTTEN SOULS MC BOOK TWO (DEUCE & EMBER'S STORY)

BY KIRA JOHNS

Prologue

"Daddy please!" I cry out as he drags me by my leg towards the cellar. As he reaches the top of the stairs, my hands instinctively go to protect my head as he begins his descent down the narrow stair case, paying no mind to my cries as my skull bounces on each step until we reach the bottom.

"Shut up, maggot!" he shouts as he yanks me up by my hair, his eyes filled with rage. He hates me. He's always hated me. I am nothing more than a painful reminder of the love he lost, and for that he will never forgive me.

Gripping my hair tightly in his hand, he marches forward, stopping when he reaches the dog crate positioned at the far end of the room. The pungent smell coming from within it is overwhelming, causing me to gag.

There is no regret in his eyes as he shoves me inside, where I will stay for an undetermined amount of time, and latches it shut behind me. "Next time you decide to help yourself to anything of mine, it will be your last!" he spews before slamming his fist on top of the cage causing me to cower in the corner of the tiny enclosure. Turning on his heel, he makes his way across the room, disappearing up the stairs.

Holding my breath, I wait for the inevitable as the door slams shut behind him. One. Two. Three. I begin to tremble as I am engulfed by darkness, not even a glimmer of light visible to offer any hope. Because there is no hope. There is only pain and misery.

Squeezing my eyes shut, I pray for a miracle, one that will never come. This is my past, present and future.

Isolated.

Afraid.

Unwanted.

Unloved.

When the door opens sharply, I jerk my eyes open in fear knowing my nightmare is just beginning. Through the tiny bars, I watch my father as he stalks across the room towards me.

My gaze is affixed to the shovel in his hand. There is no fear as accept my fate. I don't bother to resist him as he drags me from my confines, not even a whimper escaping my lips knowing what is about to come. Tonight my nightmare ends. There will be no more pain.

I feel only peace as he drags me out into the backyard, slamming me harshly to the ground. There is no regret in his eyes as I sit there solemnly, watching him struggle to dig my grave.

I am one of the forgotten.

Never to be remembered.

Never to know love.

I am desolate. Undeserving.

That is how I came into this world and how I must leave it.

To be continued...

Acknowledgements

There are so many people I want to give a shout out to for making all of this possible.

As always, I want to thank my husband. You are my rock and without you, this would all be meaningless. Your understanding and encouragement knows no bounds. I love you baby, always and forever!

To my son who would peer over my shoulder as I worked. Thank you for being so accepting when I was working hard on completing this story. Not too many twelve year olds would be so considerate. Love you!

My daughter, who listened to my plot ideas and gave input – you are one of a kind. Thank you for not being a typical teenager and for your thoughtfulness throughout. I love you!

Then there are the people who were with me throughout the writing process, allowing me to bounce ideas off them and giving me the strength to go on:

Monica Holloway – You were there from the beginning, reading each chapter as it was completed and putting in your two cents. Thank you for putting up with my annoying self and giving me reassurance when I needed it most. You motivated me to continue working (man candy always motivates me!) and made me laugh. As if that wasn't enough, you are my creative designer, making a kick ass cover and some amazing teasers! You are simply fabulous!

Tamra Simons – You are the ultimate reader, taking your time and meticulously going over each page. You were always available to bounce ideas off of and to give it to me straight. One of the many things I admire about you is your honesty. You motivate me, encourage me, and have never let me down. In other words, you are a good friend. A thank you is simply not good enough for everything you do!

Janet Brothers and Renee Santori – You two ladies have supported me in so many ways, sending me messages that touched my heart and also made me laugh hysterically. Your dedication was the reason I chose you to beta read for me and I appreciate every bit of input you both gave.

Nikki Hart – My friend and biggest fan. You can nitpick a book apart better than anyone I know, but that keeps me on my toes. Thank you for giving me a kick in the ass when I needed it, continuing to motivate me throughout the writing process and for making some kick ass book trailers! You've been with me since the beginning and I have no doubt you'll be there until the end.

Lisa Filipe of Tasty Book Tours – Thank you as always for giving me insight into my stories and constructive criticism. You are invaluable and I can't thank you enough for everything you do!

Gaele Hince – My trusty editor who always comes through for me. You are a rock star and I couldn't do it without you!

Michelle Slagan – My wonderful PA and friend. Thank you for everything you have done to get the word out about Desolate Souls and for your loyalty and support!

Last but definitely not least, thank you to every single fan I have accumulated over the last year. Your comments have touched my heart. You are the reason I do this and without you I would be nothing.

About Kira Johns

Kira Johns was born and raised in the southeastern US, where she works during the day as a paralegal in the criminal defense field. She spent her prior years working in law enforcement and before that bartending.

When she's not working or writing, Kira spends her free with her husband, children and her many pets. She enjoys spending time outdoors, whether on a boat or on the back of a bike. Kira, her husband and children are all avid competition shooters.

She is also a huge supporter of Feathered Friends Forever, the Nation's Largest Non-Profit Tropical Parrot Rescue and Sanctuary located in Harlem, GA. Not only does Kira donate a portion of all her sales to this worthy organization, she also dedicates her time to helping the many birds at the facility. For more information on Feathered Friends Forever, visit Kira's charity page on her website at: http://www.authorkirajohns.com/charity.html or visit the FFF website at: http://www.featheredfriendsforever.org

Other Titles
Available

<u>Satan's Rebels MC Series</u>

Destroyed (Satan's Rebels MC Book 1)

Destined (Satan's Rebels MC Book 2)

Deserved (Satan's Rebels MC Book 3)

Damaged (Satan's Rebels MC Book 4)

Contact Kira Johns

Email: AuthorKiraJohns@gmail.com

Become friends on Facebook:
https://www.facebook.com/AuthorKiraJohns

Facebook Author Page:
https://www.facebook.com/SatansRebelsMC

Goodreads:
https://www.goodreads.com/author/show/843
1509.Kira_Johns

Website: www.authorkirajohns.com

Made in the USA
San Bernardino, CA
08 May 2020